The Water-breather

BEN FACCINI

The Water-breather

Flamingo
An Imprint of HarperCollins*Publishers*

Flamingo
An imprint of HarperCollins *Publishers*
77–85 Fulham Palace Road,
Hammersmith, London W6 8JB

Flamingo is a registered trade mark of HarperCollins *Publishers* Limited

www.**fire**and**water**.com

Published by Flamingo 2002
1 3 5 7 9 8 6 4 2

This novel is entirely a work of fiction.
The names, characters and incidents portrayed in it are
the work of the author's imagination. Any resemblance to
actual persons, living or dead, events or localities is
entirely coincidental.

The cover image is taken from the *British Journal of Photography Annual*,
1965. Despite our best efforts, the Publisher has not been able to trace the
credited photographer, Arlette Rosa. If notified, Flamingo will be pleased
to make any arrangements with the copyright owner of the image at the
earliest opportunity.

Photograph of Ben Faccini © Emily Faccini 2002

A catalogue record for this book
is available from the British Library

ISBN 0 00 711832 5

Typeset in Minion by Palimpsest Book Production Limited,
Polmont, Stirlingshire

Printed and bound in Great Britain by
Clays Ltd, St Ives plc

To my father, who encouraged all things

He stands at the edge of the lake and rolls a dry leaf between his fingers. It crumbles apart, pieces flutter from the palm of his hand, down onto the surface of the water beside him. He watches them spin and drift in opposite directions. With the end of his walking-stick, he pushes against thin ridges of mud. They fall away. Water moves forward, running down lines of earth, filling pockets, creating pools.

He sits down on the grass. He lays his head on his knees and closes his eyes. The sounds of the lake wash against his feet.

Part One

1

We are always travelling. From country to country, from grandmother to grandmother. We spend winter and spring in the car and, in the summer, my brothers and I have bottles of water on our laps and sweets in our mouths to soften the tight bends that send us sideways across the back seat.

I am Jean-Pio, the middle child. I sit between my two brothers, waiting for the petrol sign to flash up red. It has been my place since we started moving. I either lean forward, my knees jammed into the gap between my parents' seats, or I push my head back and let my eyes drift through the metal grid of the rear window. I see onto the rushing roads with the occasional tree or lorry to block out the light. I swallow with every bump and dip to quell my car sickness, measured, like a metronome, by the indicator clicking left and right. I read number-plates, decipher stickers on the backs of cars. I play 'I spy' in my head. A for air. B for bend. C for car. D for dead-end. I add up number-plates. I count down the kilometres from town to town. I scan the billboards and signposts for new words.

Sometimes, peering into overtaking cars, I meet the gaze of a hungry dog or the empty silhouettes of strangers. I strain to see what they're wearing and guess where they might be going. They rarely look like us, eyes set on the horizon, children sitting tidily in a row, but occasionally I catch sight of a family like ours. I find parents with feet flattened onto worn down matting and children slouched behind, trouser bottoms stuck to their seats. I follow a father clutching the wheel with impatient hands and a mother severed from the world, floating like paper on a flow of water. I nudge my brothers. Together we turn to glimpse at their fleeting faces, tearing urgently along beside us, leaving sky and ground behind.

In the car, Giulio, my younger brother, sits to my right. Our father says, 'You can never tell if he's happy or sad.' I can tell because when he's sad his lips crumple and fade into the rest of his face. Duccio, the eldest, is to my left. He's so handsome that we often can't walk five metres without people stopping and staring. Our mother reckons that now that he's eleven, he's only got one or two years left until he gets a hairy top lip and greasy skin and then that'll be the end of that. Our back seat is wide enough for us not to touch each other, but if Giulio moves into my space I push him back. If I lean too far over towards Duccio, he crushes my thumb with the seat-belt wrapped around his tightened fist. If we all yell and annoy my father, he pulls the car over and shouts and our mother cries.

Our mother is Ava. Some call her Ave, others Avi. We call her Ama because it's a mix of *Maman* and Ava and she hates being called Mum. It's a bit like me. They couldn't decide on a single French, English or Italian name so that's why I'm called two names: Jean-Pio. Ama comes out with 'we' about the English, but the origins that shape her mind and flawless white face come and go on the number-plates of passing cars: England, France, Holland and Slovenia. Ama is each and every one of us rolled into one. She is a multi-purpose clasp, an all-embracing shape. She is allergic to the sun and suffers from insomnia. She has always been unable to sleep as far back as we can remember. She can never doze in the car because she develops a lingering pain between the eyes and even if she goes to sleep at night in a warm bed she wakes up with a jump and a tired head that stays with her all day.

Our father is Gaspare, or Pado to us. He's Italian, with a Sicilian father. Ama says his moods swing from singing ecstasy and smiles, to blind fury. He's an anatomist and a histopathologist, a specialist in toxins and indoor air pollution. He used to teach in England, but now he rushes around Europe, attending conference after conference, and we go with him. Children, he repeats to Ama, need to see the world. We wait for him in long car parks and he appears between meetings to gesture 'hang on' or 'five more minutes'. Sometimes he carries slides with sections of diseased lungs, or a book on rats which is kept in the glove compartment. It has the answer to many questions: peanuts give brown-brimming tumours, artificial sweeteners cause blooded pockets on the tail and nicotine spreads yellow-stained patches across white fur.

2

I'm eight years old. It's the spring of 1978. Since Pado developed his theory on how diseases spread from air conditioning, and became president of the European Board of Histopathologists, our kilometre dial has clocked into thousands and started its cycle over and over again. Our journeys, along motorways, across seas and over mountains, have to keep up with the progress of sickness from people's lungs and air conditioners. Travelling is a race against time. Every moment we pause, or complain, is a moment wasted, an opportunity for disease to take hold. Our car must carry on, always. That's the way it is. Places to get to. Lives to save. Scientists to convince.

Duccio is entrusted with the maps. He keeps these in the pocket behind our father with the stacks of papers and hotel listings for each country. Some maps you have to fold out more than others. Spain and France stretch far across my lap. We always get lost in Brussels because the guidebook for Belgium has a tear where the Flemish and French street names merge in shredded strands. Giulio has the pamphlets for the conferences stashed behind Ama's seat: '*Legionella pneumophila* and the use of erythromycin'. 'Epidemiology and the evaluation of environmental carcinogenic risks'. Giulio also has a book of jokes with two hundred reasons why the chicken wants to cross the road. Ama keeps a paperback called *What To Do On Long Journeys*. It has been fingered and thrown across the car so many times that it is tattered and scuffed like a grimy shirt collar. Duccio can tell you the make of any car from any country. Giulio and Pado can list most of the capital cities of the world. I can tell when the petrol sign is going to turn red.

In England, we stay with our grandmother, Ama's mother. She was born in London, but her parents were Dutch and Slovenian and brought her up speaking French in England. That probably explains why she married a Frenchman, our grandfather, Grand Maurice. He drowned two summers ago while fishing for crayfish in a lake in France and our grandmother hasn't been the same since. Grand Maurice thought he was so lucky to have met her that he called her '*ma chance*'. We still call her Machance even if Pado tells us she hasn't brought us much good fortune lately. I'm Machance's favourite and no one really knows why. Maybe it's because I was Grand Maurice's favourite too. Ama shrugs and goes quiet about it. Giulio thinks it's because I've got Grand Maurice's brown-green eyes and, now that he's dead, I'm the only one carrying them around.

*　　*　　*

When in Italy, we stay in small family hotels in Milan and Rome or with Pado's parents in Umbria. In Germany, we have a bed-and-breakfast near the motorway which has sticky muesli and cartoons for children on the TV. In Madrid, the owner of our hotel is so chatty that he keeps us waiting for our room keys to tell us stories we've heard a hundred times. Over the reception desk there are posters from Pado's scientific conferences coloured with microscopic close-ups of viruses and then a torn, withered photo of the owner's wife carrying dried sausages from Cantabria, the sun setting on her skirt. Ama can't sleep in the Madrid hotel because of the neon street signs outside our room so we wrap her clothes across the windows and whisper in the night. Before going to bed, Ama sniffs the sheets, one by one, to check they are clean. If she finds a hair, a scab, a toenail or even a trace of scent, she calls the reception in a small voice and we watch as astonished maids remake the beds with Ama following behind, smoothing the spreading white surfaces with her drowsy hands. When we try to help her, she gently pushes us to one side, 'Just let me do it, please.'

Pado always states, 'There's no point telling me things I know. Tell me something new', so when he pops his head into our hotel room to say 'Goodnight', you know you have to hurry to come up with new facts fast:
   'If you weigh all the insects in the world, they are heavier than all the animals put together!
   'Every single snowflake is unique!'
   'Not bad, Jean-Pio, I'll have to think about those.'
   Giulio invents a new chicken joke. It still has to cross the

road, but it makes Pado laugh all the same. When Pado leaves, Giulio asks me where I get my facts from. I don't really know. I suppose I just pick them up, here and there, glancing through newspapers in hotel lobbies, listening to Pado's colleagues, staring out of the car window. Giulio and I have a deal: if I get up before him, I have to wake him gently, ask him what he is dreaming about and suggest a good ending. He then goes back to sleep and tells me what happened later. Duccio stands in front of the mirror ruffling his shiny black hair. He hates the way Ama combs it neatly to the side, every night, before he goes to bed. If it weren't for our parents, he'd never wash his hair or change his clothes. Then no one would smile in the street or beam thirsty grins at him again. When Ama overhears our night-time whispering, she hisses a rustling 'Ssssh, be quiet!' and, in between her words, you can hear the pumping exhausts that choke her day, the sound of car doors slamming and the creasing of maps hiding roads that always carry on over the page.

Our hotels are usually within sight of the conference centres and we park the car in between hundreds of others. The rooms are teeming with fellow scientists and the foyers thick with greetings: 'Meet my wife and children', 'I read your book', 'Will you be presenting your recent statistics?'

Ama jots down notes for Pado. Her memory sweeps backwards and forwards like the windscreen wipers on the car. She collects papers, remembers dates, faces and addresses. 'Isn't that the pathologist from Stuttgart?' she nudges Pado, writing down a name called up from the depths of her sleepless mind.

Ama is Pado's translator too. She translates his speeches and articles, rolls out the languages he needs. She says the important thing is never to have an accent. That's why no one ever knows where she comes from, not even her. Pado doesn't care about accents, and whatever language he speaks, it sounds like Italian. If we have the room next to our parents, we can hear Ama correcting Pado, stopping and insisting on an intonation. Pado listens to her, running the cold bathroom tap over his toes, swollen from accelerating, foot down against the floor, all day long.

'Please Gaspare, just try once more, for me,' Ama pleads.

Then the rosary of Pado's pronunciations starts up again and coils through the wall that divides us, an echoing rhythm to sleep to.

When we don't even have time to stop in a hotel, we rush into roadside bars and hurry the waiters with 'no time to waste' sandwiches. Then we race back to the car and drive into the night, humped over our knees and our mother wide-eyed in the darkness. Pado uses the time to rehearse his speeches: 'Ladies and Gentlemen, members of the scientific community . . .' He presents his findings on smoking and the different aspects of lung congestion to the cold windscreen with Ama's lost face painted into the glass.

3

Our car rarely breaks down. 'It's a stroke of luck', say the mechanics. The outside is so dirty it has tiny furrows of green growing along the edges, and tinges of grime on the bonnet that suck up the sliding rain like silent parched mouths. Ama wishes the car would conk out from time to time, simply shudder to a standstill like a wounded car should. Behind her closed eyes, she longs for the sound of the engine spluttering, the slow, burning smell of overheating or the sudden scrape of the exhaust as it finally drops onto the road.

'Cars only break down if they're left in garages', that's how Pado sees it.

Ama has a big bin at her feet to keep the seats tidy. She'll take everything except eggshells. They smell and turn grey, so you have to wait for the country lanes and roll down your window to throw them into a bush. Sometimes we miss and Pado tells us it doesn't matter as eggshells rot fast. Ama is not so sure, she reckons they take years to blend into the earth. That means that there must be eggshell everywhere we've

14

been, a thousand jagged fragments dotted around Europe, under bushes, lining puddles in the road.

The car dashboard has dark rings of wood that project weaving patterns onto the rear window in the sun. From time to time, Ama brings out a dusting cloth and polishes it. She keeps the cloth in the glove compartment next to her music tapes. She has ten tapes in all, stacked into two piles of five. Pado keeps his tapes separate, crammed into the pouch to the side of his seat. Ama's cassettes are all of Liszt. Pado's are all Verdi. The agreement is that Liszt is for the gentle drives through open countryside, whilst Verdi is for motorways and driving fast, books fluttering in the wind. At least, that's how it's meant to be, but Pado is always in a hurry and Liszt rarely makes it out of the glove compartment. If Ama does manage to get a Liszt cassette, it's only because Pado knows that, sooner or later, as the curves and bends speed up, we are going to have to have Verdi and nothing else. As Ama's eyes are beginning to brush the leaves outside, floating to the notes of her Liszt, Pado lowers the volume until the music is inaudible, until Liszt merges with the indicator and the murmuring of the tyres against the hard tarmac. Then he pulls out his Verdi cassette, one hand on the wheel and the other on the tape machine, and plugs in opera music at top volume. Ama might be lost in tree tops, curled around distant twigs, but she sits up immediately.

'Where's my tape?' she snaps and stretches for the volume button, her ears ringing with noise.

Pado stops her, 'We have to push on.'

Ama retreats into hostile mutterings, her smothered complaints frothing out of the windows, trickling down the sides of the car.

Our parents' struggles last for a while, falling and rising, depending on the traffic ahead or the volume on the tape machine. If Pado is still shouting, 'It's bloody Verdi or nothing at all!', he speeds up to prove his point, chin up against the wheel. His foot pumps the accelerator in an outraged, stamping skip. The car surges forward, shooting ahead like a ball. We bounce over bumps, scrape along walls, hoot people off zebra crossings. Ama stares into her lap, her white hands twitch and fidget with the folds of her dress. She breathes out slowly, at regular intervals, to keep calm. After a few near misses, and as the arrow of the speedometer wrenches at its dial, she hovers her fingers menacingly above the hand brake.

'Stop Gaspare, you're going far too fast!' she yells.

Pado waits to see if she'll touch the hand brake. Ama turns to her door instead and threatens to open it unless he slows down. Pado drives on, faster and faster. In the back, we watch as Ama opens her door onto the world, widening the gap little by little, the tarmac appearing, swelling into the car until it is running like a frenzied conveyor belt beneath us. The noise of the wheels floods in. Pado won't take any notice. Duccio tries to convince him. I bow my head, so as not to see. Giulio edges away from the gaping hole, clutching onto his seat. I can feel him pressing his shoulder into me, the way it shakes when he cries. Pado nudges up to the car in front, to the point of touching. Duccio leans over us and

16

pulls in Ama's door, yanking against the force of the wind and her frozen grasp. Then the car in front skids out of the way, scared by our racing, and we screech to a halt. Ama steps out of the car. She stands silent for a while, in front of us, and then, with spat breath, she turns to Pado: 'You fucking idiot!'

Ama walks away, crosses fields, kicks dust at the side of the road. We trail behind her, Pado's window down.

'Please get back in.'

She ignores him. She stops to look at flowers, picks up stones, folds her arms or runs her hands through the air. She can cut across whole meadows, her head hung low, and disappear into woods to be alone. When she becomes a little wisp on the horizon, Pado jumps out of the car and rushes off after her. Ama can see him coming and she runs to avoid his apologies and smiles, storming over the road into the fields the other side. Cars overtake and slow down to watch our parents racing to and fro, refusing embraces and finally walking back, arm in arm.

Pado is explaining fast. 'I'm sorry, I really am.'

Ama cries until he has to shout it so loud that all the crows in the trees are thrown up like black seeds sowing the sky with their crops of regret. Then we know it's time for us to get out of the car and for them to get in. We sit together, hands in our pockets, or in the fields, scratching our fingers in the mud, watching our parents, each on their front seat, trying to sort this out again. We can stay like this for a while, the three of us lined up, a few metres in front of the car, observing the wide windscreen crammed with our parents' heads. If one of the side-windows is lowered, I creep up close. Snippets of conversation slip out unnoticed. Ama gasps out her splintered words, the rolls of reasons why she can't carry on with the endless driving, all the conferences and translating. Pado tries to convince her. Ama wraps her refusal around herself and repeats, 'It's not a life, Gaspare, it's not a life.'

I watch Pado's reaction. His eyes are twitching with arguments. He too has lists, long lists of valid reasons to carry on, lists like row upon row of microscopic slides and, on each slide, more and more reasons. Ama says she no longer knows what is fixed and what is gone. She listens to Pado, but she can't see herself any more. The never-ending motion of the car is ploughing through his lists, through the days, on and on.

We get back in the car, the seats taut with unresolved temper. To calm matters down, Pado puts on one of the story tapes he and Ama have recorded for us. Ama has imitated the pigs from *Animal Farm* and Pado has taken on *The Three Musketeers* in a special battling tone. Occasionally, in the middle of a story, Ama and Pado break into hysterical laughter, struggling to put on an accent or pronounce an unpronounceable word. Their recorded, crackling giggles fill the car, pushing back the resentment and anger. In the background of the tapes, you can hear doors banging, a dog barking and Giulio. He always insists on being present when the tapes are made. He's even managed to get a slot on a cassette to tell us a joke. Every time that tape comes on, he asks to listen to it over and over again, rewinding and rewinding, until one day it gets so chewed that the machine spits out knotted loops of music and squashed-chicken jokes.

The tapes, in the cramped swinging car, can mingle with thoughts in my mind and change into fears that stick like headaches, at least I call them headaches. There's no other way of describing them. The headaches come on stronger as the motorways rush their white broken lines into a sickly mess or when the little petrol sign suddenly flicks on red. I watch it waver for a while and then it jams on redder than before, a stain that won't go as the last drops of petrol slip away into the engine. I go to warn Ama. The sight of her tense shoulders stops me. I pull back, not daring to touch her.

I hesitate, then pat Pado on the arm instead. 'The light! Look at the petrol light!'

'It's all right,' he answers, 'I'm sure we can manage another thirty kilometres to the next petrol station. Well done for noticing.'

But how can it be all right? There's no petrol station anywhere and the road is hurtling itself further and further into the distance. I watch the kilometres tick past, hoping that Ama won't realise that we are going to grind to a halt with juggernauts and trucks flying about us like leaves in a storm. I concentrate on the stories on the tapes instead. Some manage to calm me. Others bring on a smarting-cut punch between the eyes, the blurring of shadows along the road, the memories of number-plates uncounted. I focus on my brothers' elbows skewering me. I hold on to that niggling pain, catching like a nail on my skin. I breathe softly, slowly, in and out, but my head leaks, a punctured bowl emptying. The unwanted thoughts, the thoughts I've turned back a thousand times, suddenly come, and once they've come, they're shoved aside by new ones, tumbling, falling into my head. My mouth is full of them. I try not to attach words to them. They swim, crippled without letters stuck to their sides, and then that's it. They trick me. They catch me out. They take shape and snatch words, glue them to themselves. I shut myself off from the car, the perpetual swaying, the rub of its wheels, but I can't blot out the humming of unsolicited thoughts as they dress themselves faster and faster in aching words and images. I listen to the stories on the tapes again. I reinvent new endings, swap characters with others. I create images and thoughts to wipe everything away. I stop. I start. I warn. I save. The petrol sign is redder and redder and no one is doing anything about it.

Pado looks calm. It might be all right. We might get away with it this time. I look at the cars rushing past. I follow them closely. Then that's it. A thought springs up inside me again. What if the last drop of petrol has just gone and we're about to slam to a halt right here in the middle of the motorway and we can't get out of the car and the lorry behind us swerves and hits the car in front and the car in front spins round and starts coming back the other way? Why did I think that? I didn't think that really. Look at the lorry. Quick, a word for the driver – 'Don't die' – but then the lorry overtakes and slips into the distance before I have time to say my word for it. What if the driver goes round the corner now and ploughs into the road, tunnelling into the cracked grey surface of the

tarmac? What if we shoot round the corner after him, straight
into the piled-up cars in front? I hold on to myself and it's as
if I'm pulling on a string of words, till like a chain they dance
me away. I silently repeat 'We mustn't crash! We can't crash!'
– I yell it to myself so hard that my ears are singing. I call for
help, but no one can hear. I see faces from the morning, cars
that passed us by. That staring woman, that crying girl, that
dog with a blue collar, tossing and turning its head through
the wound down window. I imagine our grandfather, Grand
Maurice, fighting and writhing against the water that choked
him. I see his face slipping, his feet digging in to the sinking
mud, his mouth, his eyes, his ears filling with the lake. Then
his face mingles with faces from yesterday and more faces
from the day before that, and number-plates, and cars and
the motorways they were on. What were the people in the
cars doing? What language were they speaking? The days and
towns slide past. I can't remember, but I must remember.
What number-plate? What car? I put my hands over my eyes.
A spiralling headache comes on full blast. The pain arrows
through my eyes and I can't think at all. I'm overturned by
a dizziness that flicks me up and down inside.

'Turn off the tape. Please!' I manage to say.

They won't. I am drifting, disorientated.

'Stop the car!'

My words melt away. Giulio shakes me, but I can't feel
anything. My voice has changed, it's an unheard, stifled
whistle.

Pado looks round in surprise and parks in a lay-by. I can see
a public lavatory in the distance and run towards it.

'Don't go in there. It's filthy!' Pado shouts after me.

I go in anyway. I lean against its wall, cars filing past and men staring at me from behind urinals. I try to find a lavatory. Most of the doors are locked. One door is open and it has a scratched outline of a mouth swallowing up a telephone number inside a heart. I sit on the closed seat, panting, trying to banish myself from my thoughts. I recite 'We mustn't crash' again and again. I can smell the rotting taste of panic everywhere. All the time Pado is hooting impatiently.

'Hurry up. Hurry up!'

I sprint back outside. Pado is beginning to pull away and, with the buttons of my head unfastened, I run to reach the car before any new thoughts trip me up. My brothers are looking at me worriedly through the rear-window. I get back into the car. Pado observes my face in the driving mirror. I know he wants to ask what's up, but the other cars are pushing past us and the picnic is getting warm. He smiles instead. He leans towards me.

'Get him a drink of water, he's dehydrated.'

His face is full of warmth, spreading into ridged lines, a map with motorways, rivers and hills. Then the story on the tape slides back in again on its way round the machine and its voice sings like a stone cast up from the tarmac.

Ama looks worried. 'Gaspare, we should stop again. Jean-Pio's obviously not feeling well. Slow down!'

Pado accelerates ahead. 'He'll be fine. Will everyone just bloody calm down, *lasciatemi in pace.*'

I gaze at the changing clouds out of the window. They have joined into one slow dragging crease in the sky. Ama turns to check on me.

'I've never seen a child stare into space so much. That's all he does all day long!' she sighs to Pado. 'No wonder the boy gets car sick.'

'I've got a bit of a headache,' I tell Ama. 'I'm fine.'

She doesn't answer. She digs her nails into the fabric of the front seat and picks furiously at the thread of the seams.

4

The trickiest thing about travelling from England to France or Belgium and back is the Channel ferry. You have to join endless queues of cars well in advance and have a ticket with an arrival time that is an hour behind or in front of where you are coming from. The last bit of the drive to the port is always silent. There's nothing to say, except that Pado hates having to be early for a boat and Ama can't stand the smells and noises of the ferry. She checks the trees on the roadsides for the slightest sign of a storm at sea. We look with her, waiting in dread, for the cutting rain, the litter-carrying gusts, the dance of cars, from side to side, along the motorway in the wind.

The signposts to the ferry seem to change constantly and Pado's shortcuts lead us to areas where there's never a shop to buy fresh bread or a place to fill up with petrol. We're always running late. When we ask someone the way, no one can understand Pado's distorted French and he drives on frustrated, leaving passers-by in mid-sentence, mouths wide open, until he finds a person who can answer him properly.

Duccio normally reckons he's worked out the route anyway. Pado is sure he's recognised the road ahead.

'It's this way,' he says.

'But that last man told us it was in the other direction!' Ama protests.

'He wasn't from around here,' Pado insists.

'How the hell do you know?'

'I do, that's all. It was obvious.'

Duccio quietly folds his map back together. He turns the top of the page inwards, just in case.

'Thanks all the same,' Ama reassures Duccio, loud enough for Pado to hear. She curls her arm behind her seat to touch Duccio's knee. He hesitates a moment, then edges away, abandoning Ama's hand to itself.

We pass at least five public lavatories, but we're not allowed to stop because Pado assures us his Italian university book on venereology is still a reference. He has it with him at all times.

'Page forty-one,' he says, pointing to his case.

Ama opens the book and scrunches up her face as she reads that 'virulent germs and potential diseases are everywhere, particularly in places of scant hygiene such as public toilets'. Then she turns the pages quickly to avoid looking at the photographs too long.

'How hideous!' she winces. 'Is that what happens in acute cases of gonorrhoea?'

Pado nods and, from over Ama's shoulder, I can see pictures jumping out at me, like squashed animals on the road, stuck between people's legs. Giulio says he doesn't care about the photographs or any disease or anything, but he is going to burst if he doesn't get to a loo soon.

Pado tells him to quieten down: 'Men can hold on.'

Ama is sure that it is harder for women and then that's it because Pado says: 'How come everything is so much more difficult for women?'

'That's not what I meant at all,' Ama protests.

'Then why say it like that?'

It all comes down to the fact that Ama was brought up in England and it's not a place to live because people don't speak their mind and have to make little, snide comments instead. It's not as if you can't make little comments in Italy though.

In fact, we used to have a potty, but that ended when Giulio made it overflow. He was telling Duccio to move over, and not looking, and then it was too late. Streams of pee were flooding the car and Ama was screaming 'Get out!' in English, French and Italian all at once. The pee made a stain on the floor and layers of antiseptic wipes won't make it go away. If the days are hot and the car is warm, a faint smell rises in your nose.

Ama likes to find her own quiet spot to pee. As the only woman in the car, she tells us she has a right to be alone. She points at trees and behind bushes, forces us down lanes. Pado always has a different spot in mind.

'Here's perfect! *Perfetto.*'

'No Gaspare, not here, please.'

'Why, it'll do fine.'

'No, not here.'

'For goodness' sake, who cares?'

'I do!'

'I'm going to stop here.'

'No, go on a bit.'

'Why?'

'There's someone coming.'

'Where?'

'There, from behind that house.'

'I can't see a house.'

'There!'

'That's not a house.'

'What the hell is it then?'

'It's a barn.'

'No, it's not.'

'Yes, it is.'

'Please drive on! Look, there is somebody coming.'

'That's a fucking cow.'

'Don't get angry with me. I can't believe this.'

'You can't believe what?'

'I simply want a pee, you idiot.'

'Don't call me a fucking idiot.'

'I didn't, I said idiot.'

'Come on, out you get. We're all waiting.'

'Carry on further! I'm not going anywhere near that cow.'

'What? Why the hell not? It's behind a fence.'

'I know. I just don't like it. I'm sorry, I'm not doing anything in front of that cow! Forget it, just forget it.'

'Right. I'm stopping here, behind this tree.'

We stop under a tree, down a lane. The air is cold, and stripped, desolate farmland stretches all about and around.

Pado turns the engine off. Ama won't budge. She refuses to look at Giulio who is tapping her shoulder from behind. Then Duccio and I tap her on the shoulder too, 'Go on, Ama, please have a pee! It's all right here.'

'Will you all stop getting at me! I don't want to go any more,' Ama yells, shrugging us off her. We shrink backwards into our seats and Pado kicks the accelerator so hard that the cows in the meadows stretch over their fences to watch the mud on our tyres being sprayed up into the air.

Crossing the Channel is not only dicey because of the rough seas, there are also Pado's glass jars of preserved lungs and the histological slides for his colleagues to take into account. You have to explain them carefully to customs so Pado prefers to slip them under his seat with all the wine he's jammed into every gap of the car.

'Don't take that much wine Gaspare, it's not reasonable. You know what they're like at customs,' Ama tries wearily.

'Bloody customs. Ridiculous limits!' Pado won't give up.

We divide the wine into 'good friends' and 'acquaintances'. The good friends get labelled bottles carefully laid out under cheese, garlic and pâtés to hide their number. The acquaintances get cheap wine shoved under the back seat, huddled up against the floating organs in their jars.

'Please tell me they are from an animal!' Ama begs when she sees them.

Pado merely mutters 'Yes, yes' to Ama.

She's not convinced, and nor are we, because it's like the time Mr Yunnan first arrived. Mr Yunnan came in a jumble of brown cardboard boxes with numbers on them. Box one goes on box two and so on and so forth, until you have a whole body, or rather a skeleton, as Mr Yunnan has been dead for some time, maybe four or five years, Pado reckons. It was Giulio and I who gave him his name. The first time he was assembled, we couldn't believe it was so complicated. Clicking the neck onto the spine was the hardest. Luckily, Pado had had delicate hinges fitted so he could rotate the bones to face all his colleagues in the back rows. He says that's how he describes the kind of deformation of the ribs that can happen with lung inflammation and something about osteoclastic pitting of the bones.

Ama was sure the skeleton was plastic. 'Look how the finger bones are joined together! Isn't it fantastic what they can do nowadays! The knees bend, and the feet!'

That was before she read the certificate, half in English, half in Chinese, which said that Professor Gaspare Messina has the right to carry human skeleton number 76455 for professional purposes.

'There's nothing to get het up about,' Pado reassured Ama. 'He's dead. I got him through a special deal with the Chinese government, in Yunnan Province. It's the cheapest and best place for skeletons because they're generally in good nick when they arrive.'

Ama couldn't look Mr Yunnan's way. She was speechless. 'What do you mean?'

'I need this skeleton for my work. It's fine.'

'It's fine to drive around with someone's bones in our car is it? What next Gaspare? What bloody next?' Ama gasped.

We looked at Mr Yunnan. This extra presence. This unassembled, severed set of bones that we had touched with our own bare hands. It was only when Pado explained that you could tell he was a young man and that he might well have been a prisoner, that I knew that the hinge at the base of his neck was fastened to the point where the executioner shot the bullet that ripped his life away. I knew it. It grew inside me, an unwanted thought that has stayed in my head ever since.

'He may have died naturally,' Duccio announced, but he wasn't convinced either.

He just said it the way Pado insists that Mr Yunnan gave his life for Science, or the way Ama quietly swallows and tells us that nothing is going to bring back our grandfather, Grand Maurice, now that he's dead and drowned in a lake in France. You only have to read Pado's books to see that there's no turning back: the organs laid out on metal trays, the close-up pinkish patterns with diagrams, the weight of a lung lying alone without a body. Most people don't give their names, Pado says. They merely die and get cut up and photographed. But the tumour, on page four of Pado's cancer book, has a name tag to the side of it. It's too small to read.

5

Once on the ferry, the oil-salt smell of the car deck clouded with car fumes, the sound of motors and creaking chains, and the gentle rock of waves get Giulio going. He complains that he's feeling sick and Ama can't answer because she can feel it too, a slow vertigo taste that rises from the stomach to lodge in the throat. Pado is convinced 'it's all in the mind'. He takes us on a tour of the duty-free shop to pass the time. Giulio is wavering. He can barely walk straight. Pado scoops him up and, as he does so, a stream of sick flies out of Giulio's mouth. It drips down Pado's front like a tie and onto the floor. Ama hurries to the cash till to ask for some tissues. She fights against the same lurching, retching urge in her mouth. She stops on a bench and breathes in deeply.

Pado is holding Giulio by the back of his jumper, out in front of him, at arm's length. '*Che schifo!* Oh no! No! Bloody hell,' he grumbles, half sorry, half irate. He turns his head away to avoid the smell. Already people are changing direction. A woman with grey hair gingerly steps out of the way and sighs something to herself.

'Sorry, what did you say? Something wrong?' Pado hurls

at her. She backs away, aghast. Pado pursues her down the corridor, carrying Giulio with him, dangling in mid air, from his sagging jumper. 'Go on!' Pado shouts at the woman, 'if you've got something to say, say it. Go on, if you dare, *ma va* . . . !' Giulio swings, crying. He hangs limply above the ground, pushing with his legs against Pado's arm to get down. Ama staggers to her feet.

'Put the child down,' she shrieks at Pado. Then it seems as if all the people on the ferry spin round and watch us, everything stopping, no one but us, perched alone on the sea.

Giulio is sick again. It splatters against the floor and slides with the rock of the ship, this way and that. Pado turns to face the glares. '*Cosa*, what? What is it?'

Ama snatches Giulio from Pado and holds him tight to her chest. She cuddles his head against her. 'It's all right my darling, calm down! How are you feeling?' Giulio shivers a little, a ring of multicoloured sick printed on his lips, and on Ama's shirt. Pado has got into an argument with one of the stewards. His shouting competes with the noise of the loudspeakers. Ama suddenly grabs me by the arm too and drags me off to find the cabins, with Giulio draped across her shoulder. 'Come on, get a move on!'

I try and tell Duccio where we're going. I wave and point down the corridor in front of us, urging him to get a move on. He can't though, he's guarding the luggage, a heap of leather and cloth shapes, as high as him.

'Hang on! What about Pado?' I say, running beside Ama.

'Well hopefully he won't bloody find us!'

*   *   *

We settle in our cabin. We each get a bunk-bed, except Giulio, who has to sleep in the middle, on the floor, in a nest of blankets and jumpers. Ama puts a bowl next to him, in case. We can hear the drinking crowds, with heavy feet, drumming the decks. The pinball machines throw up money and children run, falling between adult legs. From inside the cabin, it sounds like pots and pans knocking in a kitchen cupboard. Pado and Duccio show up, towing the luggage behind them along the corridors. They stack it up next to Giulio on the floor. Pado drops Ama's bag onto the end of her bunk. It's a shiny bag she got free from a department store. Pado reckons that's typically English liking something just because it's free. The problem with that, Ama argues, is that she's always typically something when it suits Pado: typically English, typically French, typically Slovenian, typically Dutch. Anyway she's convinced Pado is typically Italian, even if the mix with the Sicilian bit, she says, has managed to make him look Arabic.

Ama's bag is splitting at the seams with things although Pado is always telling her to travel with the strict minimum, especially clothes. In fact, he says, you only ever need two of everything because you can wash one item whilst you wear the other. It doesn't happen that way because Ama has piles of clothes she buys when waiting for Pado to leave his meetings and conferences. The car is barely big enough to hold them all and Pado has to scatter them everywhere to pack the boot, knickers scrunched under the spare tyre, tights between pages of reports, trousers and skirts rolled down the sides of bags. Ama intervenes from time to time: 'No, don't put that under that, it'll crumple' or 'I need to be able to get at that later!' There's no reply. A bit like when you lean over into the front seats and ask: 'How much further?' Then there's silence. Ama's bag is also brimming with little bundles of antiseptic wipes in plastic coating. She has kilometres of dental floss too. Before going to bed, she hands out the floss, a good length to each of us to begin sawing at our gums. She's sure there must be a bit of food stuck somewhere, lost between the back teeth, rubbing against the tongue, refusing to give. Then Ama has her books, lots of them. They are stashed beneath her clothes. She has at least five on the go at once, mostly French and English novels. That's what she's always read, ever since she was a child and Grand Maurice lent her new books each day. The two of them would spend hours reading out passages, comparing impressions. Then, as we started travelling, they would write long letters to each other, quoting lines, discussing endings. Now Ama sits up alone at night and reads whilst the rest of us doze off. She has a pocket lamp and it skips up and down the lines across the bed and into the dark with tense flicks of the wrist. Sometimes, we see her in the morning, half asleep, half awake, a book caught between her thumb and forefinger, as if the weight of the story has forced her to give up.

In Pado's case are reviews and reports bound together with wide clips and bold red writing: 'Embargo', 'Confidential' or 'Draft'. He leafs through them, making annotations, or catching Ama's eye to read a passage about a clinical trial and ask for the exact translation in Italian. Ama invents a word for him, the way she does when she can't sleep, new words to lift her away, heal the worries, pack the empty spaces of the night. She spins off idioms, chases unknown verbs, multiplies and conjugates the languages in her mind. That's why all Pado's colleagues ask for Ama's translations. She knows what's behind a phrase, the meaning that everyone is searching for but cannot find. Pado cannot dwell on translation though. There's no time to waste. If he doesn't analyse his reports and trials quickly, people across the world might start taking new medicines without realising that their lungs are being colonised by cysts and disease.

When we've rummaged through our bags and flossed our teeth, we all begin getting our beds ready, trying to make head or tail of the flimsy bunk sheets and the rock-hard pillows. Ama gives up. She's not going to sleep anyway and doesn't really care. The captain's voice comes over on the loudspeakers.

'I wish that *stronzo* would shut the hell up,' Pado murmurs half asleep. I strain to hear what is being said above the locking cabin doors and stamping corridors.

Duccio looks at me. 'I bet you there's going to be another storm.'

Why did he say that? Eventually the captain's voice trails off into an alarm noise: 'If you hear this sound, get out of your cabin immediately, leaving any belongings behind, and make your way to the nearest lifeboat station.'

I listen to the three test blasts of the emergency alarm. They stab at me, dig deep inside, indelible reminders. Three short sharp slashes of panic.

I am uncomfortable. My left foot is poking out of the sheet and blanket, and every time I feel a wave knocking at the boat, I'm sure it's a piece of jagged driftwood. The ferry mows over it and we all drink and sleep and run along the corridors not knowing that the wood is swinging its way round the motors to smash a hole in the hull to sink us. I quickly stick my head in the pillow and think of something else. Then I awake with the sound of waves again and stare into the bunks. Pado is grinding his teeth, his jaw twitching. Everyone is asleep, even Ama! I struggle out of bed and check, up close. I stand there looking at her. Her nostrils are moving softly. There is a faint band of light across her cheek from the torch she is still clutching in her hand. I study the fine lines under her eyes which, she says, grow a little deeper every night she can't sleep. I watch the hem of the sheet flutter slightly with her breath. I can't believe it. She really is asleep! I delve into Pado's bag. I get his camera and position myself near the door. The flash goes off and Ama sits bolt upright. She knocks her head on the bunk above and shouts for the light. I scramble for my bed.

Ama is screeching: 'You idiot, *espèce de crétin!*' and I'm crying because she has to be really angry to shout at me in French, even if I was trying to help her by proving that she might have been asleep. Everyone is awake now and telling me I'm stupid. Ama looks weary. Maybe she wasn't sleeping after all. Maybe she's never slept. Not ever. Closing your eyes doesn't mean anything. That's only resting, but the mind goes on and on, pleading for a second, just a second of sleep, to soothe the swelling of continual waking and thoughts. I lay my head against the sheet and crease its whiteness with my toes.

The night seems interminable now with the clinking of chains and the rush of sea under the boat. People are walking and staggering along the corridors about us. Occasionally there's a shout as my eyes are shutting or a lazily-held bag knocks against the walls. Between three and four o'clock in the morning, someone tries our door by mistake. The handle jumps up and down, followed by, 'Shit, it's the next deck up!' These are enough words to wake me completely. I shake, following the shuddering movement of the carpet-covered ceiling. I'm sure I heard a thundering wave charge against the ship. I can feel it, rising up above the others, ready to slap us out of the water. I get up and open the door a little. There's no one in sight. I shut it again quickly. Maybe they've already sounded the alarm? In the half-light of the cabin, I look at the evacuation instructions on the back of the door. All the figures are wearing life jackets. Where are ours? I peer under the bunk. I can't see them anywhere. I finally spot a bundle of material tucked away by the base of the bunk ladder. If I stretch too far though, I'll wake up Pado and he'll make me get back into bed and then no one will hear the alarm or have time to get out of the cabin as the waves turn us over. Why did I think that? My heart drums in my throat, pushing at my head. My mind inflates with television and newspaper disaster images, stories of shipwrecks, corpses floating in the sea and boats smashed against rocks with the spray of the water dancing in the air. I watch the light from the corridor under the door. I imagine the water seeping in. A drop at first, then two, then a stream and then a wave that bursts through doors and comes bellowing down the corridors and stairwells. I see the ship filling with water as we struggle to reach our life jackets and Pado yelling and Ama yanking Giulio from the floor with the sea currents curling over us.

'We can't sink. The ferry mustn't sink.' I start saying it, slowly, continuously.

I'm thinking of Grand Maurice and how the water of the lake must have pushed open his mouth, poured between his teeth and flooded through his body down under the reeds. He lay at the bottom of the lake for a week, with his eyes and ears and nose clogged with water, before they found him. I know that if I'd been fishing with him, it wouldn't have happened. He wouldn't have slipped in the water. He couldn't have.

'We mustn't sink. We can't sink.' Over and over again, I trip out the words.

I feel the door quiver a little with the long heavy corridor silence. Is there anyone on the ship? Maybe we are the only ones left as the boat drifts out of control towards the convulsing open sea. Maybe everyone is already jumping onto the lifeboats, scrambling and screaming for help? My head is pumping. I push against the door with my feet. If I hold the door back, we'll be all right. We'll be saved.

I'm shivering and I don't know if it's the cold or the rush off the top of the waves that are about to come and drown us. I pull a blanket over me. I shove my back hard against the door, my eyes peering down at the gap underneath it, waiting for the trickle of water to begin. My head hurts so much.

Suddenly Ama is stroking my hair. 'What are you doing there my love?' she says with bleary eyes.

'I don't like my bed,' I stutter, but then tears well up inside me and I have to say I have a headache. A searing, aching one.

*   *   *

38

When day breaks, the corridor becomes alive with slamming cabin doors and running children and groggy morning voices. The loudspeaker makes a few announcements about the car deck, the opening times of the shops and immigration requirements. Pado has a shave in the oval basin. He splashes a lotion on his face and the cabin fills with his familiar smell. He carries us off to the restaurant. He guides us across the newly-cleaned, slippery floor.

As we're grabbing our trays, Giulio tells me: 'Ama says they're going to take you to a doctor!'

'What doctor?' I gasp.

Giulio steers me behind the breakfast stand where the cornflakes have toppled out of their bowls. 'Ama told Pado you don't sleep enough and that's why you're always staring into space and getting headaches. I heard her saying it this morning.'

'What are you two whispering about?' Pado shouts. 'We have to hurry. You can talk in the car.'

I'm not hungry. Not now. There's nothing wrong with me. I saved the ferry from sinking.

The drive back down the ramp is slow. It's like that coming into England. You have to wait for hours as they check every car and passport. It makes Pado furious. He joins the 'Nothing to declare' queue. Ama asks whether that's wise, but there's no way he's budging. Our mother is the only one allowed to talk at customs. Pado is too dark to speak. Ama inherited our grandmother Machance's Slovenian and Dutch white skin, but she still doesn't answer the way she should. As we approach the customs checkpoint, Pado rehearses a few lines for Ama to repeat: 'We're on a private visit', 'No, we only have the allowed limit of alcohol', 'I'm a British citizen'. Ama checks her face in the car mirror. She sweeps her hair to one side. She whips on a quick layer of lipstick.

'Clear answers. Clear and direct,' Pado stresses. 'And remember for the French customs, we're resident in England and for the English customs we're resident in France. Okay? Did you hear what I said? *Hai capito?*

Ama lowers her window.

'Passports please!'

Ama thrusts out five passports. The officer reads through each one. He comes to Ama's and opens it to find a long string of floss stuck inside its pages. The floss clings to his fingers and winds itself around the passport cover. 'Sorry,' Ama stammers, embarrassed. 'I don't know how that got there.'

'Mrs Maseenou? Messounah? Mishina?' the officer starts, flicking his hand to free it of floss.

'Messina!' Ama corrects him, politely.

'Italian is it?'

'The man's a genius!' Pado mutters to himself.

'Where is your place of residence?' The customs official hands back the passports and waits for an answer.

'Well, um. It's . . . um.' Ama looks at Pado, unsure, panic crossing her face. Pado glares back at her, eyes wide-open, dumbfounded. 'Ah! Um, here, England! I mean France, sorry France, yes France,' Ama strives on.

'France? You have an Italian car!'

'No.'

40

'No, what?'

'Yes.'

'So when were you last in England?'

'Oh, um . . . two weeks ago, I think.'

'Business or pleasure was it?'

'. . . um, that's . . .'

'Where are you going now?' the officer fires quickly.

'Around,' Ama makes a wide gesture with her hand.

'Around where?'

'How's the weather been recently? Lovely day for this time of year!' Ama suddenly tries.

The customs officer looks at her astonished. Giulio asks what's up. Then the officer starts circling the car with renewed zeal. 'Great, absolutely fucking great. Thanks for that, Ava!' Pado huffs. He's so irritated he flicks through the ferry brochure to keep calm and mumbles, '*Stronzo*,' 'bastard' at the customs official, loudly. He hates the way they look at him. He loathes their facetious smiles, the simple voice that explains, in basic English, that this is England and nowhere else.

'Did you see the way he looked at me?'

Ama tries to ignore Pado's mounting rage as the customs officer gets more and more curious.

'Keep quiet, darling. This is not the time to get paranoid.'

She's struggling to maintain a composed face, but Pado is off: 'He probably thinks I'm some jumped-up "dago" just off the boat, some peasant looking for work! Well I can tell him and all these bastards that I used to teach in their bloody country, at their bloody universities!'

'For goodness' sake, control yourself, Gaspare. Shut up! Please!' Ama begs.

'I mean, look at this idiot,' Pado rages.

We can feel Pado's raven hair twitch with indignation. He's no foreigner to this place. He has our mother and she has pale untouched beauty chalked all over her face. We smile to soothe him. His jaw is set in fury. His hands are dancing across his lap, boiling with a desire to wipe this moment away. Ama is edgy. The customs officer looks into the car. Pado can't smile, not at him. Ama smiles too much, much too much.

'Could you open up the car please, Madam!'

'*Figlio di* . . . Fucking . . .' Pado growls.

Ama hoists herself out of the car to try and resolve this on her own. The customs officer leans into the boot. He begins lifting wine bottles out. So far he has counted twice the limit. Then he discovers the jars of lungs. Ama blushes, coughs and sniffs. Pado can't bear it any longer. He's out of the car too, waving his certificates. He has had enough. On the back seat we shrink into nothing. Giulio curls into a closed, tight ball. Duccio rearranges his maps into separate country piles, making sure the corners meet. I feel myself sliding down, further under the seat. I clench my teeth and wait, trying to help Pado in my thoughts. Ama goes to stop Pado, but his eyeballs are fixed. She stands in front of him, supportive and pleading. It's going to be all right. She knows he can do it. He's got to do it.

He's doing fine, explaining calmly enough, then he says it – the word he can never pronounce – 'innocent'. It is innocent like 'inno+scent' not 'inno+chent', we've told him a hundred thousand times.

The officer says, 'Sorry, what?'

Pado raises his voice, 'Why bother innochent people?'

The officer takes it badly and they're off.

'Please follow me, Sir.'

'Listen . . .'

'Kindly do as I say!'

Another officer comes and joins the first. They lead Pado into a room. Ama gets back into the car, crying. She bangs the door shut so hard that we all freeze. She sits holding her head in her hands, then she gently switches on the tape machine for some music, something to take her away from here, from this. Instead of music, the tape is still stuck on Giulio's joke. His distant voice coughs and laughs. Ama punches the eject button furiously. The tape flies out onto the floor. She picks it up and hurls it onto the top of the dashboard. Giulio fiddles with the biscuit packet beside me, pushing his face up against the glass so no one can see his eyes. Then I hand Ama a biscuit to calm her. She absently takes a bite and throws it out of the window. A seagull snatches it up and deposits a large white dropping on the car in exchange. Pado returns a while later with a heap of clipped receipts.

'What the fuck is this shit doing on the car?' he shouts.

He starts up the car again. Ama leans out and tries scrubbing the bonnet with a tissue. The white stain won't go. She scrapes at it with a piece of paper. It rubs onto her hand. We drive off into England, Pado yelling about customs officers and seagulls that shit everywhere. Duccio leans against the head rest in front of him. I can see he is watching Ama clench her dirty finger, two layers of antiseptic wipes wrapped tight around it.

6

From Portsmouth to London and then on to Machance's is always busy.

'Left-hand side darling,' Ama reminds Pado at every cross-roads and roundabout.

By the time we get to London, Pado has to turn and say: 'Yes, I've understood it's the left. Thank you.'

Our drive is going to take a little longer than usual as we're stopping near Regent's Park for a doctor's appointment. Ama gently tugs at my sleeve.

'Jean-Pio, we've arranged for you to pop in on a colleague of Pado's. He's a headache specialist. A very good doctor.'

'What headaches?' I complain.

'Come on. Please darling. It'll only take a moment and we'll all feel better.'

There's no point arguing as Pado has already parked the car and started reading the door numbers. Giulio looks at me as if to say, 'See, I told you.'

Pado helps me out of the car and Ama waits behind.

'I'll only complicate matters, really I will. Your father is much better at these things. I'll stay with your brothers,' she assures me.

Pado pushes a button on an intercom. A woman's voice shouts back, out of the wall: 'Fourth floor!' We go up some brown-carpeted stairs. As we're about to go in, Pado sits down on the sofa on the landing. He leans his head on his arms and takes a long, deep breath.

'Are you all right Pado?' I say.

He looks up and pokes me in the stomach, smiling. ''Course I am. I'm just a little tired today and I can't see when I'm going to find time to do my research for the next conference. Anyway, we're here to sort you out. Not me. Come on *caro! Andiamo!*'

A secretary opens the door and the doctor emerges from behind her to greet us. He can't wait to talk to Pado about his latest book. Pado would prefer to get straight to the point.

'We're in a bit of a rush, sorry, but if you come to my next lecture . . .'

The specialist is disappointed. He pulls his chair up towards me. Talking to Pado, he shines a torch into my eyes, takes my blood pressure and checks my knee reflexes.

'You don't have to bother with all that,' Pado intervenes. 'I've already checked him over. I think you just need to get him to describe his symptoms.'

I don't know what to say except that I get headaches in the car and on the boat.

'Describe us the feeling?' the doctor asks. I can't. 'Where does it hurt?' he adds. I don't know.

45

Pado breaks in to avoid the silence. 'He's been having these headaches and dizzy spells for some time now. He gets some form of vertigo or migraine. It seems to come when he is tired. Maybe he's a little dehydrated from time to time. My wife says he's easily distracted too. Personally, I don't see the connection.'

'How often do you drink water?' the doctor questions me.

I give him the same answer I've given Pado: 'Every morning, lunch time and in the evening and, since I've been told to drink more, at tea time too.'

'He probably gets travel sickness like most children!' The doctor reaches for his prescription papers. 'There are some very good new pills,' he promises Pado.

'No, really,' Pado stops him. 'I don't think we would have come to see you if it was just to get some travel sickness pills. Besides, I recently read some research into the side-effects of those pills. They're not too great.'

I begin to shift in my chair because the specialist seems to be quickly searching for ways to impress Pado.

'I tell you what,' he says to Pado, 'could you leave us alone a few minutes. I'd like to ask him a couple of questions.'

Pado now looks like he thinks this whole specialist thing is a bit of a waste of time. He gives in anyway.

'If you think that would help. But remember, he's only eight.' Pado pats me on the back. 'It won't take long, try and tell him what it's like.'

'Yes,' I smile. As Ama said: we'll all feel better afterwards. I'm left facing the doctor, who has taken out a writing pad. I imagine Pado walking down the stairs to join Ama. Perhaps they're sitting in the car together, with music slowly suffocating in the machine. Or maybe Pado is in the room next door, trying to fit in some work, reading through magazines or rewriting his book with the photos of white rats, fleshy pink stumps growing out of their backs and cut-open lungs.

'Well, Jean-Pio, what can I do for you? Why don't you tell me how the headaches start?'

I begin to tell the doctor again that sometimes, in the car, with the swerves and dips, I get a bit sick, but that instead of feeling sick in the stomach I get a headache and that if I get a headache I have to close my eyes to make it go away. Then, when my eyes are shut, I feel even more sick. And that's that. I can't tell him any more. He wouldn't understand that I have to stop the car from crashing or the ferry from sinking or that if I'd known Grand Maurice was going out fishing on his own, I would have thought about it all day so that he didn't drown and leave us with a gap in everything. And now that Grand Maurice has gone, and we're all stranded for ever, I have no choice but to swap bad thoughts for good thoughts all day long because I can't think that someone can just go out fishing and never come back, or that hundreds of people, all across the world, are drowning and dying every day and no one is trying to stop them, or that all the air conditioners are spewing out diseases that kill and no one knows.

*　　*　　*

'Are there any other pains? Do you get stomach aches? Can you sleep?'

I look at the ceiling. I don't want to be here. I don't want the specialist to talk to me any more.

'No, nothing,' I say.

We both fidget in our chairs.

The specialist gets up and calls Pado in. There's no reply.

'I bet you he's gone down to the car,' I tell him.

We look outside and there's Pado leaning through the car window talking to Ama. He notices us and makes his way back up to the doctor's. It's my turn to be alone now, whilst Pado listens to what the specialist has to say.

Pado finally emerges, 'Thanks for your time,' and points me down the stairs.

'Well,' Ama says, as we arrive back at the car, 'what did he say?'

'We'll talk about it later Ava. You know as well as I do that it's not that simple. Travel sickness, he thinks, maybe.'

'Oh that's a surprise!' Ama sneers. 'I wonder how he could have got that?' She strokes my face. 'What about the water though? Does Jean-Pio understand he's got to drink more water?' Ama carries on. 'We can't go on like this. It's getting ridiculous.'

Giulio is prodding me to know what happened. I'm counting time away, nothing to say, nothing to think. Duccio has a map on his knees and is drawing in the precise route we took from the ferry to London.

7

It's an hour's drive to our grandmother's house from London. Machance isn't old, but she looks it because she hasn't really eaten very much since Grand Maurice died two years ago and she moved back to England from the house in France. She sits in her bare dining-room and tells Ama that it's hard being alone.

She spends most days dead heading the flowers in her garden and, in the evenings, she extracts the fine hairs from her chin with a rapid pull of her fingers to pass the time. By nightfall, she has a tiny nest of thin hairs in her palm. On windy nights, she casts them from her window into the breeze and by morning they have gone. I imagine them gathering in the bark of trees, forming rings of wiry softness clinging to the trunks.

Soon after we arrive at Machance's, Ama sets to work, going through urgent bills and clearing up untidy rooms. She stops as soon as Machance appears, not wanting to get in the way, not able to explain. She glances over the sparse furniture and sagging paintings, confused by the disrupted order of the house.

Then people start turning up to see Ama and Pado. These friends and guests come and go, sad at the fact that we're never in one place.

'Why don't you stay a while? We never see you!' 'Why are you always rushing off so soon?'

Ama answers them all with the same empty expression, her bag for the next journey already packed and prepared in her head.

Two visitors, Michael and Joan, stay a little longer. Pado rolls out medical stories and cases he's heard at his conferences, like the one about the woman who smoked so much that her lips went yellow and grew into grapes of tumours that clustered like chandeliers from her mouth down into her lungs. Michael listens to Pado in horror.

'Enough! Enough!' he begs: 'You're going to put me off smoking!'

Joan urges Pado to carry on. 'Keep going, Gaspare. He's got to give up one day. He already can't breathe properly going up stairs!'

Michael tells her to stop being so ridiculous and gets up, pointedly, to light a cigarette. Machance brings him an ashtray. He balances it delicately on the window sill, blowing his smoke outside. I watch him from the table, inhaling, sucking in the smoke in big gulps. Pado and Ama move on to another subject. Machance explains something to Duccio. Isn't anyone going to say anything to Michael? Isn't anyone going to show him Pado's book on lung disease? I look at Michael again, rotating the ashtray with his finger. Now he's knocking the grey ash off, with precise little taps of the cigarette. The smoke snakes into his mouth and sticks to his lips, like deadly air flowing in and out of an air conditioner. The tumours. What about the tumours? His lips will swell and rot. He won't be able to speak or swallow and the scabs and stubs sprouting from his lips will turn into blisters of blood. I picture him dying and the doctors waiting to cut out his lungs for a photo or a microscope slide, with his finished life etched in its dulling colours. I feel a headache mounting, a sickness in the back of the eyes. I stare back at Michael, transfixed.

Machance interrupts my gaze and asks me to help her lay out some glasses. I reach across the table. I spot a pack of cigarettes, inside Michael's jacket, draped over the chair. I can't stop looking at it, poking out of the grey material. I carry an empty bowl to the kitchen. What if Michael ends up like Mr Yunnan or Grand Maurice and all the other dead people? We have to stop him! I corner Giulio near the fridge: we should do something quick! Giulio says if I can grab the cigarette packet, he'll divert everyone's attention. He starts running up and down asking Ama for a sip of coffee. She tells him to calm down, plonks him on her lap and roughs up his hair. As she curls strands of Giulio's hair round her fingers, I dig into Michael's jacket. Pado looks at me strangely. He is wondering what I'm doing, but he's too busy waiting for the next joke or smile to mind. Michael laughs with Pado.

*   *   *

I can feel the cigarette packet burning in my hand.

Giulio and I rush off to the bathroom. We pass Machance turning last year's apples from the garden on the window ledges. She rotates each apple, every day, to check that it's not rotting. Not that it matters much: she'll never eat them anyway because she is thinking of Grand Maurice. In the bathroom, Giulio and I run the warm water and fill the basin to the brim. We have to move fast before Michael tries to light up again. We tip the cigarette packet into the water. The cigarettes take up the basin like felled tree trunks on a river. They gradually fall apart, shavings of paper and shredded leaves. Giulio pulls out the plug. The cigarettes clog the hole and gargle. Machance is walking by outside. We don't have long. The cigarettes won't go down. I push and prod them unsuccessfully into the plug hole. Then I open the lavatory. They'll have to go down there instead. We drop them in the bowl and pull the chain, a lengthy throttled flush. Some cigarettes float back up to the surface and linger for a while, others go straight down and never return. Then we realise we still have the packet itself. We drop it into the loo as well. With the brush we crush it up and dilute the water with blue antiseptic. Clean smells drench the bathroom and the packet vanishes.

They haven't noticed that we left the sitting-room. Duccio is on his own. No one's patted him on the head. Ama says that we have to protect Duccio. It's not often that people are born like him. Not even the photographer who came and took pictures of him in his suit could get it right. 'He's too good-looking,' Ama sighs and no one can do him justice. 'Beautiful children aren't always beautiful adults though,' so we have to be careful to appreciate it now. Her friends do. Ama has one friend who kisses us hello and Duccio swears she once touched his lips with her tongue. It was like a warm, wet piece of ham. Giulio and I don't understand. He has a nose and eyes and mouth like us, but they always look at him, the same way as they look at Ama.

Michael goes to light another cigarette. He pulls the ashtray off the window sill. Giulio tugs at my sleeve. We sit down and do something. Something nothing. I try and think calmly, smoothly. Michael searches from one pocket to another, knocking his head to remember. He gets up and looks in his coat, in Joan's bag, in his trousers. He's frantic and he doesn't like it when everyone carries on talking. He has to find his cigarettes. Now! It has to be now! Joan tries to calm him, but Michael says, 'The cigarettes can't have just got up and walked out of the room on their own.'

Machance comes to the door and coughs a little to announce that the loo downstairs is blocked. If we need a lavatory, we'd better go upstairs and be careful not to use too much water, as there's only a small tank. Ama and Pado don't understand how the loo could be blocked. It was working ten minutes ago. Lavatories don't simply block like that. 'Another thing to fix for my mother before we leave,' Ama worries. Pado apologises to the guests and fetches some tools from the boot of the car. He begins hacking away at the tap behind the lavatory drain with a spanner, then a hammer. Michael is like a dog, rushing, searching. Pado, with his legs poking out from behind taps, tries to prise the lavatory pipe open. Giulio and I know he'll never make it. Machance has never opened her pipes and there is rust all around the house. In her bedroom there is a photograph of Grand Maurice shaded with so much dust that it looks like a hoover filter with an old face in the middle. I must never think of what Grand Maurice's face is like now, dredged from the lake and swaddled in weeds, sealed in his tomb.

Then the pipe loosens, with Pado suddenly saying, 'What's this?'

He's about to pick it up, when Ama warns: 'Don't touch it, it's disgusting!'

She hands him a plastic cup. We always have them ready in the repair kit. He scoops up a lump of shredded matter.

'Put it down Gaspare, please! It's revolting,' Ama fusses.

Pado is not so sure. He points the cup towards the light and swivels it in the palm of his hand.

'Looks like vegetable with bits of paper.'

Michael hasn't calmed down. 'I could swear I had them. I had them there in the sitting-room!' He squints into the cup of shredded mass and then looks again. He asks for a screwdriver or something from Ama.

He picks around inside the cup. 'That's strange!'

He extracts a little white paper. It has disintegrated, but he knows it's a cigarette filter. He asks Pado to have a look inside the pipe and he scours it with a rod. Giulio and I are just retreating when a heap of filters comes out in an avalanche of matted tobacco. Michael is speechless.

Joan says, 'How did they get there?' and that's when I'm thinking Michael's lucky to be alive, to have avoided the tumours, otherwise he wouldn't even be able to speak.

Michael is so angry that he starts packing up his things. He puts his coat on and tells Joan they're off. Pado attempts to sort things out. He proposes to go and buy some cigarettes. There's no point wondering how they got there, he'll pop into town and get some more. We have to stop him! He can't just go and buy more. We can't let Michael die.

I shout: 'He has to stop!'

Michael is astounded, 'What! You little brat.'

Ama is so embarrassed. Pado is stunned. He ushers me out of the room. 'You can't do things like that! Those cigarettes didn't belong to you!'

I call for Ama. She glares at me across the room, offended, disappointed. She shakes her head: 'Jean-Pio, how could you? I can't believe it.'

Michael is gesticulating at us. Pado gently steers me towards our bedroom. He asks me how he's going to explain all this to his guests, and locks the door behind him. From the bedroom, I can hear everyone arguing and apologising. Giulio is trying to tell me something through the locked door. Pado yanks him away. I have to be left alone, otherwise I won't learn.

There's nothing to do in the bedroom. I gaze out at the farms beyond. There are cows scattered everywhere. On the drive, there is a little white car shooting off with Michael and Joan inside. I can't see their heads from here, but I want to tell

Michael that I tried my best to save him. Now he's going to buy more cigarettes and Joan is going to collapse when he's gone with swinging lumps of cancer strangling his throat. I lie on the bed and stare at the ceiling coming and going, shrinking down on me until the room pushes back its colours. I get up and pace round the bed. I shake the door from time to time. I look at the cows in the fields. I can't even count them because the sixth or seventh sometimes slips away and then runs back and looks like the others. I feel dizzy, even without the motion of the car, the solid stillness of these four walls marching down on me. I have to get out. I start hammering at the door. There's no reply. I don't want to get a headache in here, not here, on my own. I fight against painful thoughts and images, creeping into me because they know that I'm locked in a room with no way out. I kick at the door again and fall on the bed. I breathe like Ama does when she's upset. One, two, three, and out. I must stop a headache from coming. One, two, three . . .

There's a knock at the door. It's Machance. She wants to know why the door is locked. I say Pado has the key and it's my fault because I flushed Michael's cigarettes down the loo. She sits down on the carpet on the other side of the door. Through the wood, I imagine her gently pulling out the hairs from her chin. A soft sound like a blade of grass sliding from the earth.

Machance tells me she doesn't know what's happening to our family. Always tired. Always travelling. And now me misbehaving. 'It's really not what Ama needs. She's already at the end of her tether.' When Machance was young, she says, things were different, you had to be strong. There were no televisions or radios or cars. You couldn't just switch on some music to brighten up your day, or jump in a car to have a change of scenery. In those days you had to have your own little television screen in your head to click into, turn off this, turn on that. But that was long ago. Now nothing is the same anyway, since Grand Maurice drowned in the lake in France.

She tells me that Grand Maurice looked a little like me. He had hair that you couldn't keep down and he never stopped walking and thinking. From morning till evening, he pounded up and down the countryside. That's why, one day, about four years ago, he set out for a stroll and got his foot caught in a jagged rabbit trap. At the time, Machance and Grand Maurice were living in their house in France and farmers often laid traps in the meadows and woods for game. But Grand Maurice had forgotten, because that was the way he used to walk, head in the air and eyes stuck to the sky. The trap sliced his ankle and clasped itself shut around his foot. He yelled out in agony, but no one heard. He tugged at the trap with his hands and picked at it with a large stone, but it only dug deeper into his flesh. The harder he tried to prise the trap apart, the worse the wound became. And so he waited. He waited three days, three whole days until the man who laid the trap came to pick up a crushed or squealing rabbit and saw Grand Maurice with his nearly-severed foot full of rusting metal, dried blood in the furrows of the soil.

During those three days alone, as Machance longed for news of him, Grand Maurice had to keep his mind. He counted trees and ran his tongue around his mouth until he knew all of his teeth in size and shape. He found that the back ones had holes with smooth tops and that the front ones were uneven. He could tell that some were going black and others had roots which wouldn't let go. When he was bored of his teeth, and the pain was too much to bear, he called upon his memories of journeys, sights and sounds, and each time that he felt himself slipping, he came charging back in with a face from his past and a story to jolt the mind. As he watched his foot fester and swell, he thought hard of Machance and how they'd met on a warm cloudy day in September in London. He spoke to his remembering and chatted to himself. He went back to his childhood and pictured his mother, his father, his school, his friends and clothes. He tried to recall every moment that had been. He started with his earliest memory, year by year, then month by month and, finally, week by week. There were gaps, huge unaccounted-for absences, empty months, patchy years, faces without names, names without people. He tried harder and harder, until he felt his mind might burst, until he had managed to remember almost everything. Then he watched the skies. He invented new words to describe each different kind of cloud. He listened to the birds. He whistled back at them. He picked up leaves from the ground, felt their shapes and ran their surfaces across his hands. By the last day, his mind and body were so stretched that the past and present had merged into one.

Machance was so happy when they freed him from the trap and brought him home from hospital, with his foot stitched up and plastered, that she put together a dinner for all his friends. The pain in Grand Maurice's foot only grew worse during the course of the dinner and he had to stand up and keep moving so as not to think about it. He dragged himself round the room with eyes full of seething sadness. The heavy plaster on his foot rocked him back and forth, gouging ruts in the parquet. Machance encouraged Grand Maurice to sit down again, but he couldn't stay in his chair. He went to bed before the guests had left. He could hear them saying 'goodnight' to Machance through the bedroom window. As they went down the steps outside, they turned and asked: 'Is he going to be all right?' The noise of their cars leaving filled the house. Machance cleared the table on her own. She blew out all the candles lining the table. She climbed into bed alongside Grand Maurice and held on to him through the sheet.

Machance shuffles a little on the carpet on the other side of the door.

'The doctors never managed to get his foot to mend properly. The bone didn't really heal. Do you remember how Grand Maurice always limped? That's why he needed you to help him when he went fishing.'

She taps at the door with her long hands. I can feel solid dry tears rolling down her fingers into the wood. She tells me to hang on. Pado should come and get me out of here. She'll tell him, enough is enough. I wait a while, lying on the bed, my head swimming with Grand Maurice's suffering. Thoughts eat into me.

Pado turns the key and swings in. He doesn't smile. He still looks angry. I won't talk to him. He sits on the end of the bed.

'*Ma Jean-Pio, cosa facevi?* You do know you shouldn't have done that, don't you?'

I don't care if he doesn't understand. Anyway it's his fault. He said everyone who smoked was going to end up dead. The photographs are in all his books. Now I can't tell him anything. If Michael dies then it's not my fault, because we all could have stopped him, but instead they laughed with him and all that whilst Grand Maurice was battling with a rabbit trap in his head.

Pado tells me it's time to go again, to move on.

'*Andiamo!* Pack your things! Everyone is waiting in the car.'

It's a slanting wet afternoon and the rain is bouncing off the car bonnet. 'It won't last long,' Ama says, almost to persuade herself.

We have visits to do: friends, and the annual international conference of specialists on legionnaires' disease. Pado explains to us again how microbes and toxins collect in air conditioners and then expel themselves into rooms and grip in your mouths to kill you. In one company, in New York, the only person who didn't get ill was the doorman and that's how they found out because he spent his time outside and wasn't silently sucking in germs to die. I imagine all those people sitting attentively at their desks, working away, and then, gradually, one after the other, they begin to cough, splutter, sag and turn grey. And then that's that, they're gone.

We stop at Elizabeth's on the way to the conference in London. She's Ama's artist friend. We're thinking of dropping off Duccio to have his beauty captured in a painting. Elizabeth looks Duccio up and down. She declares she's never seen a boy quite so good-looking.

'Here we go,' Giulio mumbles to me.

Duccio doesn't notice though. He never really notices because he doesn't care any more. He's too busy with his duties. Maps to read, cities to identify, trips to plan, cars to name. Pado needs him because Ama no longer knows the difference between motorways, dual carriageways, side roads and main roads. It's all the same to her: one long journey across nowhere. Duccio though has little notepads in which he writes long lists: all the routes we've ever been on, the restaurants, the cities in alphabetical order, the value of local currencies. When he's finished his duties, he reads books about great sporting geniuses. As Pado says to Ama: just being good-looking won't get you very far in life.

Elizabeth thinks she can do a portrait of Duccio. It's going to take some time however. Not an hour here or there – maybe two or three weeks of posing.

'We don't have that kind of time,' Pado objects bluntly.

Ama seems annoyed. How are we going to get Duccio done? He's coming up to twelve soon and then that'll be that, he'll be thirteen and fourteen and then his beauty will have vanished. Elizabeth takes some Polaroid snaps of Duccio. He looks uncomfortable and he is sighing heavily. When the pictures come up, slowly appearing like blue sky amongst dispersing clouds, you can see he is sighing so we have to start again.

'Darling, make an effort for us,' Ama pleads. 'This is not what we need.'

We go off nosing through the paint tubes and turpentine. We find a canvas covered in cloth showing a naked woman reclining on top of a red table. She is motionless and holding a flower to her mouth. She looks like she might be sniffing or even eating the flower. Giulio fetches Duccio and I remain, running my eyes across the pink shapes and breathing in the smell of acrid oil colours. Duccio takes one look at the naked painting and tells us it's horrible.

'Stop poking around, come over here!' Ama orders, exasperated.

This time the Polaroids are all right, but Duccio is refusing to say a word.

As we're all getting back in the car, Duccio slams Giulio against the head rest and steps over him to get to his seat. Giulio lets out a scream and I can't sit down either because Duccio keeps on shoving me away with kicks. 'Behave!' Pado shouts. Duccio settles down. I try to lean as far as possible towards Giulio, to avoid touching Duccio. He is packed with fury, bubbling, ready to burst. I know that if I even brush his coat, he'll shower me with punches. I sit upright in the middle. I watch the raindrops drifting across the windscreen. I'm sure the wipers could go faster. They haven't caught that drop, nor that one. That one, there, the big one! I'm about to make a wish on a raindrop when Duccio explodes. He can't keep silent any longer.

'I'm not going to be naked in the painting!' he yells.

Everyone is a little astonished.

Ama leans into the back. 'Darling, whoever said anything about being naked?'

Pado is grinning to himself. 'Where did you get that idea from?'

Maybe I should tell Ama about her friend who stuck her tongue in Duccio's mouth, but she doesn't look like she wants to hear that now. Our mother calmly explains that no one will be naked and that's that. It's only a portrait of Duccio's face and it's a nice thing to have.

'We'll hang it on a wall somewhere,' she adds calmly.

I don't know where because we are always moving and I can't see how we can stick it on top of the car as it won't last with the rain and certainly not with the conferences outside Rome where they even steal the tyres off you. Pado is sure that's an exaggeration though and that others are just as deceitful and clever at stealing.

Ama brings out the sandwiches Machance had made for our lunch. Salmon, avocado and tomato. I open mine up to make sure there's no chin hair tucked away inside. I examine the fish for germs lost inside the pink pleats. I hold it up to the light. 'Stop fiddling and hurry up,' Pado tells me. We have to eat fast. The 'legionnaires'' conference starts soon. Pado wonders whether he should quickly update his diagram of an air conditioner water tank. Ama thinks that it would be clearer if he's going to bring in recent theories on cooling systems and airborne microbe reproduction. We drop Pado off outside a large grey building. He rushes up the main stairs. Giulio shouts out that he's forgotten the rat book from the glove compartment.

'Doesn't matter,' Ama shrugs, because he has all that stacked away in his mind.

We drive on, not knowing what to do in Pado's absence. Ama buys a newspaper and flicks through the film and exhibition pages. She keeps on checking her watch, but there's not enough time to fit anything in. She starts up the car, with a resigned turn of the wrist, and we push on to a park. Ama stops at the entrance and tells us to get out and play on the bit of lawn in front of her. It's still raining and we come back after a few minutes. Ama is looking at her newspaper again. She's ripped out sections, book and theatre reviews. She lays the strips of paper across the dashboard and reads them quickly. When she sees us, standing in front of her, she begrudgingly folds them into a wad in the glove compartment, stacked reminders of occasions to be missed.

We get back in the car and Ama wearily drives on past a few shops. She asks Duccio to get out and see if they have any dresses in the windows. He runs alongside the car, stopping and peering into each shop. He points at a dress. Ama leans over the steering-wheel and shakes her head at him. Duccio tries the next shop and then the next one, till we get to the end of the street and have to turn into another road. Eventually we find something for Ama in a decorated window, two streets further down. We park and Giulio is instructed to wait in the car. He's sulking at being left behind. He says it's not fair that it's always him who looks after the car, but Duccio reads the guidebooks and I have to watch the petrol gauge.

'Don't you bloody start. Don't make me angry Giulio! Not today! Everyone has to help with something,' Ama warns.

She waves back at Giulio as we enter the shop: 'If a traffic warden comes then pretend you don't understand. Speak French or something! We won't be long!'

In the shop, the assistant is all smiles. Ama tries to find something that Pado might like too. Duccio and I tease her by repeating what Pado says about her bottom being dipped on one side. Ama doesn't find it funny at all, especially in front of the shop assistant and she whips a '*Ça suffit. Assez*' at us in French so that only we understand.

It doesn't work because the shop assistant says, 'Where are you from?' and Ama replies 'England' rather pointedly.

Then a man comes in and he is drifting across the shop looking for some clothes for his wife. The wife apparently likes red so I point him to a pair of reddish trousers I've seen on a rack in the corner. He has hardly started walking across the floor when he notices Ama. He compliments her on the dress she is trying on. Ama pulls back into a changing-room to get away. The man carries on talking to her through the curtain.

I can see her head coming up over the curtain. 'Kindly leave me alone,' she says in a curt voice.

The shop assistant intervenes and asks what kind of red clothes the man wants. He can't answer because he's got Ama in his mind and he can't think of his wife's shape and size any more. Ama pushes past him holding a black-grey dress. She wants to pay. The traffic wardens are coming and we have to go. The clinging man, who wants red clothes, follows us outside and pats me on the head. He hangs in front of the car and tries to help Ama get out of our parking space.

Giulio keeps on asking, 'Who is that man? What's he doing?'

Ama refuses to answer. She's in a fluster. As we are leaving, indicator clicking down, the man blows a kiss at Ama.

She shouts, '*Petit con*,' and we all laugh because the man doesn't understand he's just been insulted.

Giulio doesn't like him either even though he didn't see him leering over the changing-room curtain.

'Not a word to your father,' Ama begs, as we are all afraid that he will drive bumper to bumper at top speed if he finds out.

We arrive in time to pick Pado up outside the conference hall, before it starts raining again. He's only been waiting a few minutes, so he's happy. He has a colleague with him from Denmark. He agrees with Pado: 'It's a clear international policy on the regular maintenance of air conditioners that is needed.'

We're going to be late for our next meeting at the Association of Toxicologists. We get away without anyone blowing kisses and speed across the city. Pado is in a good mood and he still can't stop laughing about the fact that Duccio thought that he would have to strip off for Elizabeth.

'Used to be a pretty woman in her day,' Ama tells us.

'What's happened to her now?' Pado wonders.

Ama explains that Elizabeth has been a little unhappy lately. Things haven't worked out for her. 'She even takes Polaroid photos of herself every day to see if she's growing old. She has two years' worth of photos stashed away. A photo for every day, and if you look at the first photo two years ago and the ones this month, you can tell her face has slipped and the wrinkles have appeared. But if you look from day to day, there's no change at all.'

Giulio wonders whether she takes her photos in the morning or the evening. Ama doesn't know. I'm thinking that she must take them in the morning, so that the thoughts that make up a day don't weigh down her face.

Pado is convinced that this photo business goes to show Elizabeth still hasn't got over her husband leaving.

'Why did he leave?' Duccio asks.

'It's a long story,' Ama sighs. 'Her husband told us he simply couldn't cope, that's all.'

'How do you not cope?' Giulio demands.

Ama glances sideways at Pado. 'It's a bit long to explain!' but now Duccio and I want to know too. 'Okay, okay,' Ama says, 'basically, one day, Elizabeth's husband was sitting having breakfast with her and he noticed that her jaw clicked every time she chewed.'

We're all a little taken aback. 'Her jaw!'

'Yes, her jaw,' Ama replies. 'He'd never really noticed it before. Anyway, he tried not to mind, but the more she ate, the more her jaw clicked away.'

'Then what?' Giulio is as curious as me.

'Well,' Ama continues, 'he thought he'd be able to ignore it, but he couldn't. Even when she stopped eating, her jaw clicked as she talked. It sounded like a bicycle chain against pedals.'

'Why didn't he tell her?' Duccio objects.

'There are some things you can't say,' Ama answers.

'But then what?' Giulio demands.

'So,' Ama carries on, 'one night, after a supper when he'd listened to Elizabeth's jaw click and click, he realised that he was always getting up to clear dishes, to go to the loo, sort out papers, anything just to avoid the noise. Elizabeth got angry and said if he kept on getting up and down, he might as well go and do something useful like walk the dog. He thought about telling her, but he couldn't. How can you tell someone their jaw clicks?'

'You say it!' Duccio protests. 'You say: excuse me, your jaw clicks!'

'But he couldn't,' Ama argues, 'because she would have said sorry and that would have been that. She would have explained that a clicking jaw is a clicking jaw and that's not a reason to be angry.'

'Well, exactly,' Duccio answers. 'Isn't that what he wanted?'

'I said it was more complicated than that.' Ama can't wait to get this story over and done with now.

'So what happened?' I ask.

'He left,' Ama snaps rather abruptly. 'He just left. He got up, cleared her plate, put the cheese in the fridge, opened the door and walked out. She shouted after him, "Where are you off to, what are you doing?" but he couldn't hear anything except the clicking of her jaw, opening and shutting like a window caught on a broken hinge.'

'And that's why she's looked tired ever since,' Pado adds.

'All that for a click in the jaw!' Giulio can't get over it. Nor can I.

I press my forehead against the seat in front and go over the story in my mind. The car engine sounds loud behind my closed eyes and I can't hear what Ama is trying to say to Pado.

8

Each spring, we drive to Italy and stay two weeks with our Italian grandparents. That's the way it's always been: two long weeks of heat and open space. Soon after we've crossed the border into Italy, Pado gets out of the car and stands on the verge taking in the air.

'It's the same air as over the border in France,' Ama sighs impatiently.

Pado turns to us and in a singing voice smiles: '*Siamo arrivati!* Welcome to Italy, *Benvenuti in Italia!*' He gets back in the car and announces that he's in a better mood.

'Maybe we should move here just for that,' Ama laughs.

Ama never enjoys staying at our grandparents' and, on the way there, she says to Pado: 'I still don't understand why we have to stay a whole two weeks. It's far too long and it's just another journey, as if we haven't got enough on our plates as it is!'

'My mother loves seeing us, and I can catch up on my reading,' Pado explains. Ama says that's not enough of an explanation for her. 'Well your mother certainly doesn't love seeing me,' she adds, 'I can tell you that much!'

'*Ma dai*, nonsense, it's all in your head!'

'I tell you she doesn't like me,' Ama insists. 'She never has. She thinks I've taken you away from her or something. Anyway, the sooner we leave again the better.'

'That's positive! Really what the children need.'

'Don't tell me what the children need Gaspare!' Ama stops Pado with a glare.

From the border to our grandparents' is a stretched-out journey of narrow motorways and cypress-tree bends. If the driving gets too much and the windows rattle with Ama's stifled complaints, we head off into villages and towns in search of churches with cold stone floors. We stand in the aisles soaking up the cool air. Pado tells us the tales of the local families and the names of the popes. We stop and run our hands along carved tombs or strain to see fading frescoes tucked away behind altars. With a torch darting over the church walls, Pado uncovers the lives of saints and describes biblical stories. He sits us down to recite and memorise the cities of Renaissance Italy. Giulio gets stuck somewhere down south. I stall on the name of Ferrara. 'Come on *ragazzi*,' Pado says, 'you can do better than that.' We try again and reach the end of the list without any mistakes. 'Nothing worse than a lazy mind!' Pado reminds us as he leads us off into the crypts. The names of Giotto, Benozzo Gozzoli and Masaccio mingle with those of Jesus and the apostles.

Ama slips off and lights a candle.

'What's that for?' Giulio asks.

'It's for Grand Maurice,' Ama answers, grabbing our hands. We form a circle. We watch the flame flutter and struggle against the draughts. Ama stares down at the polished floor. She suddenly looks the way she did two summers ago when Machance called up from France to tell us that Grand Maurice had gone missing whilst out fishing by the lake. For a couple of days Machance kept us informed and then gave up. For a week no one dared think anything and we all sat silently waiting for news until a French policeman rang to say that a drowned man had been found. Ama put down the phone and left the room with Pado following her. Hours later when Pado came back in, he sat us down and made us understand that we wouldn't see Grand Maurice again. We wanted to find Ama, we wanted to check it was true, it couldn't be true, but Pado said Ama wouldn't be coming down. I waited outside her bedroom all afternoon and listened to the walls crumbling with Ama's cries. I tried the door several times, it was locked and, every time I called out, Ama couldn't hear me because my voice had gone. No one made any food that evening and Ama didn't join us. We took the biscuits from the larder and ate them dry. Pado sat with a book on his lap, reading and re-reading the first page. Each day after that Ama shrunk a little into herself. Pado tried to comfort her and then us and then no one could comfort anyone any more. Ama never made it to the funeral in France. She could barely leave her room. Then Machance came over and the loss we felt threaded itself through all of us.

When the Italian sun weighs down too hard on the car, we adjust the windows until our sounds are muffled in a constant jostling of fresh air. Ama brings out her four picnic containers, sniffs them and insists that we stop to eat. Pado can barely hear what she's saying because of the wind whistling about the car like a battered kite. Anyway he can never believe that our food can go off so quickly.

'We haven't got far enough,' Pado insists in a loud voice. 'We have to be past Pisa before we can stop and eat. You know that!'

'Well we're going to get food poisoning unless you stop!' Ama warns him.

Pado switches into another gear instead. The car is cata-pulted forward. I try and focus on the trees lining the road, but we're going too fast. They flicker like railway tracks under a train, then they're gone, lost into the background. Pado asks Duccio to check something in a guidebook. Ama shifts nervously in her seat, turning to face Pado again.

'Do you want to kill us or what?' she asks. Gently at first, then louder. Her hair is swept upwards by the air pouring in through the open window. She brushes it violently to one side. 'Do you want to kill us or what?' she yells a second time.

'What are you on about now?' Pado sighs, exasperated, searching for a gap to overtake.

'You know exactly what I'm "on about". I'm asking you how you intend to kill us: driving the car like a maniac or poisoning us with off food?' Ama shrieks.

That's it for Pado. He pulls the car over, clears his throat and goes into a long lecture about the decomposition of foods and the spread of bacteria. Ama is not impressed. She may not be a scientist like him, but she can tell if food is off or not. She brings the sandwiches up to her nose, screwing up her face.

She puts one on the dashboard. 'That's definitely off,' she fusses. 'It's hot. The children need to eat.'

Pado stops her half-way, fighting back his rage: 'Why can't we have a fucking freezer-box like everyone else?'

Ama is astounded. 'Well if I had a fucking life like everyone else, I wouldn't even need a fucking freezer-box, because I wouldn't be sitting in this damn, fucking car!' she rages. 'Besides,' she continues, rooting through the glove compartment, 'you're the one who told me about the danger of freezer-boxes in the first place!'

Ama pulls out a yellowing newspaper article which describes the diseases affecting freezer-box users. She reads in a clipped voice: 'Freezer-boxes are havens for germs unless they're washed with boiling water,' and that's precisely what you can't do as it ruins the insulation, which, moreover, the article goes on to say, contains carcinogenic material because that's how it maintains the cold.

Once we've decided the food might be going off, we have to find a picnic spot rapidly. Finding the right picnic spot is rather like finding the right peeing spot though. We always have to make sure it's far from the traffic, in a beautiful meadow, near a river, and most importantly, that no one's deposited a puddle of urine, or something worse behind the trees or in the grass. We do this because we once had a nasty surprise in the middle of a picnic in Italy. We were sitting with our white-fresh *panini* of goat's cheese in a lush poppy patch whilst Ama got up to rinse the salad. She was checking each leaf for grit or slugs and decided to pour the rinsing water somewhere useful. She found a little pink flower, not far off, and was about to comment on its petals and the fact it needed water, when she felt her foot stick in a mass of brown excrement and white tissue paper. She let out a yelp of revulsion and slipped over as she tried to yank her leg away. Pado rushed to her rescue and we all stood up to protect our sandwiches from a shower of shit as our mother shook her foot in desperation.

'Stop moving your bloody foot,' Pado bellowed, but she wouldn't. She was so disgusted that she trembled and trembled and shook her foot up and down. 'Take your shoe off,' Pado ordered her. She couldn't bring herself to do it. So Pado had a go.

'Don't get your hands dirty. Whatever you do, don't touch it,' Ama was pleading. 'Has it gone on my ankle? Is it on my ankle?' she panicked.

Pado eventually managed to drag Ama away, without her shoe, and she sat shuddering on a tree trunk. Meanwhile, Pado was busy moving the picnic rug: 'Come on, help me boys.' We pulled the blanket down the hill and the only thing left behind was our mother's soiled shoe, a little grey island of elegance decorated by strands of filthy white loo paper which were beginning to blow into the bushes and trees. Pado crept back to fetch the shoe whilst we tried to finish our food. Ama refused to eat anything and Giulio decided that he wanted something else for lunch. Pado couldn't quite bring himself to pick up the shoe so he plucked a large leaf from a tree and used it to rub the shoe against the grass. As he did so he noticed that the shit had traces of blood in it. He couldn't stop staring at the smears of brown in amazement.

'What are you doing Gaspare?' Ama was getting impatient and wanted to leave.

'Come and have a look,' he beckoned to her.

She covered her face with her hands. 'I can't believe this, give me my shoe back.'

'No, seriously, look at this,' Pado insisted. He had broken off a long twig and was flicking bits of turd off the shoe onto the ground. Duccio, holding his nose, had joined Pado. 'Look at these traces of blood,' Pado was saying. 'See how they have coagulated in the faeces. It's the most amazing pattern.'

That was it for Ama. She was hobbling back to the car screaming, taking us two with her. Giulio threw his sandwich under a bush and said he didn't want to eat ever again. Ama had a pinched face that meant that she could easily start up the car there and then and drive off leaving Pado and Duccio studying grooves of shit on a grey leather shoe beside the road. We waited at least five minutes in the car.

Ama began hooting and banging her hand against the seat. 'What the hell are they doing?' Pado and Duccio turned up carrying the shoe at arm's length on the end of a branch. 'Just get rid of the damn thing,' Ama implored.

'No, wait,' Pado said, leaning into the car. 'Look at this blood!'

He brought the shoe up towards Ama's face.

'Take it away, take it away, immediately. Don't come near me with that fucking shoe!' Ama screamed in a shrill voice.

Pado stood back. 'Will you listen to me.' He was irritated. 'Look at the traces of blood,' he insisted.

Ama wouldn't, so Giulio and I stared out of the back seat and saw the circling rings of winding red liquid in amongst the fibrous brown.

'That,' Pado declared, 'is either a very serious case of

constipation, cancer or even something highly infectious like gastroenteritis.'

'Get rid of that fucking shoe then. Please!' Ama repeated.

Pado jumped in the driver's seat and we were off, leaving the shoe on the roadside.

Pado didn't look any calmer in the car: 'Maybe I should notify someone?'

Ama was hysterical: 'I touched the shoe, didn't I? I touched the shoe?'

'Maybe I should warn the health authorities that someone here poses a serious health risk,' Pado worried.

Giulio was anxious. 'Are they very ill?'

'Very ill, maybe dying.'

Suddenly Ama wound down her window and threw her remaining shoe into a pond. It smashed against the water. The car sped on so fast, I couldn't see the ripples opening up around it. Then Ama held her hands out in front of her like two filthy rags.

Pado thought maybe we should try and find the ill person, search the lanes for a face with pale eyes and streaming forehead: the tell-tale signs. We observed all the passers-by, the people having picnics in lay-bys and even the farmers toiling away on their tractors. We shot past a huffing man on a bicycle with a tatty-looking blue jacket.

Duccio turned and glanced at him: 'He looked pretty ill, didn't he?'

'Keep going!' Ama cried, 'We don't want his germs near us!'

'But what if it's him?' Pado protested, slowing down.

'We can't just stop someone and ask them if they've laid a turd behind a bush two miles away!' Ama blasted.

'Well why not, if he's a threat to public health?' Pado said.

Duccio warned us that the man was catching up. Pado slowed down to a crawl. The man wondered why we were stopping and pulled over too: '*Buongiorno!* Can I help you, are you lost?'

'Don't touch him, don't breathe in, whatever you do don't go near him,' Ama whispered, from the edge of her seat.

Pado lowered his window a fraction and, with his head tightly inside the car, politely told the man through the thin gap that we didn't need any assistance.

'Okay, *va bene*, have a nice day.' The man smiled and cycled off.

'He looked ill,' Duccio started.

We all agreed, yet it was more the redness of his eyes and the thick clotted hair than signs of some hideous disease.

'No, I don't think it could have been him,' Pado declared.

'Let's get the hell out of here,' Ama pleaded.

We had no choice but to pull into a garage and take it in turns in the bathroom with Pado. He rolled our sleeves up to our elbows and showered us in soap and scalding water. Ama went to the bathroom alone, for a long time, and came out with a new pair of trousers on.

'I managed to wash my legs,' she said, pleased to have shed the risks of disease. 'What shall I do with my socks and trousers, maybe they have a bin?'

'No, we should throw them somewhere else,' Pado insisted. Leaving them in a bin, he said, might mean a child finding them or, worse still, a dog could lick them and then lick a child's face and the chain of disease would be set off, hurtling down the motorways behind us.

I searched high and low for bits of shit and blood in the car. When no one was looking, I studied the soles of my shoes and those of my brothers. They all seemed clean. My hands were still red from the scrubbing. I began to gaze out of the window thinking of all the people who might go for a walk in that wood, sit down and then, in the middle of their sandwich, simply keel over. Their friends would think they choked on their bread, but the real cause, hidden to all, would be the stringy threads of minuscule blood and germs eating away at them from inside the brown-stained grass. What if someone tried on the shoe? What if the disease crawled up their leg into their heart? Then what about thoughts? What if germs are like thoughts and thoughts like germs, and if you think something you can contaminate a person, a place, the whole world?

9

We are exhausted by the time we arrive at our grandparents'
in Umbria. They have a rambling solid house with walls so
thick that three large people can sit across the window ledges.
A burnt-green vineyard stretches in front of the building.
Its descending paths engrave the landscape with a deep
criss-cross pattern. Nonno, our grandfather, spends most
of his time up on the balcony, staring into the vineyard.
Around October, as the fruit is a rich purple and bursting
against its skin, he gives the order for the grapes to be picked.
If you look at Nonno when he is there, up on the balcony,
you can't really see him at all. All you can see is a brown face
with rows and rows of vines streaming into the reflections of
his eyes. Ama says he is so dark that it's better, for his sake, if
he never comes to England, especially where Machance lives.
There you have grey-haired women who teeter along in high
heels saving insults in their mouths and minds for the first
foreign face to turn up. Anyway, Pado adds, Nonno loathes
leaving his house in Italy and he'll never make him come to
England because he can't speak English and the sky is so low
that he might feel he can't cope, and waste away.

*　　*　　*

Our grandmother, Nonna, has a meal ready for the first evening. She hands me a spoon to lift off the sauce that sticks to the sides of the bowl when everyone has been served. Afterwards, she holds up the scraped-out bowl to Ama. 'See how they love our Italian food! A change from all those sandwiches.'

Ama nods dully and searches the room for Pado.

The evening is hot. Nonna opens the dining-room door. The noise of crickets, in the long grass outside, bursts in. Nonna fans herself with her hands, she brings them up from behind her back and spreads her fingers to rake the draught. Her hands whirl about her head and push at the night. Once she's started she doesn't stop. Her gestures carry on throughout dinner, and the darker the night, the more the candles on the table dance with her hands as they gather up garlands of air. Even in winter, Ama tells us, Nonna sits on the steps of the house and throws up her hands to chase away the damp skies and rain.

Nonno welcomes the rain. 'In Sicily we never had good rain,' he explains. 'Umbria,' he is convinced, has the perfect climate and, because of that, he has one of the best vineyards in the region. That's why the mayor keeps on increasing his taxes to make him join the local wine co-operative. 'I won't give in!' He thumps the table.

Pado is busy describing our travels. He tells his parents and their guests about our recent stay in England and how he's going to ask for further funding from his old university in Rome for research. He fishes his latest book out of his case and hands it across the table. He recounts how, during our visit to Brussels two months ago, he met America's most prominent pathologist.

Nonna admires his book, its coloured, gleaming surface. 'What a clever husband you have,' she whispers to Ama and passes her the book.

Ama hands it straight onto the next person. 'Oh, I don't want it. I know the whole thing off by heart, back to front,' she sighs.

Nonno is sombre. He has his two friends sitting next to him and they are both deeply preoccupied too. Pado asks to know what the problem is. Nonno tells us about Aldo Moro, the former prime minister, who's recently been kidnapped. He's being held hostage by the Red Brigades. Pado knows a bit about it. He shakes his head in disbelief as they describe how his five bodyguards were killed. Nonno adds that the government doesn't appear to want to give in to the kidnappers' demands.

'It's a dreadful thing for Italy,' he worries.

'They might well kill him unless something is done soon,' his friend joins in.

Then they talk about the letters Aldo Moro keeps on sending to the government and how his wife is writing letters back in the daily newspapers because that's the only way she can communicate with him.

'Do you remember that other kidnap where they sent bits

of the hostage's ears and fingers to make sure they paid the ransom?' Nonno's second friend adds.

As everyone talks of the kidnap and their stories soak up the room, I concentrate on a gecko crawling near the light over the window outside. It passes round the window and through the door. It grips the top of the hinge, then slides down the gap. It pauses, awkwardly, between the hinge and the wall. Nonna stands up. She walks towards the door. She's about to shut it. I half close my eyes. I say to myself that no one will save Aldo Moro if the gecko is squashed. Nonna pushes the base of the door with her foot. The door slams. I jump up and rush to the window. I watch the gecko scurry off into the climbing plant on the wall. Aldo Moro will live!

'*Cosa fai?* Come and sit down,' Nonna says, leading me back to my chair and handing me more food.

'Oh don't worry, he can go outside if he wants,' Ama tells her.

When the weather is very dry, and Nonno is worried about his fruit trees in amongst the vines, the farm workers come over the hills with a tractor, dragging a tank on wheels full of water from the stream below the vineyard. The tank floats like a ship at sea with a pipe as a mast that gushes litres of water onto the bare roots of the trees: apricot, nectarine, pear, peach and plum.

Nonno directs the workers from the balcony. 'More water for that tree. That's enough for that one. That doesn't need any. On the roots! On the roots! *Ancora!*' he shouts.

I sit behind him, seeing which tree is more deserving and which one will be left dry. Nonno explains each tree to me.

He picks off leaves and runs his fingers round their shapes so that I remember their names.

'If only I had an almond leaf to show you,' he tells me. 'That is the tree of Sicily.'

Nonno calls Duccio and Giulio over. Together we walk across the garden until we reach a clearing amongst the trees. Nonno quickly checks no one is looking and then lifts me up by the forearms and swings me round and round until I feel dizzy. The branches and leaves skim my feet, wrapping my ankles in sharp flicks. I focus on the ground below me, curving and bending between Nonno's shoes. My thoughts overturn and tumble through my mind, bouncing away the painful sequences that turn each day into a string of threats and missed opportunities. I want Nonno to keep going for ever, until the thoughts settle and fix, until Grand Maurice never died, until Aldo Moro is released and no more ferries are going to sink and all the diseases that are going to kill stop spreading. Keep going Nonno! Keep going! My mind soars and drops, nothing is in place, nothing is fixed. I fade into a circle of moving air and there is no meaning to be felt. I hear Duccio's voice, like a song, coming and going. He wants a go too. Nonno grounds me to a halt. I can't stand up and I fall onto the grass watching the clouds surge above me.

Nonno gives up after one go with Duccio. 'You're too big. *Sei troppo grande caro!*' he apologises. Then he says it's probably my last year too. 'I certainly won't be any stronger next summer!'

Nonno sweeps Giulio off his feet. Giulio's hair lifts into a horizontal pattern, a scarf rolling through the air, a wave over his head. I watch Giulio's eyes blinking, filling with images: house, vineyard, trees, stream, hills, sky, round and round, again and again. Nonno is lost in the movement too, held to the earth by Giulio's swinging. He closes his eyes so as not to fall.

There's always so much commotion during the fruit-tree watering that Nonna tries to keep us inside. There are maybe ten men, and the noise of the running tractor, stopping and starting, by the trees, and then the burst of litres of muddy water. The dog is frantic and manages to get out to follow the tractor, barking. Nonna can't bear the noise. With each bark she looks like she might turn mad.

She rubs her hands along the kitchen table and pleads, 'Stop that dog, someone please stop him.'

I run off after him. Every time I get close enough to grab him, he slips away, tail wagging.

'No, not like that, call him gently!' the farm workers laugh.

So I beckon him softly, 'Lorenzo, come here, please.'

Then I think he doesn't understand, so I say it in Italian, but he digs at the base of the fruit trees, rolling in the mud and eating small black things.

'What's he eating? Stop him at once!' Nonna yells from the kitchen window.

I rush and realise that everywhere about me are hundreds of tadpoles gasping for water, shrivelling in the sun and slipping into death, their soft backs drying up in the mud or being eaten by the dog. I stand bolted to the spot, panic transforming me.

I run to the men spraying the trees and yank at their shirt sleeves, 'Stop! Stop!'

I point to the tadpoles, some nearly frogs, spurting out of the end of the pipe with their minuscule hind legs crushed by the weight of the water, kicking out at the air as they are sent dashing against the earth. Some hit the trees, others fall into temporary puddles, swim about for two minutes and then sink as the water slides into tunnels of crumbling earth. The men seem unconcerned by my worried face and push me teasingly. I desperately put the survivors in puddles.

'There are plenty more where they came from. *Non importa!*' the men say.

They carry on firing flows of tadpoles across the fruit trees.

I forget the dog and run to the house. Ama asks what's wrong. Nonna wants to know where the dog is. I don't answer. I can't answer. Not now. Thousands of lives are being shot like bullets into the dry ground. I dart around for a bucket and fill one with tap water. Back in the vineyard, I throw the tadpoles as fast as I can into the bucket and watch them spin to the bottom, soaking in the water, then rising up, bellies to the surface, or writhing a little with their tails to show a sign of life. I'm crying because I hate the men who are doing this and because I can't seem to get the tadpoles into the bucket fast enough. They are in the grass, sliced up in blades of cutting green, stuck to the bark of the trees, unseen and unheard. They are everywhere. I can't get them all in the bucket at once. I begin choosing the biggest and the least dry. Then I regret that I'm ignoring some and picking up others, so I race back gathering them up too, just in case. But the 'just-in-case ones' plunge like stones to the bottom of the bucket and their heads nod dead against the plastic sides. Others swim crippled shapes in the palm of my hand and then fall still. I've been at it for a while when Nonna comes to pull me away: 'They're only tadpoles, stop it and come in,' but she hasn't seen their tiny mouths opening and closing, silent pleas to be saved. I carry on. My knees are covered in mud and my hands cut from scrabbling away at the earth.

I sprint down to the stream below. My bucket is full to the edges with the dying. It's ten minutes down to the water that slides past the vineyard walls. I thump my feet against the earth to scare the vipers, the way Nonno told us, but I can't beat my shoes too hard for risk of the tadpoles slipping out of their bucket. Suddenly Aldo Moro is in my mind. I say to myself that if I get to the stream without thinking of him, and no more tadpoles dying, he'll be saved. But then, within a few steps, I've started thinking about Aldo Moro and why they haven't released him. The thoughts are all around me now, in the bushes, under the stones and wrapped inside the trees. They are coiling themselves around my feet. I delve my hand into the bucket. I try and awaken the dying tadpoles. I plead with them. I keep them moving.

The stream runs beneath me, through the low branches. My heart is in my belly because more and more tadpoles look dead. I release them into the pools at the side of the stream. I can see the traces of tractor tyres sunk into the mud. I imagine the tractor pipe and the sucking noise as it draws up water and tadpoles by the dozen, hoovering them up regardless, ripping off tails and heads, whirling up the stones and sending havoc into the clear moving stream. I fish the lifeless tadpoles out of the bucket and run them through the stream with my fingers. Its water is fresh with bursting bubbles. Other tadpoles die in the stream and drift along, carried like limp twigs, only to get caught in nooks of reed or swept under stones. I scoop some of them up and cushion their death in the folds of my pockets for safety.

Nonno tells us that this stream marks the end of his land. If you look over to the other side, the trees are different, the fields are different and there is a white shade of light that soaks into the earth. It forms a belt across you and grips you tight. Nonno is convinced that 'no one could ever grow vines over there'. The cypress trees along the horizon sway to the splashed rush of the stream. I wonder which way the tadpoles go when they become frogs. Do they go up towards the shade of the cypresses or do they stay on this side, in the vineyard and rocky earth? There is a fallen tree trunk across the stream. It slides and rips into the water. I know that we're not allowed to cross the stream. I know that this is the end of the land, yet my pockets are packed with the dead and I have to bury them on the other side. A place no one will disturb.

I run along the tree trunk and jump down on the other side. I walk up the hill, the stream shrinking behind me into the distance. I make for the big cypress trees dividing the horizon. They reach as high as the blue of the sky, their branches curving inwards like flickering flames. My grandparents' house is a fading dot down below me. I see the point where the vineyards end and the shimmering grass begins. You can see the stream trailing a watery line, but not the fallen trunk across it. Everywhere is the same now, the same white-spreading light, the same hills tumbling one into another, forgetting the house behind. I go from cypress tree to cypress tree, and under each one, I bore a little hole with my thumb for each tadpole. I push the earth over the crumpled drying bodies and stamp the ground. I run back to the stream, stumbling and falling in the uneven grass. I have no problem crossing back over the water. It's as if the path I walked earlier has remained, with footprints to guide me. I splash the water with my feet. I wait for the gentle current to fill my shoes, over my socks, down onto my toes. The stream comes in currents of cold and warm. Ripped weed rushes past. The earth sinks under my feet, a little with every move, gravel slipping gradually, gradually down into the mud. I look back at the leaning grass hill painted with trees. The air is weighted with heat.

10

Nonno rarely leaves his garden and he comes up with excuses when we ask him to accompany us into town. The only reason he'll come, he repeats, is to go to church or if we can help him persuade the mayor to stop hassling him with plans for the wine co-operative. Pado has been trying to convince the mayor to give up for years though.

'They simply can't accept that I have the best vines in the area,' Nonno sighs. 'Besides, you can't mix everyone's wine together like they do at the co-operative. What if some grapes are from a vineyard of clay and rocks and others are from the sunny hills on the way to the village? That's not the same taste at all.'

I know that Nonno's wine is fruity and dark because of the tadpoles that find their way into the secret furrows of earth. They die curled up round the vine roots to feed them over the winter with their rotting black shine.

There's a shed at the bottom of one of the vineyards, in a dip in the landscape. From there you can get a view of the garden behind the house. I only know because I went under the shed and it had a crack in its bottom wall. I told Duccio not to make me go under there, but he did. He said that maybe there were some tadpoles left in a drying puddle and this was their last chance. I hesitated two days. I circled and circled the shed, refusing to slide under. I sat in the sun and tried to catch a whiff of damp earth or the sound of tadpoles as their hind legs grew, but I couldn't see or hear anything. Then Duccio said that it had to be the last hiding place for dying tadpoles because it's the lowest point in the vineyard and the waters run there, and if the waters run there then it had to be festering with tadpoles and, the longer I waited, the more they were dying. So I squeezed through the farm tools and cut my knee. It took a while to get right under the shed, but when I did I couldn't hear my brothers' voices or feel the earth, all I could see was a tunnel view of the garden below. In the garden, I saw Nonna and Ama sitting opposite each other on wicker chairs. Ama was trying to read her book, but Nonna kept on interrupting, pointing at her with big gestures. Ama was staring at the ground beneath her, with an expressionless face. Nonna's shouting voice sprayed words into the air, over the top of the house. I strained to hear what she was saying, then suddenly Ama got up, pushed over her chair and ran out of the garden without looking back. From where I was, I could see her racing through the vegetable garden, scaling the low stone wall and storming down the path towards the stream. She stopped for a minute to catch her breath, bending over, reaching out in front of her. Then she set off again and disappeared into the landscape, the colour of her clothes fading into the dry, brittle yellow of the grass. I waited for her to reappear, then gave up. I forced my way back from under the shed and came up into the light to face Duccio and Giulio waiting expectantly.

'Well, where are the tadpoles?' they asked. I didn't answer. I didn't explain. They both turned and looked past me down the vineyard, as if they knew something was wrong.

On Sundays, we make the steep walk, beginning at ten, to reach the church at half past ten. Nonno and Pado prefer to follow in the car later. Ama has a coloured parasol to protect herself from the sun. We don't take the dog with us. Nonna makes sure he's tied to the kitchen table even if Ama thinks it's cruel and that you wouldn't begin to get away with that in England but then again, this isn't England and you can't take a dog to church anywhere. Half-way to the village, and about fifteen minutes from the church, Nonna goes silent. She always stops talking at the same place, slightly before the turning to the wood, when she sees the vine with the twisted and twirled wire like a halo. From then on, we have to whisper or walk far behind her. She recites her prayers, her fingers rushing round her rosary. I follow the way her lips move up and down with each step and whispered vow. By the time we get to the church door, with the carved angels bunched onto its handle, she is ready to look up again. She enters the church and her eyes drink in the multicoloured light from all the stained-glass windows.

During Mass, Nonna rocks from side to side. Ama holds my hand and, with a finger, runs along the lines of prayers so I can read too. Pado and Nonno show up late and find a place standing at the back. Ama turns to find their faces in the crowd and waves discreetly. The priest's voice mumbles and rises as he bows and chants.

Ama looks at us, 'Are you all right?'

We hope no one has heard her speak English. I think that boy over there has now and he's nudging someone and, together, they're thinking: who are those children?

'*Allez*. Concentrate darling. Please!' Ama urges, in French this time.

Now the old women over there are really staring too. I know who they are. They are the women who, as we leave church, congratulate Pado for having three sons and pinch our cheeks and squeeze the flesh in their wrinkled hands until it's the worst twisting pain. I'm looking at the priest and the two boys in white, standing at his side. They ring the bell, bring on books and kneel when it's time. Nonna wants Duccio and I to be like those boys one day. What happens if we ring the bell when we're not meant to though, or if Giulio tries to make us laugh from his pew?

'You don't make mistakes like that,' Nonna is sure, because, when you're up there, 'it's different, you're in another world.'

On the way out of church, Nonna takes us to the cross in the side chapel. She bows her head and clasps her rosary. She touches the cross and kisses her hand. She lines us up to do the same. I struggle to clear my mind quickly. I mustn't touch the cross with a bad thought in my head. If I do, it'll stick to the cross for ever and every time I see it I won't be able to think of anything but the bad thought.

Once we've chatted to a few people in front of the church, we head down the main cobbled street to the market stalls. Ama examines all the fresh produce, picking up fruit and smelling it. She strikes up conversation with the cheese woman and asks for a recipe. The woman offers to sell her some cheese to take back home. She refuses and walks away. She gazes bewildered at everyone else's shopping bags and packed baskets, her own hands light and purposeless. She grabs Giulio and clutches him by the sleeve. He pulls away and dashes to Pado. I stand back from the noisy market and watch my family walk on ahead. I feel like slipping under a stall and letting the stampeding crowd pass me by. Something in me wants to watch my parents' feet, desperately rushing around trying to find me and then washing away, blending into the mass of people, gone. Under a stall, completely alone, I could turn into this open space, calm and sheltered. My brothers are lucky. They sit on the sides of the car and can rest their elbows on the doors. They are propped up and sturdy for the long trips. I'm floating with nothing to hold me down. I want to be like the farmers in the market who return, week after week. I want to stay here, now, and never move.

Nonno and Nonna decide to walk home together. We leave them to head off down the hill and cram back into the car. All the vehicles leaving the market make their way down the narrow lanes with us. A truck halts in front and then a van comes in from the side. We come to a standstill.

'Why we couldn't walk, I really don't know,' Ama complains.

Pado is hooting and the car behind also.

'*Si! Si!* Hang on!' the driver ahead of us shouts back.

93

'*Ma guarda questo cornuto! Cosa sta facendo!* What an idiot! What the hell is he doing?' Pado whacks the dashboard with his fists and hoots again.

Ama turns to look out of the window. The man in the car, to our side, is gesturing something to her. She quickly sits up straight, trying to shield her window with her elbow and shoulder to stop Pado from noticing. It doesn't work.

'Bastard!' Pado shrieks when he sees. He reaches for the door.

'Stop it, Gaspare. For goodness' sake. Calm down!' Ama beseeches him. 'Ignore him! Please!'

'This is my home! I'll do what the hell I want for once.'

The man gets out of his car. Ama buries her face in her hands, her foot kicks the floor repeatedly. Pado is thinking of all his favourite insults in English. He swills them round his mouth, savouring their bite. He is launching into 'Son of a fucking . . .' when the man stops dead.

'*Ma ciao* Gaspare! *Come stai?* How have you been? Good to see you back!'

'Alessandro!' Pado beams. 'I can't believe it!'

He jumps out of the car and shakes the man by the hand. The two of them step onto the gravel verge and exchange news. The cars behind are hooting even more angrily, over and over again. The minutes swell with the noise of waiting.

Without a word, Ama climbs into the driver's seat and sets off down the hill. Pado doesn't notice at first, then he starts sprinting behind us, yelling at us to stop. Giulio and I can't help laughing. Even Ama and Duccio are in fits. Pado shouts and gesticulates wildly. His running legs fracture the wing mirrors with reflections of disjointed dancing steps. Ama

94

peers, from side to side, into the small squares of silver glass to look at Pado. She smiles to herself and, with her smile, she draws the chasing figure closer and closer to her. Pado is right up behind us. His face appears between the lines of the metal grid on the back window. His eyes are blinking in the sun. We slow down and pull into the entrance of a house. Pado swings open the car door, breathless and sweating.

'Very funny,' he pants. 'Very bloody funny.'

'Serves you right,' Ama giggles.

We try not to laugh again all the way back to Nonno's and everyone knows not to catch Ama's eye in case we do. I fit this moment into place. I save it, an image to hold up against the headaches.

As we enter the drive up to the house, Ama gently whispers something in Pado's ear.

'What?' he asks.

'Remember to tell your mother to stop getting at me,' Ama repeats. 'I'm really not in the mood. I'm not going to sit and take her snide remarks any more!'

Pado looks at her, unsure of what to reply. We glance at each other across the back seat. Maybe Pado's waiting for us to get out of the car. He slows down and parks up against the barn. We rush out to leave them alone, but Ama steps out with us and closes her door. Pado remains in his seat, staring into the cracks of the barn wall.

That night, in bed, I'm looking at the geckos rushing about the arches of the windows outside. It's almost the beginning of daylight. I can see someone out in the garden, by the large cluster of prickly pears on the steps down into the first vineyard. It's Ama. She's wearing a long night dress and some broken straw shoes that Nonna uses to pick herbs in. She is checking to see if there is any fruit on the plants. She examines each plant, gently, careful to avoid the spikes and the rip of the brambles underneath. She holds her head low, with her chin lost in the folds of her night dress. From here, in the half-light, she has the same profile as Machance. I hope she's all right. I put on my shoes and run out to join her, dressed in my pyjamas.

'What are you doing, Ama?'

She raises her eyes, startled.

'Oh no, Jean-Pio, don't tell me, you've got one of your damn headaches?'

'No, I just . . .'

Ama cuts in, exasperated. 'Listen, the doctor in England said there wasn't anything wrong with you. Please go back to bed now. Go on, off you go.'

'But, I wanted . . .'

'Do as I say for once!' Ama pleads with me.

I stand there speechless, stuck to the ground.

Ama looks at me straight in the eyes. She waits a couple of seconds for me to go. I still can't move, I'm stuck staring at her. Then she shouts, her voice stings the air. 'Tell me, Jean-Pio, do you really think you're the only one round here with bloody headaches? Go on, tell me! Do you ever think what it's like for other people? Have you any idea what it's like for me with my mother's health and Grand Maurice gone? And all this bloody travelling to and fro, and staying in this damn place with your grandmother following me around like a dog all day long. That's a fucking headache! That's what it is. A fucking headache! A bloody waste of life!'

She kicks at the ground, harder and harder, until the shins of her legs are covered in fine brown earth. Her voice grows smaller. 'A bloody waste of life that's what! Do you understand that, can you understand that? An utter waste of life!' she repeats.

Ama is dazed by her own words, stunned into a short silence. She watches me as I turn and walk to the house. Then she dashes after me. She grabs me and pulls me backwards, towards her. She clasps me so tight I can hardly breathe. She nestles her head in my hair. She cries, slowly, tenderly. I can feel her wet eyes against my scalp. She holds on to me, pushing me further and further into her chest. We stand there folded into each other. Then she lets go and kisses me.

'I'm sorry my love. I'm so sorry.'

I open the door at the back of the house. Ama disappears down the garden steps. I make my way through the kitchen. My head is knocked by her words. I fight for something to replace this moment. I try and dredge something up. Nothing comes.

Nonna is suddenly standing there in front of me.

'Thanks for waking me up,' she says. 'What a racket you were making! What's wrong with your mother this time?'

'Nothing,' I say, 'it's me. I couldn't sleep.'

'One of your headaches again! Your father told me about that. Honestly, what a way to bring up children. My poor boy.'

She ruffles my hair and takes me by the arm. She drags me along the corridor. She bangs with her fist on Pado and Ama's bedroom door.

'No! No! Pado's asleep,' I try and tell her.

Nonna doesn't care. She knocks again and, when there's no reply, she pushes open the door and switches the lamp on. Pado throws up his arms and shields his eyes from the light.

'The boy has a headache!' Nonna says, pointing at me.

Pado looks across the room, barely awake.

'What? Who? Where's Ava?'

'How should I know? She's your wife,' Nonna huffs. She turns and leaves, telling Pado to do something for me.

Pado sits up in bed. There are a few open books lost in the sheets at his feet.

'What's wrong? A headache?' he says, squinting at me. 'Go back to sleep, that's the best thing for a headache.' Pado leans against the wall with a pillow wedged behind him. 'Find your mother and ask her to come back to bed,' he adds wearily.

I want to tell him Ama is walking about the garden in broken shoes. I want to tell him I didn't have a headache. It's Ama who isn't well. I just switch the light off and leave.

11

It's time to head off towards England again via Lyon for a meeting of the European Histopathologists. Giulio and I don't want to leave. We chase through the garden, prolonging every minute and second until we have to get back in the car. I want to go into the vines one last time. I want to chase the tadpoles further down the stream into the part where it crosses the woods and the tractor pipe can't reach them. I try persuading Pado that I have left something in the vineyard. He hands me bags and boxes to carry instead, to make sure I stay put by the car. Then Pado tells me we should bump into Alberto Devoti, a scientist friend of his, in Lyon. Apparently he has made enormous breakthroughs in the treatment of headaches.

'He will sort you out,' Pado assures me.

He passes me Professore Devoti's book. I look at the photo of the author on the back page. He is sitting at a desk, legs crossed. He has a microscope on a shelf in the background. I don't want to meet him.

*   *   *

We have to get into the car. Nonna grabs Pado. She holds his head in her hands and kisses him on the forehead. She leaves her lips pressed up against the long shallow wrinkle above his eyes. She mumbles, 'Goodbye, *figlio mio*, take great care of yourself. Come back soon. Please!' She hugs us all. When I hold on too long, she gently pushes me away with a smile and adjusts her shirt. Pado packs up the rest of the car under Nonno's worried gaze because today is Ama's thirty-third birthday and no one's mentioned it yet. Ama hasn't really spoken since breakfast. She barely answers if you ask her something and she merely nods if you call her name. We set off, with Nonno waving goodbye from the edge of the vineyard, and my eyes stuck to his disappearing figure, keeping his silhouette in my mind for the journey, for always.

Ama curves inwards on the front seat and closes her eyes. Pado reaches out and searches for her hands. He tries to break her tight fists. She won't give in. She has her eyes, hands and jaw firmly clenched. There is no music, no game to distract, no churches or cows to point out, just a relentless sense of exasperation. Finally, when Ama gets out for a pee at a clean motorway station, Pado turns the engine off and calmly explains to us that there is to be no talk of birthdays. No one is to say 'Happy Birthday' or 'Congratulations', nothing like that at all. Only a smile, if we need to, but at the right moment, nothing else. We all want to know why, as birthdays are normally for cakes and presents, Ama told us so herself. Pado does his best to explain that Ama isn't too happy about driving around all the time.

'She probably would have preferred something a bit cosier, not spending the day in the car. You understand? *Capito?*' he tells us.

Ama emerges from the petrol station with an 'I know you've been talking about me' glare. She gets back in the car and pulls the door shut. She watches the passing trucks and the pupils of her eyes quiver with the outside world. I sink back into my seat. Duccio is reading the index of his book. Giulio is dozing off. Pado overtakes the car in front, desperate to reach somewhere different.

Maybe it's all my fault, this travelling to reach a doctor who can't help because no one can understand about the headaches. Maybe it's the thoughts that have seeped into the car and which I can't clear away fast enough. Maybe it's them turning Ama's life into a waste. 'A bloody waste of life,' she screamed. I want Ama to be happy like before, the way she laughs with Elizabeth, the kind of smile she has when Pado turns up after a conference. I store up happy memories and send them to her in my mind. I imagine her walking along the beach before we get onto the ferry, her toes curling over the pebbles, hands reaching for the skies. I think hard and fight against the bad days, the days when the threaded seams of Ama's front seat have been picked bare by her agitated fingers and the worry of Machance alone in England. And then Grand Maurice who sank to the bottom of a lake with Machance expecting him back home, looking through the window into the vines. Perhaps she'd poured him a glass of wine. Maybe it was never cleared away. It stood there waiting for ever. The liquid turned a mouldy brown and dried, an unbroken rim of loss round the glass.

Ama told us that Machance had only really got nervous when evening came. Grand Maurice often stayed out until supper, stopping in hamlets and villages on his way back from fishing. But that night, he didn't return. Machance went out with a torch along the vineyards shouting Grand Maurice's name. She walked up to the hill above the house and watched the paths disperse into the ringing night. She listened for the familiar noise of his walking and the tapping of his stick on the dry ground. She left the kitchen door ajar and sat on a chair waiting. She didn't eat. She couldn't reach the food piled high in the cupboards, her arms too fragile with fear. She folded and re-folded her clothes, up in the bedroom, and stared at the trees outside, begging them to distract her. She left the shutters open and the night insects knocked, frustrated, against the glass. Then in the morning, when there was still no sign of Grand Maurice, Machance informed the police. They sent out search parties over the vineyards and grasslands and took a dog to help them. Machance drove down the lanes with the village mayor, stopping at the places Grand Maurice loved. She thought of the rabbit trap and how something like that might have happened again. She asked the farmers to check their ditches and traps. The police went to the lake and found nothing. No one found anything, only deserted roads and absence. Machance kept going the first two days, hoping that Grand Maurice would turn up. She stuck to her daily habits, and walking to the post office to call us in England gave her another routine. By the third day, she stopped. A feeling of sorrow broke in. It swept along her week until a policeman turned up at the door to say Grand Maurice's body had been found by a fisherman, snagged and wound in reeds, washing to and fro across the mud of the lake. Then Machance locked all the doors and windows and sat alone in the house until she could talk again, but she only had enough words to get through the funeral and make her way to England.

I stare at the back of Ama's head. I watch her hair gathered together and pressed up against the seat. Then Pado shouts at me: '*Ma non è vero?* You haven't been doing your job Jean-Pio! Look at the fucking petrol sign! *Merda!*'

The light has suddenly gone red. I can't believe it. When? How?

'Don't get angry,' Ama snaps curtly. 'It's your own ruddy fault for not checking when we filled up! You can't expect the boy to do everything!'

Pado would love to be thankful that Ama has spoken at last. Instead, her words infuriate him.

'We'll get some petrol in the next town,' he mutters.

'You do realise that it's Sunday, don't you?' Ama adds.

Normally Ama would have told Pado that we're not in a hurry, that there's no point taking the back lanes to save one minute here or there, but today was a day when she couldn't speak. Now it's too late. Maybe we should stop and talk about it, work out a plan, because we are definitely in the middle of nowhere. The last village or town was at least ten kilometres away.

'Pado,' I splutter, 'maybe we should turn back!'

He glances down at the petrol dial. 'Don't worry. There's bound to be some town soon.'

'What town would that be Gaspare?' Ama wonders.

I can't believe I didn't check the kilometres. That's what I usually do each time we fill up with petrol. I work out how many kilometres we can do for the amount of petrol. I always get there before the red petrol sign. I fall back into my seat. Duccio and Giulio are looking at me strangely. Duccio doesn't make mistakes in working out the routes and Giulio always keeps his conference papers in order. I desperately search out of the window for the next town. Wherever I look, there are only more and more plains of crops. Each time we pass a bend, I'm sure there's going to be a village, but each time it's only an isolated hamlet without a soul in sight. Pado asks Duccio to check the distance to the next town. Duccio spreads out his map and measures the distance with his thumb. He reckons it's about twenty kilometres.

'We should make it,' Pado sighs, relieved.

We turn into the main square of a small town. People are streaming into church. The bells are ringing above us. All the pavements are tightly packed with cars. The houses have their shutters folded inwards and bolted against the sun. The petrol station, on the furthest side of town, is closed.

Pado is concerned, but he immediately suggests we drive to the next town which is only another eight kilometres away. 'There has to be a petrol station open there,' he hopes.

'There is no way we're setting off into the wilderness with

only a few drops of petrol left. Be reasonable!' Ama spits, arms folded, leaning against the car.

So Pado walks to the church to find the garage owner. He emerges with a large man, Gino, who explains that he would love to help Pado, but he hasn't had a new delivery of petrol for days. He's still waiting. He doesn't even have any cans to give us either. We thank him kindly and get back in the car.

Pado is adamant. 'We have to carry on to the next town. Maybe there we might at least be able to buy a can.'

Ama hisses something about 'stupid shortcuts' and 'everything always being shut in Italy'.

We drive into the countryside beyond the town. Pado turns the engine off and lets the car roll every time we get to the top of a hill. After a couple of kilometres, the engine dribbles to a halt next to a vast cornfield. Pado smashes his foot down on the accelerator. The car won't move. Ama is seething.

Pado gets out without a word. He searches through the boot for a petrol can and walks off, towards the next town, with a semi-apologetic, semi-'don't you dare say anything' wave. We watch him march briskly down the lane. He disappears into a dip, emerging again further on, even smaller. I can't believe I didn't check the petrol sign. What have I done? Ama orders us out of the car. She sits with the windows wound up. After a while, we can hear her crying and blowing her nose into her remaining tissues. She shoves on a Liszt tape and her gaze knocks against the inside of the windscreen. Pado says that playing the tape machine without the engine on runs the car battery down, but Ama obviously doesn't care. Not now. She leans her face against the side-window, her skin crushes a soft white shape on the glass. I step round

105

the car, trying to grab her attention and get her to give me a sign, any sign.

In the field next to the car, Duccio and I work out a way of turning wilted corn stalks into catapults. Giulio shreds grass into bundles. In case, he says, Pado doesn't come back in time and we need something to sleep on. Ama finally emerges from the car and finds some shade under a tree to read her book. Giulio is sure that Ama would cheer up if he sang 'Happy Birthday' to her. I dissuade him. We shouldn't mention her birthday. Pado told us so. Duccio reckons that was before we broke down. Now she's really having a bad birthday. We have to come up with something fast. What if Pado can't find any petrol? What if we have to stay here? Giulio decides he's got to do something for Ama. He starts pulling some leaves off the lines of cabbages next to him and flicking the mud-covered bits onto the ground.

'What are you doing?' we ask.

'Making a cake for Ama,' he says in a soft voice.

I join in and strip the cabbages of their leaves. The leaves are hard and tough with white edges. I rip little bits and crush them into a pulp on a flat stone. We pat it together into lumps. We put the lumps onto the middle of a large leaf and squash them down. We decorate the edges with dry sticks.

We carry the cake over to Ama in procession. She doesn't notice us arriving until we are right up in front of her. She looks up with a start and we burst into song.

'Happy Birthday to you! Happy Birthday to you! Happy Birthday dear Ama . . .'

She scrambles to her feet, bewildered. Then she grips the tree beside her and turns, her forehead against the trunk. We pass the cake to each other, waiting for her to face us. She doesn't. Duccio steps forward and tugs at her shirt, 'Ama what is it?'

Ama clutches the tree even harder. Her hunched back trembles, tears break into her words. 'Sorry boys. I'm sorry.'

She moves in a ring round the tree without letting go. She takes the cake from us with one hand and whispers, 'What would I do without you?' Then she says, 'Go on, go and play!' We stand there for a while before retreating slowly, looking back over our shoulders. Then we run, each in a different direction, trying to think of a game to carry us on our way.

Ama wanders to the car to fetch something to drink. The bottle of mineral water has practically boiled in the boot. Ama leaves it in the shade to cool down. A truck stops in front of us. It's the first vehicle to go past since Pado left.

A large man with a dog gets out and walks towards us. '*Signora Messina!*' he shouts. It takes us a while to realise it's Gino from the last town. He tells us Pado phoned him about half an hour earlier, exhausted, from the petrol station in the next town, which was also shut. Gino has already picked him up and brought him back along the fast road. Now he has come for us. He ties our car to his truck with a rope and we swing our way down through the bands of crops. Ama holds on to the wheel, going through the motions of driving, noiselessly. Gino explains that the tanker is finally going to deliver the petrol later. As soon as it does, we can set off again. We leave the car in front of Gino's fuel pumps. Then Ama catches sight of Pado, inside the house, seated at a long table with Gino's family, tucking into a bowl of food. There's a sprinkling of parmesan cheese on the tablecloth by his plate. Gino asks us in, but Ama remains outside and settles down on a bench next to the car. She pulls a book out of her bag and reads. We run to the house and plough into the lunch put in front of us. People are watching the news in the room next door. The television blares out announcements. Aldo Moro has written another letter from his captivity. My whole body tenses.

Everybody carries on eating, listening to the screen. I can't eat any more. I drop my fork onto the table. I watch people come and go on the television, explaining, despairing, shunning the camera to hide their anguish. I must think of something else quickly. I spring across the tarmac to the car. I clamber into my seat and sit staring at Ama on her bench. I can't focus on anything. What are they doing to Aldo Moro? Where is he? Maybe he's near here, somewhere, tied up and gagged in a cellar, in the back of a shop. Maybe he's in a cave, tucked away in the countryside, lost to the world. What does he think about in the dark on his own? How does he know if it's morning or night? I run through my head to find a thought, an image to rub all this away. Giulio comes and knocks on the window. Duccio, he says, wants to finish my food.

We fill up with petrol, thank Gino and his family. Ama

gets in the car and slams the door shut. Pado looks at his watch.

'Good, we should still get to Lyon on time.'

He asks Duccio to help get us across Genoa. Duccio studies the route. Pado drives fast. The full tank of petrol has given him a new burst of energy. Ama lays her neck back on her head rest and closes her eyes. She clasps her hands together on her lap. From time to time, she takes a little gulp of air. I watch her chest rise and fall with every intake of air, contorting with her trapped silence. Factories tower over us, encircling the car. Genoa appears in the distance. Columns of lorries, packed to the top with cement and gravel, clog our way. We crawl in their wake. They cover the windscreen and windows in a fine layer of grey dust. It slips through the air vents and chokes the car with a smothering fog. Pado overtakes the lorries, darting in and out of their thundering wheels. They shower us with more and more grey powder. It swirls inside the car like a storm. Giulio coughs and Ama doesn't stir. Her eyes are firmly shut now, refusing to open.

We leave the lorries from Genoa behind and enter a town. We are driving up its main street, with the windows down to let out the dust, when Ama suddenly opens her eyes, sits up straight, rearranges her dress and screeches: 'STOP!' at the top of her voice. Pado slams on the brakes and we all look at her, astonished. Thumping the dashboard, Ama explains to Pado that that's it! She can't carry on. She is having no more driving, no more conferences, no more filthy hotels, no more sandwiches! 'I want a life Gaspare! I want a fucking life!'

She cries huge, breathless, bursting tears. They cut a clean streak down her cheeks through the fine powder of dust on her face. Duccio asks whether we should get out of the car. Pado says it's better if we keep going.

'Don't ignore me! Don't bloody ignore me!' Ama screams. To make her point clear, she springs open the glove compartment, scrapes together its contents and throws the whole lot out of the open window. 'No more!' she repeats.

From the back seat, I can see Ama's favourite Liszt tape lying on the tarmac in a confetti of blowing newspaper reviews and cuttings. Pado drives on, slowly, hesitantly at first, checking for a reaction, then he pushes down on the accelerator and we speed off through the town. Ama warns Pado that he'd better stop: 'Gaspare, didn't you hear me? I said stop! Now!'

We shoot on, clipping pavements, ignoring signs. We come up against a red traffic-light and some waiting cars. Pado hoots nervously. Ama kicks open her door, turns to us in the back and shouts, 'Come on boys!'

We stare at her, then at Pado.

'Have it your way,' she sighs and steps onto the pavement. She walks purposefully down the street. Pado quickly pulls into a parking place.

'Where's she going?' Giulio stutters.

I jump out of the car and run after Ama. Giulio joins me and the two of us are charging down the pavement, spluttering for Ama to stop. We throw ourselves at her legs. She grips us tight and her shaking hands crush and envelop us in the pleats of her skirt.

*   *   *

Pado catches up with us. He bars Ama's way. Duccio stands beside him, clenching the map awkwardly, not knowing where to look.

'What has got into you Ava?' Pado snaps, 'What do you think you're playing at? We're going to be late for our meeting in Lyon.'

Ama looks like she might break in two.

'Are you bloody deaf Gaspare? I said Stop! Enough! Can't you understand that? *Basta!* That's it!'

Ama pushes Pado to one side. 'Enough. That's it. *Je n'en peux plus!*' she bellows, close up to his face. She sets off again, turning to us: 'Hurry up boys. The sea shouldn't be too far away!'

We dash after her. Duccio passes the map to Pado and follows us, hastening his pace.

'Come back Ava!' Pado yells down the street.

Ama stops to look in some shops. She goes inside one and buys towels and sun cream. She asks for directions down to the sea and says to the shopkeeper, 'Can you imagine, these children have never spent a day on the beach!'

The shopkeeper looks at us weirdly. There's a big market in the square opposite the shop. We wind our way through the stalls. Hotels rise up between palm trees and billboards. Ama cheers up. She tells us to breathe in the smell of the sea. Giulio notices the first seagull.

'Come on!' he shrieks excitedly, twirling his new towel above his head.

Ama says he's going to take someone's eye out if he carries

on like that. She spots the sea ahead of us, a patch of blue rising between two buildings. We race down the street, Ama swearing she can run faster than all of us put together. The sea bursts open in front of us.

There is hardly anyone on the beach. The shopkeeper had warned us that the sea might be a little cold. It is icy.

'Maybe May is a little early to swim,' Ama laughs, dancing from foot to foot in the shallow water.

Duccio and Giulio want to swim. They dive straight into the water, wearing their pants, squealing in agony. Giulio disappears in a wash of waves. Ama tells him to stick near to her. It's so cold when I get in that I have to keep on swimming so as not to scream. We get out and lay our towels on the sand. Giulio and Duccio collect hermit crabs. They stack them up in a crusty tin can they've found buried on the beach. Ama filters sand through her fingers. We're all wondering where Pado is, but no one dares ask Ama.

Ama's face has gone blotchy. She plasters sun cream on. A man stops and asks her if she needs some putting on her back. He stands above her, grinning.

'Will you please leave me alone,' Ama pleads. '*Per favore!* Can't you see I'm with my children?'

Ama grumbles something at him when he's gone. Giulio says that was a strange question he asked about the sun cream.

'Not worth thinking about!' Ama reassures him, tying a towel over her head. Another man goes past selling Pepsi and ice cream. We watch people come and go. Ama's face is swelling in the heat.

'Damn this,' she complains, 'I thought my sun allergy had got better.' We stand over her, creating shade with our towels, but the sun is too hot. 'I'll have to get a parasol,' Ama decides. 'You can't stay here though.'

We move together down the beach front. I run back to get the tin of hermit crabs. When Duccio and Giulio aren't looking I throw them back into the sea, one by one, along the shore. Duccio sees me and chucks some sand in my face. I don't care. The hermit crabs are safe, each sent out with a thought into the sea. We pick out a bar in the distance. It has a blackboard, with a menu written on it, planted in a pot. Ama leaves us at the counter whilst she goes off to get a parasol: 'Stay put! Don't move!'

The barman gives us three lemonades and assures us Ama can pay when she comes back. We've never done that before and Duccio is rather wary about the whole thing. Still, 'We have to try' we say to ourselves, sucking the fizzy liquid through straws.

'It's disgusting,' Giulio winces and spits, handing me his bottle.

I'm not sure I like it either. The barman comes and asks if we want another drink instead. He'll give us anything we like, 'for free this time.' Giulio says he would prefer an ice cream and I do too. Duccio is the only one who wants a second lemonade. Another man saunters in, throws a crate onto the floor.

The barman sits Duccio down on another chair and asks him all sorts of questions to which he doesn't know the answers. Finally, when we're getting to the end of our ice creams, Ama returns carrying a huge parasol with 'Pepsi Cola' written across it.

'Where did those come from?' she protests when she sees our ice-cream packets.

Duccio tells her the barman kindly gave us ice cream and lemonade.

She's furious. 'It's very bad for their teeth!'

'Oh but they're so lovely, you have to spoil them,' the barman smiles.

Ama throws a few lira on the table, '*Grazie*,' and ushers us out hurriedly. When we're back on the beach, she gathers us together anxiously. She seems frantic all of a sudden.

'Did he touch you? Did he touch you?' she asks Duccio.

'Touch what?' he answers, confused.

'You know,' she says, pointing at her bottom. We fall about laughing at her gesture. Ama is relieved. Giulio sticks his bottom in the air too, slapping it, again and again, imitating Ama and then charges up and down the beach screeching in hysterics.

A car parks behind us on the beach. It's Pado. He's found us. He sits on the bonnet of the car watching. He has his arms folded across his chest.

'Do not look at your father!' Ama warns.

We gaze out to sea, concentrating on the waves, not daring to turn round. Slowly, out of the corner of my eye, I see Pado lay his files out on the low wall in front of the car. He reads his books and marks his pages with a pen. He keeps on looking up, hoping that Ama is going to walk over to him. She doesn't. She shows us how to skim pebbles across the waves and how to split open seaweed so that it pops with a loud noise.

Eventually, Pado jumps over the wall and trudges towards us through the thick sand. Ama lets out a sigh of exasperation as he gets near. Pado looks aghast when he sees Ama close-up.

'What the hell has happened to your face?'

'It's fine,' Ama replies. 'Leave us alone!'

'It's completely swollen and red. Your little beach holiday has obviously been a great success!'

'It has. Thank you,' Ama snarls. 'In fact, we thought we'd stay here!'

'I think your little joke's over now, Ava. We have to be in Lyon tomorrow morning!'

'We don't *have* to be anywhere!' Ama spits.

'In case you've forgotten, I wanted Jean-Pio to meet my friend Alberto Devoti in Lyon! Or don't you care about your children's health?' Pado throws in.

Ama is put off for a second. She looks at me apologetically. 'Sorry darling, yes, how stupid of me. Well, anyway,' she says, cuddling my head in her arms, 'it doesn't really matter. What he needs is a good holiday, like the rest of us!'

'And what do you think we were doing at my parents' for two weeks!' Pado shrieks.

'Some holiday,' Ama mumbles back.

Pado reluctantly agrees to finding a hotel.

'One night only,' he keeps on saying as we get back in the car.

'We'll see,' Ama threatens.

We drive along the sea front, stopping and starting, letting Ama out to ask the prices of rooms, from hotel to hotel. We reach the edge of the town. We turn back and try the hotels along the back streets. Ama thinks *La Spiaggia* hotel looks all right. She disappears in through the door, under a plaster lobster hanging from a geranium flowerpot. We struggle in with all our bags and papers.

In the bedroom, Ama chucks a used-looking pillow in the cupboard. She pulls back the blankets and runs her hands across the linen. There's a patch on Duccio's bed.

'Look at this. It's disgusting,' Ama complains.

Pado bends over and inspects the spot, 'Seems fine to me, maybe some rust from the washing line.'

Ama isn't convinced. 'Could be blood or sick.'

'The sheet has been through a washing-machine,' Pado starts explaining. Then he gives up before he's ended his sentence. 'Okay, I'll call reception.' Within minutes the hotel owner has arrived with his wife. We're all very apologetic and so are they.

'What seems to be the matter?' the owner inquires. Ama is rather put off by the fact that it's the owner and not a maid, so talking about dirty sheets is not too easy.

Eventually Duccio blurts it out as it's his bed anyway: 'Can we have clean sheets as mine have a stain?'

The owner's wife is mortified. She takes the sheet to the window to examine it closely. 'Oh, no, it's a little bit of dust.

There, it's gone,' and she shakes the sheet vigorously before putting it back on the bed.

Ama turns to Pado in English, 'Go on, tell her, it's blood, not dust. I'm not having Duccio sleep in that fetid bed.'

'So that's settled is it, Professore Messina?' The owner smiles before Pado has a chance to speak and he and his wife leave, wishing us a pleasant stay.

'I'm sorry that's not good enough!' Ama shouts. 'They'll have to sleep two to a bed. I'm not having a son of mine in that blood-stained sheet.' She sits down on the end of the bed, a good distance away from the stain.

'Calm down. It's only a fucking sheet,' Pado explains.

'Well, that's precisely what it might be,' Ama sneers. Then she starts muttering to herself. Pado says, 'Speak up!' and we're off.

'Well it's just the last straw that's what it is!' Ama yells.

'What is?' Pado gasps.

'All this!' Ama screams at him.

Pado is not going to take it. Not after today. 'It was your bloody idea to come here. Your great idea to waste an afternoon in this pit of a town! And now all this fuss about some petty sheet. You were a pain all morning in the car. Always bloody exaggerating, always complaining. *Sei una . . .*'

Ama is furious. 'Exaggerating, is that what it is? I suppose it's also exaggerating to say I traipse around Europe after some obsessed scientist. Is it? Go on tell me, Gaspare! Is this a normal life for a family?'

The word 'normal' makes Pado shudder. It's what he hates the most: 'normal', 'normality', the average, people living dull, ignorant lives. He goes to usher us out of the room, but Ama says no.

'I think they should stay, it's their life too. I think we should ask them if they enjoy this life of seedy hotels, celebrating birthdays in a car, filthy sheets, weeks with your parents, constantly staying with friends, sandwiches, car sickness, sea sickness and all the bloody rest.'

'Sounds like a pretty good life to me. I wouldn't have minded being brought up like that.'

'Oh, come on, you had everything. What have they got? Nothing. That's what they've got. Nothing but a few grimy books stuffed under a car seat. Is that a childhood?'

'There you go again! They speak more languages than any other children I know. They're cultured. They're mature. They're seeing the real world.'

'Mature! They're only bloody children, Gaspare, and unless you've noticed, they're a bit worse for wear. I mean do you think it's right that an eight-year-old child like Jean-Pio should have permanent headaches, or that Duccio should sleep in filthy beds?' Ama begins to cry. Not her usual bursts of angry tears, but frightened sobs of tiredness, of nights unslept and sorrow that she can't suppress.

Pado doesn't talk. He walks up and down hesitantly before laying his hand on Ama's shoulder. She shakes him away violently. Giulio throws himself onto Ama's lap, unsure whether to cry or not.

Pado turns to Duccio. 'Well, what do you want?'

Duccio looks at Ama for a reply. She doesn't move. Duccio swivels and stares at me. I close my eyes. My mind melts into the room, jumping from Pado to Ama to Duccio and Giulio and back, seeking a grip to hold on to, to stop the thoughts from caving in on me.

'I don't know,' Duccio stutters.

Pado throws a roll of lavatory paper onto the bed, expecting Ama to pick it up. She wipes her eyes with the pillow instead. Deep damp patches in the plump whiteness of the linen. Pado struggles on, facing Ama.

'Well, what do you suggest? Do you honestly want to give up on all of this? What about the conferences, the research? I know this will pay off in a few years' time. It has to.'

'I don't care any more, Gaspare, I don't care. All I know is that I can't go on. Really. I'm so tired of all this. Could we not go to my mother's for a while and stop this travelling?' Ama suggests.

'I can't and you know it. We might have at least two conferences coming up in Paris and you've got that translating job in Germany. Anyway we can't stay with your mother very long. I mean, let's face it, that's another problem. What the hell are we going to do with your mother?'

'What do you mean, "do" with her?'

'Well, she can't live on her own for much longer. She's losing her maples.'

'The expression is "losing one's marbles",' Ama snaps. 'Anyway she's not losing anything, imagine what she's been through with my father's death. She is suffering from intense grief, can't you see that? Actually, probably not with your sense of scientific precision. Besides, staying with your mother, if you don't mind me saying, has become a bloody ordeal.'

'So what are you saying? We can't carry on like this, we can't visit my parents any more, we can't stay in hotels, but we have to deal with your mother's depression!'

'She is not depressed.'

'Sorry, she has bad days!'

'Can we stick to the subject. I just want to stop all this travelling, do you not understand? I want somewhere to go. Is that too much to ask? All I want is a house to live in. A simple house.'

'Look, we can talk about it later. Now is not the time.'

'No, that's what you say every time. How many times have we had this conversation? How many times have we got back into that damn car without a decision?'

'Well, we can't afford a house. So that's out. How am I suddenly going to conjure up a house? Anyway I've told you. There's no way I'm living in England.'

'I don't care where it is. I want somewhere to live.'

'Well, in that case, why can't we go to your father's house in France for a while? It's completely empty.'

'You amaze me! You know full well that neither my mother nor I want to go back there for now. It's too painful after all that's happened.'

'Beggars can't be choosers.' Pado waits for Ama to correct his expression. She doesn't. He pours himself a glass of water from the bathroom tap. 'If you want a house, you've got one right there in France. It's beautiful. It's perfect. The children used to love it.'

'Well it's not that simple Gaspare. That house is not just any old house. It has a lot of memories.'

'Well, it's mad to leave it empty . . .'

There's a long silence. Ama leafs through the guidebook next to the telephone on the bedside table. Pado reckons we should go outside and play a while in the *piazza* in front of the hotel. He takes Duccio to the window and shows him where he means. Duccio leads us down the stairs. Giulio wants to stay and listen to what Ama has to say through the door. Duccio pulls him away.

'But maybe we should?' I protest frantically. 'What if . . .' Then I don't know. I don't know at all. We walk into the square and sit by a fountain. I peer inside and count the coins at the bottom. Giulio flicks water at a statue of a lion. People come and go. Pigeons skip about our feet. None of us feels like playing. A shopkeeper peers out of his door at us, wondering what we're doing. Time drags on, slowly.

About three hours later, Pado opens the window and leans out.

'Where the hell are you? *Cosa fate?*' he shouts down.

He sees us huddled together on the steps to the fountain. He calls back to Ama, 'Come and look at this miserable bunch! *Che tristezza!*'

Ama stretches over Pado, poking her head through the window too. She bursts out giggling. The two of them laugh and screech, holding their sides.

'We've been here three hours!' Duccio breaks in angrily.

Both Ama and Pado are surprised. 'Oh sorry, so you have! What were we thinking of?' Then they're off laughing again. They sprint down the stairs.

'Let's go. Quick, quick!' Ama sings, tugging us down the street. Then Ama and Pado start cuddling and kissing and it's the first time we've seen them like this in a long time. Duccio doesn't understand. We're all too worried to ask what's happened. There's a pizzeria on the same street as the hotel and we settle down at a table in the corner, away from the smokers. We order.

Ama is smiling, 'Looking forward to your pizzas?' She gives Pado a knowing nudge.

The waiter comes to take our orders and when he's gone, Pado gently corrects Giulio's Italian. 'But don't worry about it. Your French is more important now!'

'Why?' Duccio asks first.

'We might be moving to France!' Ama and Pado say in unison.

Duccio, Giulio and I stare at them, astonished. What about the car? What about Nonno and Nonna, Machance all on her own and Mr Yunnan in his boxes? What about the conferences and maps?

'When?' I say.

'Not quite yet, but soon. Your mother has some translating work to do in Germany and we have to check with Machance if we can use Grand Maurice's old house in France.' The mention of Grand Maurice's name startles me. The conversation is full of new thoughts I dare not think. I tap my fork gently against the side of my plate, a hidden tune to keep me going.

'Grand Maurice's house?' Giulio is amazed. 'We haven't been there for years.'

'I know,' Ama interrupts, 'I couldn't face it. It was all too much. But your father's right. We have no choice now.' She smiles at us sadly, but determined. 'Anyway, it's the only way I'll get your dear father to stop this travelling,' she adds, poking Pado in the ribs.

Giulio says he remembers the house. Maybe he does, maybe he doesn't. I remember everything, because Grand Maurice died and the way he walked, his garden, his clothes, his face and the way the two of us went fishing together are in my head for ever.

Then Ama sits back and looks at me with a surprised face.

'You're very brown darling!' she says, examining my skin so closely that I feel her breath across my cheek. She gets her make-up mirror out of her bag and shoves it in front of me so I can see for myself. 'Amazing,' Ama giggles as my eyes appear in the mirror. 'A few hours on the beach and look at you. There's no keeping that Sicilian blood down!'

'What about them?' I protest, staring at Duccio and Giulio, but they, Pado says, haven't got Nonno's Moorish skin.

Ama stands up and asks the waiters for telephone tokens. She wants to ring Machance in England. She gathers together ten tokens by swapping coins with a neighbouring table. She piles them up, one on top of the other, by the telephone in the corner of the restaurant. We watch her as she dials and then rearranges the tokens, waiting for a reply. Suddenly her hands and face plead with the wall, explaining words in elaborate, determined gestures. She feeds the machine several times, glancing at us each time, urging us to carry on eating without her. She looks away. The tokens run out. She comes back to our table. Her walking is heavy and slow.

Pado asks her how it went.

'It's not going to be easy,' Ama sighs as she pulls up her chair. 'Machance is not happy with the idea. I think we should go ahead and visit the house though. Let's see what we feel like there, just for a day. Machance gave me Madame Joignet's number. She has the keys.' Then Ama scrapes the cold cheese off the top of her pizza and pushes it to one side. She squashes it with her fork. She picks up the cleaned dough with her fingers and rolls it delicately into a ball. 'I'm not sure I'm ready for all this either. It's going to be very strange for me without my father being there,' she whispers into her plate, offering Pado the dough.

We get up early the next morning. Ama is nowhere to be found. Pado is anxious. He asks the woman at the reception desk if she's seen her. The receptionist says she saw Ama pop out earlier. She even cashed a traveller's cheque for her. Pado tells us to settle down on the sofa in the hotel foyer. He keeps on checking his watch and peering out of the window nervously. Then Ama abruptly bursts through the revolving doors of the hotel, out of breath. She's laden with things, spilling out of her arms: bread, cheese, soap, fruit, some tins and a large straw hat. She throws the whole lot on the sofa next to us, in a heap.

Pado looks at Ama and then at the mountain of goods.

'For the house in France! It'll save us some shopping.' Ama grins at him, before he can say anything.

'But you're not going to wear that are you?' Pado gasps when he sees the hat.

'Why not?' Ama protests, 'I think it's lovely!'

Pado can't believe it. He turns to her, amazed. 'Well it's not exactly *cheek*, is it?'

Ama swipes Pado over the head with her hat. '*Chic*, Gaspare, not *cheek*! When will you bloody learn?'

Part Two

12

We're not going to Lyon. From *La Spiaggia*, we cross the French border at Ventimiglia and head up towards the centre of France. We've driven through France countless times, stopped in motorway hotels, attended conferences in Toulouse, Bordeaux and Paris, but this time it's different. It's no longer a vast floating space between England and Italy, but a place that might become our home.

As soon as we leave the coast, Giulio and I are leaning out of the windows, staring at all the houses: 'Are we nearly there?' 'Isn't that the wood next to the house?'

Duccio has the map of France spread across his knees and is running his fingers along the creases as if none of this were true. Pado whacks on the music. Ama doesn't care because the mountains are rising above the car in warm blocks of light and because all her tapes are lost somewhere on a road in Italy. It's further than Pado remembered, much further. The car travels on for hours.

'We're heading,' Ama says, 'to the southern Touraine.'

Houses and villages gently disappear and stretch into strips of deserted dry green with forest after forest drumming out the distance for the car. We're going to the centre of the land in the middle and the three of us in the back have all given up pointing at houses.

Ama takes the map from Duccio and crunches it untidily in between the seat and the hand brake. Suddenly she is telling us the names of the villages, the woods and vineyards. She shows us a couple of churches she used to visit, the Loire river and damp-patterned houses carved deep into the rock. We carry on, down straight narrow roads, cutting through vines and cornfields. Ama directs Pado into a hamlet through a back lane. There's a farmhouse on the left. It's Madame Joignet's house. Ama pulls on a bell chain and disturbs the dog tied to the post. It spins around its kennel, barking wildly.

'Remember Casimir?' Pado says, pointing at the dog.

An old woman appears, dressed in a long blue apron. Ama doesn't know whether to kiss her or shake her hand. For a while they stand awkwardly in front of each other then hug. Madame Joignet guides Ama into the house. When she reappears, Ama is rubbing her eyes with the corner of her sleeve and carrying two years' worth of post. Pado jumps out to help her. The house keys are delicately balanced on top of the piles of unopened post. I glance at the first envelope. It has Grand Maurice's name written across it in black.

Ama says she would prefer to walk to the house. Pado tells her we'll park the car and go with her, then.

'No,' she gestures. 'I need to be alone.'

Pado takes her to one side. 'Ava, I think it's important for the children that we all go together. This has to be a positive thing. Please. For them.'

'It is positive. Very positive,' she tries.

'Well, try and show it,' Pado insists quietly. 'You said you'd be all right here.'

Ama reluctantly clambers back into the car. On the drive to the house, she doesn't look up once. Instead she sorts through the post, putting the letters addressed to Machance to one side. She packs the ones for Grand Maurice in a bundle with her elastic hair grip. She flicks the elastic with her finger. It whips at the brown envelopes. She does it again, then again and again.

We turn down a thin, stony lane. There are no houses, only the occasional brick shed surrounded by meadows. Tarmac fades into bumpy mud tracks. Then there are vines everywhere, an unbroken sea of wooden stakes and taut wire and nothing else. We come to a sharp turning next to a chestnut tree and then that's it: the house. A spreading jumble of oat-coloured stone, like a child's building blocks knocked down and resting in front of a hill. No one says a word, as if we've all known that we would come to a standstill here at the bottom of these slopes covered in vines. Pado stops the car between the trees and vines. The engine carries on running, the exhaust dyeing the overgrown grass a murky brown. Ama winds up her window and keeps her hand tightly on the handle. We gaze at the sudden immobility around us. The roads no longer whirl past black and white. The shooting faces that shine through windscreens, with mist across their mouths, have gone. The trees, the houses and skies have rooted themselves in our stillness.

One of the house shutters is nearly off its hinges. A gutter is full of slipped, damaged tiles. Pado hops out of the car first. He steps onto the carpets of new space before us and almost topples over. He picks at the grass, taking in his new ground, beckoning us to join him, but the familiar hum of the engine and the trapped air keep us tight inside the car. Pado walks up the garden to inspect the house. Ama follows him, clutching the heavy keys, her feet ripping through flower-beds where the stems of struggling plants have matted together. By the time she's reached the door, we can tell she has already invented a different garden with flowers to keep her bearings and herbs to crowd the alleys. She tramples the nettles covering the steps to the front door, fiddles with the lock. Before opening the door, she turns and calls Pado. She repeats his name two or three times. Pado has slipped off behind the house. Ama pushes the door with her foot. It catches against some grit. She scrapes it away. She rests her head against the door and it opens gently in front of her. She walks in.

Soon shutters start cracking open on the first floor. There's a whip of wood against stone as they hook to the wall outside. Ama waves to us from each successive window, her face framed in the chipped shape of open shutters. She melts backwards and forwards in the rooms, bending down to pick things up, fingering the peeled wallpaper, anything to keep busy.

'Come on boys, get out of the car!' she yells.

The grass is so high it smothers the vines hemming in the garden from all sides. Pado is staring blankly at the mud blocking the bottom of the gates. He is floating, hesitant, caught between the rush of roads and this quiet steadiness. I'm imagining no more open-eyed drives through the night, no more hotel rooms filled with untucked white sheets, no more picnics with plastic containers that open and close like half-formed intentions, started and unfinished. Ama shouts at us again to get out of the car. We can't move, as if stuck, transfixed by the enclosing garden. Ama charges down towards us, annoyed.

'After all this, you don't even want to get out of the car? This is for you, boys. This could be your new home!'

I'm staring at the garden, the rolling lines that head out into the vineyards, Grand Maurice's garden.

'I don't understand you,' Ama sighs. 'Anyway, your father certainly won't let you stay in there.'

Sure enough Pado heaves us out of the car. 'Come on, you lazy *cretini*.'

Giulio is pulled out first and falls flat on his face in the long grass. When he stands up, he can only just see above the crowns of stems and blades. I feel as if the earth is still moving. The same as when the car drives off the ferry and the ground in the harbour is rocking with the waves. I can see the overgrown lawn running past, folding and turning, flowers like traffic-lights, coloured images to retain, to lodge deep inside me.

*   *   *

'Why didn't Machance sell the house to someone?' Duccio asks Ama.

'Well, it's very difficult to sell something like this darling.' Ama lists all the problems of the house, the electricity, the plumbing, the draughts, the heat in the summer. 'Besides,' she finishes off, 'this is our house. This is where Grand Maurice was brought up. He loved it here. He loved the vines, the wilderness and light. Machance couldn't sell all this.'

'How far is it to the lake, Ama?' Giulio asks. Duccio and I look at him. We don't know why he said that. He doesn't know either. It just came out.

'We'll talk about that another day darling,' Ama answers, confused. 'Today,' she adds softly, 'we have things to do.'

I know how far it is to the lake. I'm the only one who used to go there with Grand Maurice to catch crayfish. We had our own special fishing method with bits of meat attached to a bicycle wheel. It was the best method in the world. He told me so himself.

Giulio calls me down a trail in the grass. I set off behind him and Duccio follows me. We reach the vineyard. Beyond is a wood thinned by dry mud tracks. We watch the lizards disappearing over the garden walls, their tranquillity broken. Every inch of the garden has cut itself off from the world outside. The odd gardening tool, left under a tree or bush, has turned a rusty brown. The fruit trees have sprouted saplings about their feet. The well is tangled with clumps of climbing brambles. Giulio invents a game. We have to crawl in the grass and try and catch each other. The grass is so thick that it bites into our clothes and binds itself across our knees, pulling at our ankles. I feel as if I'm under the sea, ensnared in drifting banks of seaweed, waiting for the rays of light from above to call me up. Duccio and Giulio scream my name to tell me the game's over. I'm still crawling, alone, taking in the smells and insects of the hidden world. I don't want to be found. I want to spread myself out into the garden and merge with the ground until the thoughts and remembering that make up a day disappear into the earth.

Ama opens up the boot and brings out a few snacks. She lays a blanket on the grass in front of the house. She rips some bread into pieces and hands us a plate from the kitchen. I imagine Machance and Grand Maurice passing these same plates, their blue china rims and cracked surfaces glinting in the evening light. Night time comes fast. Pado is surprised to find the electricity still connected. He runs to an upstairs room and plugs in a light. An insect-flecked stream of brightness prises open the darkness of the garden. Ama lies on her back looking at the stars.

'I want to sleep here,' she says. 'Right here, listening to the night.'

'It might be a little chilly,' Pado warns.

We follow Pado into the house. Duccio opens up a tall sweet tin in the kitchen. There's nothing in there. Giulio asks how come we can remember where everything is and he can't, but he was only four when he was last here.

'That's almost too small to remember anything,' Pado tells him.

We walk through the kitchen, up the curling, wooden steps

into the sitting-room, dining-room and hall. I can hear the sound of stairs shifting and Grand Maurice's laugh as he played hide-and-seek with us in the cellars. Then the noise of his walking-stick as it dropped into a crook of his chair, waiting for the end of dinner. Pado opens a door and splutters at the billowing dirt. We climb up another floor. None of the beds in the upper part of the house can be used. They are caked with dark grey crusts of damp. The terracotta tiles on the floor have little holes pressed with grime. Giulio asks where we are going to sleep.

'Good question,' Pado replies. 'Probably on the back seat of the car.'

Ama is still lying on the blanket in front of the house. Her arms are lost in the thickness of the high weeds. Occasionally she pulls a hand up to examine a wild flower or shake away an insect. Pado accompanies us to the car. I jump into the front and wrap the gear stick in a duvet to stop it jutting into my back. Giulio climbs down into the space behind the front seats, the way he sleeps when we are driving through the night. Duccio spreads out on the back seat and uses his jumper as a pillow. Pado waits for us to settle down and then makes his way back to the house. We can hear him talking to Ama and then knocking about the kitchen. He comes out carrying a wide wooden bench and several blankets. He puts them down next to Ama on the grass. He lays his head in the warm curved arm rest of the bench. His legs stick out over the other end. Through the rising lawn, and in the beam of light streaming from the upstairs window, I can see Ama reaching out for Pado's hand. Their arms curve in an arched bridge above the grass. I try to feel the rush of the car, the gentle rocking motion of the swerves and bends of the journey, but we are dug into the field without a driver to carry us. The house is still wide open, the kitchen door held back by a stone. The garden is full of Grand Maurice, still and hastening silence.

13

Ama wakes us in the morning with croissants and *chaussons aux pommes* from the village. She hangs them through the car window, letting them drop onto our laps. Pado is by her side. We eat our breakfast and watch them, through the windscreen, as they discuss whether to take on the house or not. Ama has already walked to the post office to ring Machance. She has said we can have the house if we really want it, even if Ama still isn't quite sure. She says we could maybe look for something to rent in the area until she feels ready to move in.

'We don't have any money to waste on renting, Ava, don't you see?' Pado explains. 'Anyway, if you're not ready now, when will you be?'

Ama doesn't know what to think. She goes off into the house. She carries a chair out onto the grass. She cleans it with a cloth. She stops and starts. She folds the cloth in two. She tucks distant images inside. Pado comes up behind her and envelops her in his arms. She turns and buries her head in his shoulder. The cloth falls from her hand onto the lawn. It catches on a tall plant, spilling and coiling down its stem, not quite touching the ground. Pado talks to her, leaning his chin against the top of her head.

'You're right,' Ama whispers back, then louder, 'You're right, we should stay. We have no choice.'

Pado lifts her head up and, with one finger, gently parts the strands of hair covering her face. 'Looks like the decision was made for us anyway,' he laughs, pointing at Giulio. He is carrying a bundle of twigs. He wants to build a hut for himself at the back of the house.

'But what about my translation work in Germany?' Ama suddenly remembers, extracting herself from Pado's arms. 'I can't cancel now! It's far too late.' She looks disoriented. 'You'll all have to come with me. You can't stay here!'

'We'll be fine on our own,' Pado assures her.

'No, I can't leave you here. Why don't you all wait for me in England? At least my mother can help you with the children.'

'I'll cope. I'll be fine.'

'No, Gaspare, you won't manage. My mother's great with the children. Besides, you have masses of research to do.'

'The children want to stay here now,' Pado says.

He takes Ama by the hand. He carries on talking to her.

Madame Joignet arrives on her bicycle. She brings more papers and letters for Ama and some fresh vegetables from her garden. She wants to know how long we're staying as her son, Marc, would like to come and see us all before we set off again. I race off down the garden to the point where the lawn halts and flows into the vineyard. I stand with the heat of the cracked earth rising up into me. I want to stay here, for ever. I tear the tops of the grass with my hands. I crush the seeds. I breathe in the air. I have to stay here. I have to. We can't leave Grand Maurice's house, with his garden growing on without us.

The morning sun gets hot quickly. Ama ushers us under the mess of creepers and vines to the side of the house. Climbing plants, sagging in the shape of a roof and propped up by sticks, hang over a wooden table. On an iron bench lies a cushion, as stiff as parchment. Pado is trying to straighten the kitchen door. He bashes away at the warped wood with the hammer from the car. Ama finds a basket she had as a girl. She tells us Machance bought it for her from the gypsies who came to pick grapes during the *vendange*. The echo of the hammer bounces over the garden. Ama sits on the steps flicking through her diary. She tells us that she's decided to go to Germany alone for a few days, she's got no choice.

'It's not going to be easy, but I'll get Machance to come over to help look after you while I'm away.'

She reaches for her handbag and jumps to her feet. 'I'm going back to the post office to ring my mother,' she shouts at Pado. 'Come with me boys. I need a hand.'

We follow her to the village along a gravelled track bordered by clumps of wilting flowers. Ama points out the school and the *Mairie*, then the cemetery in the distance. It rises up out of farmland, the yellow wheat jabbing at its square walls. We skirt past the church and down towards the post office. We enter under a big yellow sign. The post office is one long room with a door in the corner, leading onto a kitchen. A man greets Ama. She introduces us to him. He leans over the counter and shakes us all by the hand. Ama goes into the telephone booth in the corner. The man behind the counter fiddles with a machine and tells her she can pick up the receiver. Ama starts talking to Machance. She turns, from time to time, to tell us to be patient. She's in the booth for at least fifteen minutes. Then she calls us in, one after the other, to say a word to Machance.

'Tell her something nice,' Ama insists, ushering Giulio in first.

He clings to the receiver, waiting for Machance to talk.

'Speak!' Ama urges him. Giulio stutters a 'hello'.

'We love it here!' Ama mouths at him. 'We love it here!' She twists her lips around the words silently with big open eyes. 'Go on, say it!'

Giulio doesn't understand what Ama's trying to say. 'What?' he asks.

Ama drags Giulio out and it's Duccio's turn. He says a couple of sentences and waits for a reply, then I go in.

'Hello Machance! It's me, Jean-Pio.'

I can't hear anything at the other end.

'Machance! It's Jean-Pio. We're at your house.'

Ama is telling me to hurry up, but there's still no reply.

'Machance! Are you coming to see us?' I try. I rattle the receiver a little, from side to side. I push it hard against my ear, till it etches a circle of pain. Then I make out a rasping noise, a murmured crack. Ama grabs the receiver from me and listens too. She quickly pushes me out of the booth. She points us to the door. We scatter off towards the exit.

'Mother! *Maman*, are you all right? Are you all right?' Ama repeats. 'I'm sorry. *Je suis desolée.* I thought it would cheer you up to speak to the children.'

I stay by the door, watching. Ama holds the receiver to her chest and its distant sobbing merges with the pounding of her heart. She hangs up and makes for the counter to pay.

'Doesn't look like Machance is going to come,' Ama says to us on the way out, then she walks ahead, without us, all the way back to the house. Giulio runs after her. 'Leave her alone!' Duccio stops him with a shout. Giulio hovers, waiting for us to join him, then he drops back, trailing on behind.

Pado is still dealing with the kitchen door when we get back. Ama clears more furniture out of the rooms. I follow her into the house. The rooms downstairs are covered in chipped parquet and the corridors are tiled black and white. The windows have cracks and blemishes from rotting leaves, smooth stains where lizards come to heat themselves on the glass. Ama opens the sitting-room door; its warped frame creaks to the point of nearly snapping. 'There's another thing for your father to do,' she thinks aloud.

Everywhere she goes, Ama opens the windows and lets in the fresh air. She pauses to look at things, putting them back in their exact place. I don't touch anything. Everything as before. Thoughts and images undisturbed.

Then Pado calls us out to help him unpack the car. He carries the three boxes containing Mr Yunnan to the shelf in the sitting-room. He stacks them up, one on top of the other, until they nearly reach the ceiling.

'He'll be safe here,' Pado reckons.

This room is Mr Yunnan's now, I say to myself. Ama

suddenly bursts in with a massive hoover. She stamps on the power button and the dust swirls and runs away from her. She chases it, slamming the hoover against the skirting board. I look at Mr Yunnan's boxes. They wobble and quiver slightly.

'Out the way!' Ama shouts over the noise, but I can't leave now. I walk under the shelf waiting to catch Mr Yunnan's boxes in case they fall. I can't imagine what would happen if they do.

'I've never known anyone spend so much time doing nothing!' Ama says, exasperated, when she's finished. She points out of the window at Giulio and Duccio. They are cleaning the seats of the car with Pado. 'That,' Ama tells me, 'is useful!'

By evening, Ama realises she hasn't even thought about supper or cleaning the bedrooms for us. Pado reckons we should go to a restaurant quickly and think about the bedrooms later. Ama reminds him of the restaurant they used to eat at with Grand Maurice before the turning off towards Poitiers. She tosses a book out of her suitcase, searching for some clean clothes, and disappears into the larder to change. She comes out wearing a white dress that fans out at the sleeves. Pado puts on a dark jacket. We pile into the car.

'Looks pretty seedy,' Pado starts when we draw up outside the restaurant, but then he stops because he remembers it was his idea to eat out. A waiter leads us to a table and hands us some tired-looking menus inside plastic covers. We all start reading through the lists of food. My eyes drift across the room thinking that Grand Maurice must have sat here many times, maybe on this same chair. I could be touching the chair he touched, the menu he touched, the fork he ate with. Giulio is picking at the corner of the wine list, sliding his nail between the see-through coating and the paper. Duccio is trying to work out the difference between two dishes. I need to go to the loo. I tell Ama and wander off upstairs, following the sign. There's a room, along a corridor, at the top of the stairs, next to the lavatory. There's a thin man and a woman in the corner watching television. They have their backs turned to me. The man grumbles something from time to time. I walk up behind him to see the television screen. It's the news. A newsreader sits, with a solemn face, behind a desk. Then suddenly there's a shot of a street filled with cars, flashing lights and policemen. They're speaking Italian. Then there's an open car boot with a man curled up inside. The camera closes in on his face. The newsreader announces that Aldo Moro has been found murdered, dumped in a car boot. Murdered! The word pours out of the television. It sweeps into the room like a scream, pushing everything else aside. I clamp my hands over my ears. The thin man mutters something. He gets up and searches for a button. Please switch it off! Please! He turns the volume up instead. Stop! Stop!

It can't be true. But the newsreader speaks to a member of the Moro family and the television shows people in the street. A young woman is howling something, swinging her arms up and down. Then the camera homes in again on the crushed face in the car, the folded limbs crammed as if in a box. I have to get out. I have to stop listening to this. I turn and walk towards the stairs. I follow the black lead of the television along the wall. I yank at the plug. The television fizzles to a stop. The screen shrinks to black. He didn't die! He can't have died! My head is churning. The thin man shouts at the draining screen. The woman next to him tries pushing some buttons. I close the door behind them and make my way along the corridor towards the stairs. I can't go into the loo now. Not now. I get to the top of the stairs. My knees are weak.

Half-way down the steps, I freeze. Aldo Moro's crumpled face springs back at me. The stairs swim in visions of his packed-up body. Maybe it wasn't him? The only way I can get down the stairs is to believe that. But the newsreader said it was him. I can still hear his name being read, a short name that has come to an end: Aldo Moro. I hesitate between one step and another. I can't get down the stairs. Each step is a thought more dreadful than the last. What if the Red Brigades take more people? What about Nonno now? Then all the cars in Italy are hooting and crashing with bodies in their boots. I can see Aldo Moro's wife. Her silent mournful face. I have to get off these stairs. I try putting one foot on the step below me. I can't. I pull it back and put it on the step two above. Then I jump down two, quickly, before another thought comes to get me. I'm suspended, alone, clinging to the wall for support. I try to think about something else. Nothing else will come. I'm stuck. I'm going to capsize, drown in thoughts like the young woman who swung her arms and screamed on television. I run my fingers along the banisters. The polish on the wood smears onto my hand. I can't budge.

Giulio has been sent out to see what I'm doing.

'Where are you? Come on. Hurry up!' he yells from the bottom of the stairs.

'I'm coming,' I shout back. I don't want him to see me. He mustn't see me. He starts walking up the stairs.

'Get a move on!' he says. I can't. Giulio reaches my step. He is standing next to me.

'Well, come on!' he repeats.

I manage to get down three steps then it all fires back. All the next steps are full of thoughts, each step wrapped and marked with images of Aldo Moro.

'My shoe hurts,' I tell him. I sit down, panting. I fiddle with my shoe so that he'll go away. He just stands there, waiting.

'What's the matter?' he asks. I show him how my shoes are too big. He doesn't see it. He catches my sleeve and pulls me down.

'No!' I shriek. Giulio stands back, surprised. I'm frightened now and he can't understand that this step is so bad you can't put your foot on it and this step is good and that one over there is in-between.

'Have you got a headache?' Giulio asks. I can feel the steps falling away, the building crumbling beneath me. I want him to stop asking me questions.

'It's my shoes,' I tell him, again and again.

He says he's going to fetch Pado.

'No, I'm fine. It's nothing. Please!' Maybe if this step won't do, I could put my foot on that one three steps down? I leap and tumble down the stairs. Giulio chases after me, shouting at me to stop. I jump again, avoiding the big curved step of the corner and any sadness that might contaminate the three in between. I'm down. I've reached the bottom.

Giulio leads me into the dining-room, confused.

'What's got into you?' Ama says, 'You look dreadful!'

'My shoes hurt,' I say quickly, shuffling into my chair.

Ama looks down at my feet. 'Look fine to me. What are you talking about?'

The first course is salad with cheese.

'Imagine! I'll be able to do this when I get the kitchen going!' Ama beams at us.

Giulio says he doesn't want cheese. He wants tuna salad. Pado says he's not sure the tuna is fresh.

'I'm sure it's all right,' Ama nods, ordering it for Giulio.

I don't feel like eating much salad. Pado makes me finish my bread instead. A few more families start coming in when we are on our pudding. There's a cassette player in the corner of the dining-room and one of the waiters puts on a song. Ama hums along to herself, remembering the words and clicking her fingers to the tune. Suddenly she jumps up and stretches her hand out to Pado.

'Would you like to dance with your wife, *Monsieur l'Italien?*'

Pado looks at her in amazement and so do we. Ama slides round the table, moving to the music. She gives Pado a wiggle of the hips and tugs at the lapel of his jacket. Pado hesitates. He glances across at the people in the restaurant.

'Come on! Don't tell me you've gone all shy?' Ama teases him.

She brushes against Pado's knees with her thigh. He stands up and takes her by the waist. He puts his other hand on her shoulder. Ama rests her head on Pado's chest. Together they flow through the room, skating across the gleaming, tiled floor. We watch them without a word. The cassette player stops, garbles a few noises, then starts another tune. Ama lifts her head up. Pado kisses her, once, twice, until their mouths join them together and their arms let go.

Duccio reaches for the car key, stands and pushes his chair back under the table: 'Let's go outside.'

We follow him out of the door. Ama's white dress turns in the restaurant like a tablecloth blowing in the wind, wiping everything clean.

We get into the car and wait for Ama and Pado. There's hardly any light in the car, only a trickle from a lamp outside the restaurant. Duccio swings the car key round his bored fingers. Then he picks up a guidebook and squints at the columns of script. He marks a couple of spots with a pencil. He doesn't have much to do now that the maps have come to an end. Then we watch Ama and Pado emerge from the restaurant. We drive back home. The lowered windows let in noises of all kinds: crickets, night birds and the spraying-clicking sound of irrigation pipes washing the cornfields with water. Pado rushes the car up the drive through the vineyards. The bumps and holes throw us from side to side. Pado jumps out and tugs at the broken gate. It only springs back. We sit and watch him, digging his heels into the crumbling night earth. Ama tells him to give up. We leave the car where it is on the edge of the vineyard. Giulio has fallen asleep. Ama doesn't want us to spend another night in the car. Pado tells us to settle down somewhere in the house. Duccio and I carry Giulio, half asleep, to the corner of the room Ama cleared in the morning before going to the post office. The clean area of floorboard shines in the light, a contrast to the dirt on the other side.

'I'll be back in a second,' Pado reassures us.

We lie down on the creaking wood. Pado reappears a few minutes later with some blankets and cushions. He drops them onto us. One falls half across my face. I leave it there, breathing in the rough itchy material.

Pado shuts the door behind him. I can see dust, in the night draught, gathering into small bundles, racing across the parquet floor.

Then he opens the door again and walks over towards us. 'You've all done so well today,' he tells us, bending over to kiss each of us in turn. 'I'm proud of you. *Buonanotte ragazzi.*'

'Why did the chicken cross the road?' Giulio asks. I can hear Pado smile in the darkness of the room because he can't think of an answer. As he's closing our door, I whisper, 'Pado.'

'What?'

'Aldo Moro is dead. They killed him.'

Pado is saying something to Ama in the corridor outside. Then Giulio suddenly leans over his blanket and throws up on the floorboards. His sick is full of little bits of tuna. Duccio turns on the light. He tosses a cleaning rag over to Giulio to mop up.

'Better not disturb Ama and Pado now,' he says.

I help Giulio with the rag. He doesn't look at me. Ama and Pado won't know about this and I'm sure he'll never tell anyone what happened on the stairs in the restaurant.

14

Ama disappears off to the post office again, first thing after lunch. She can't stop worrying about us staying behind at the house with Pado whilst she's in Germany: 'It's no good, Machance is just going to have to come out.'

Pado soon has us out in the garden digging up clumps of thistle and removing ivy from the orchard trees. We carry the ripped-up roots and ivy to a pile under the walnut tree. It smells like a million tadpoles there, a warm, steamy smell of rot. Pado tells me to dig faster, but I can't because each worm I find has to be put back in its hole and each unwanted thought that springs up has to be smoothed back into the earth. Then Pado needs a rake. He hunts the house and stable. He can't find one. He is sure they sell them in the village shop. Giulio says he'll buy one, but Pado won't let him go alone. I'm sent off to accompany him.

It's quite a way to the shop, down past the church and

post office. We keep on thinking that we'll bump into
Ama, but there's no one on the track except us. Once we
reach the village, the houses become long and narrow with
white shutters, the doors and windows in different places in
each house. The shopkeeper asks why we need a rake and
we shout 'Thistles!' simultaneously. He says he's not sure a
rake is the best thing, but he sends us off with the only one
he's got and I hand him the fifty-franc note Pado gave us.
On the way back, I lift the rake up like a flagpole and Giulio
picks leaves and stabs them onto the sharp spikes. We soon
have a spread of leaves, green, yellow and red. I try to stick
an old crisp packet on too. I know you can't put plastic on
the compost heap, but I want to do it anyway.

Giulio insists on going down to see the river, so by the church
we take a different route. We run down the lane, swooping
the rake at overhanging branches. The crisp packet falls off its
spike and we are fighting over who is going to stick it back on
when we hear a group of loud voices. We peer over the edge
of the path, through the reeds and grass, and see a minibus
parked by the side of the river. There is a gathering of maybe
eight boys packing up a dinghy. Giulio and I watch them for
ten minutes at least. The minibus has camping equipment
in the back and the name of a school or something written
along the side. There's a sticker with 'GB' on it above the
number-plate. Giulio wants to go and see the dinghy so we
clamber down the bank and walk up to the boys. They stop
what they are doing and turn to face us.

'*Bonjour*,' we shout, '*on peut voir votre bateau?* Can we look
at your boat?'

The tallest boy steps forward. He says something that sounds like French but isn't.

'*On peut voir le bateau?* The boat!' Giulio repeats.

'*Nous Anglais* . . . We're English!' the tall boy replies in a hostile voice.

Giulio and I look at each other, amazed. They're English. We can't believe it.

'Can we see the boat?' we shout loudly in English, rushing forward.

The boys stare at us, taken aback. They form a closed wall in front of the dinghy.

'Are you English?' one of them asks, suspicious.

I look at Giulio. He's still trying to peek through them at the dinghy. 'Sort of,' I say back.

'So why do you speak French like that?'

'Because . . .'

'Can we see your boat,' I repeat. No one replies.

They're looking at us strangely now. Giulio backs away and comes and stands beside me. The tall boy has moved further forward, right in front of us. A long minute goes by. He studies me, up and down.

'You know what they are?' he calls out to the group behind him. He smiles to himself. 'They're Pakis!'

The boys fall about laughing. One of them laughs so much he has to sit down on the dinghy. The pebbles on the edge of the river make a crunching noise under his weight. Giulio and I don't understand.

'We only want to see your boat,' Giulio tries again.

Then the tall boy gets angry: 'You can't see our boat. Fuck off! Go on, fuck off you filthy Pakis!'

He picks up a stone and hurls it at my feet. It ricochets off the ground and hits my shin with a sharp pain. I grab Giulio and together we scamper up the bank. A boy snatches me by the shirt and pulls me down. I manage to get up, but Giulio falls beside me. I scoop him up. Another boy grabs me by the collar and yanks me down again. He kicks me in the back, the stomach and punches me in the face. 'Paki bastard,' a boy is chanting with a strange sideways jiggling of the head, in an accent I've never heard. Giulio is crying and they push him to the ground too. Finally the tall boy scours the depths of his stomach and throat for a large pile of laughing spit and splashes it on my face between my eyes. It slides, with a smell of chewing gum and beer, onto my nose and, by the time the tall boy has gone, it has begun dripping onto my mouth. Giulio is holding my arm and I'm holding him. We sit for a while, not moving. Then I can hear the sound of a man walking through the undergrowth. He doesn't see us. He walks down towards the dinghy and gathers the boys together. The minibus leaves with the dinghy strapped to a trailer. My knee is shaking against the grass, like chattering teeth. Giulio picks up the rake and starts walking back home. He pulls it by the handle so the metal head scrapes and screams against the earth. Its grating snares on roots, flicks them up. Giulio's head rocks more and more.

Pado is bent over a terracotta pot, cleaning out earth and roots.

'Thanks for the rake, *grazie*,' he waves, without really looking up.

When we don't answer, he straightens up and lets out a shout. Giulio carries on walking towards the house. I stop to look at Pado, my cut forehead driving blood down my nose. He hurries towards me, tripping over the grass. My eyes are still bulging with panic. I can't say why we left running and joking to get a rake and came back stunted and broken. Ama catches up with Giulio and takes him by the shoulders into the kitchen. 'Giulio! Giulio!' she screams. Pado demands an explanation. Ama is so frantic that the room can barely contain her. I describe what happened. Giulio breaks in. He had noticed the boys before I did, down by the river. They were English, so we spoke to them.

'Let me see your knee,' Pado asks Giulio.

I show them my forehead and my stomach, swollen with patterns of red bruising. Ama cleans my mouth with antiseptic wipes because Giulio has said how the spit shot out onto my face and dripped onto my lips. I can still feel the smell rubbing against my teeth. I fight hard to stop it entering my throat, my body, my mind. My head is racing with thoughts, thoughts puffed up with blood. I concentrate on the pain to keep me from straying. I mustn't remember any of this, no sounds, no words, no images, no nothing. It all has to be driven away.

'What were they playing at?' Ama wonders. 'Why would anyone do a thing like that?'

That's all Pado needs to shout for silence and to tell Ama that she comes from a country of savages.

'Which country?' Ama protests. Then she realises it's not the time and place to argue with Pado about who comes from where. Ama says it's maybe something we did or maybe we were too friendly with them.

'Too friendly!' Pado is out of his mind. 'Does being friendly mean you get beaten up?'

Ama backs down. 'No, of course not, but there must be some reason.'

'Did they say anything?' Pado asks.

'They put on a funny accent,' Giulio tells him.

'A funny accent? What kind of accent?' Pado demands.

'I don't know. A funny accent! Then they said, "Fuck off Pakis!"'

'What's Paki?' I ask, but Pado has turned away and is kicking the door. Ama goes to stop him because if he carries on the house will fall out of its windows. He kicks and kicks and kicks. He repeats the word, 'Paki!' He hurls it against the walls, splattering the room with names. 'What kind of fucking people would do that?'

'Don't get angry,' Ama begs, 'we'll call the police.'

'Call the police, what bloody good will that do? What do they care about my children being beaten up because they're Pakis?'

'Well, we have to report it somewhere! I'll go to the *Mairie* now.'

'Come off it, they'll laugh. What's a fight between children for them?'

'Don't be ridiculous, they weren't children. They were teenagers. Besides there can't be too many English school minibuses in the area.'

Pado won't listen to her or finish punching and kicking the walls. I can see a tomato on the window ledge is going to fall and that's all I can think about. If it's hard, that's all right. But if it's ripe, then it will squash and flatten onto the tiled floor.

Pado grabs me by the hand. 'Come on!'

He pulls me off to the car. Duccio wants to come too. 'Stay and look after Giulio,' Pado tells him.

*   *   *

Pado pushes me into the car. We speed off through the vineyard and down towards the river. He burns round corners and all the time he says: 'Keep an eye out for them.' He drives down lanes, backs into clearings where fishermen have built wooden huts.

'Is that them? *Ti ricordi?*' he says, pointing at a couple of men.

'No,' I say.

'How about those three?'

I don't want to see them anyway. I have nothing but fear inside me. I rub my mouth and I sense the taste. Pado won't calm down. We drive faster and faster. We head towards Châtellerault. Someone shouts at us as we swerve out of the way of a truck.

'Fuck you!' Pado yells and the driver shakes his fist. We slip down a hill into side roads bordered with poplar trees which measure the land like pins on a map.

'They have to be here somewhere.' We go from lane to lane.

'Please stop,' I say to Pado. I can feel my stomach hurting and thoughts pummelling away at my temples. My mind is giving way. 'Please stop!'

He won't. We carry on. I say, forget it. I say we have to go home and anyway perhaps Ama is right, I shouldn't have been so friendly with them.

'It wasn't about being too friendly. It was about being too bloody brown,' he tells me.

'Well maybe I am too brown,' I answer.

'Don't you even think anything like that ever again! *Mai!*

Mai!' he bellows, irate. But I didn't say anything, I only said that I shouldn't have been in the sun, like Ama said, because now look at the result.

'You are who you are, never forget that!'

I have little chance of forgetting as it's written across my face for ever. I think of Nonno and how he could never leave his land. I see his face travelled like a path, a path that has ended at the edge of his vineyard. Pado accelerates. He tears through blind bends and spurs me on from time to time: 'Are you sure it's not that lot?' I can't think what he would do if it was them. Would he get out and kick them? Would he scream? Would he shout? Would he sit still and wait for them to tell him they hated him too?

It's getting dark now. There is no one left outside. Lamps come on in houses. The outlines of rooms appear out of nowhere. People close windows, pull shutters together. Pado takes a left turn out of a village.

'Let's go for a drive,' he says, ramming down on the gear stick.

We dart off into the countryside. The reddening sun is dropping down in the sky, leaving a vague dab of light behind in the wing mirrors. Pado rolls down a window and the evening air comes smashing in. He belts down the straight lanes. I watch his hands on the driving-wheel, chasing each other through the turns. Pado switches on the headlights and the lanes flick open before us. Every turning becomes wider than the last. Every tree looms larger. The headlights know the way. The road slips onwards and we go with it. An insect comes crashing into the windscreen and its eyes slide apart, emptying its body. Its antennae go this way and that. Its tongue curls up and round. Its wings fall away and whistle off behind.

'Sorry,' I mouth to it. Sorry for this.

An occasional farmhouse jumps out at us, poking its roof above the sparse hedgerows. Trees crowd over us now. Branches rain on the roof of the car, wooden drops tapping away. Moths hover in the lights. A mess of beaten, transparent, fragile wings and legs twist and turn across the windscreen. A new world is created as the headlights carry us forward. Their beams spiral and trap another moth. It spins towards us, welcoming the light. It spreads across the glass, cut down the middle. Little clouds of yellow liquid streak our vision. A wing stays. It won't give way, stuck, imprinted. 'Sorry,' for always, 'sorry, sorry, sorry.' A deadened dense silence fills the gap between our seats. I'm floating alone, wrapped in thoughts of torn, brittle insect bodies and wings.

'Sometimes it feels good to drive,' Pado murmurs, laying his head on the seat rest behind him. The rushing air sucks at his shirt collar and I can see he wants to cry and it's only because of me that he won't.

15

Machance is going to come over. Ama has managed to make her agree, after ten phone calls. She'll only stay a while though.

'If I can cope with coming back here, I'm sure she can,' Ama assures Pado. He has organised for one of his colleagues, John Betlam, to drive Machance to us in his car.

Ama has to prepare Machance's room. She walks through the garden picking wild flowers to put in a vase. She gathers together a broom, a dustpan and some clean linen.

She hands me a dustbin bag. '*Viens.* I could do with some help.'

I follow her hesitantly up the stairs. Ama stops, from time to time, to lift up bits of grit she's missed on the wood of the banisters. Her footsteps are uneasy. No one's been into Machance and Grand Maurice's room yet.

Ama puts her things down in front of the closed bedroom

door. She takes a little breath. She squeezes my shoulder, then grabs the door handle and twists the room open. We both stand on the threshold, peering into the stale air. Then Ama marches past me towards the window. She pushes it open and fixes the shutters to the wall outside. Two years of darkness evaporate slowly. Ama and I stand watching the light reclaim every corner of the room, spreading like spilt water across the floor and down the walls.

The bed is unmade. The sheets and blankets are still gathered in folding mounds and coils the way they were left. A few books are stacked on a shelf near the window. By the side of the bed, a decorated table holds up a bowl of objects: a whistle, a torch, a pencil and notepad. Next to the bowl is an unstamped postcard of Notre-Dame-La-Grande in Poitiers. Ama picks it up and flips it over. She looks at it without expression. She puts the card back on the table, face down. She turns and gazes out of the window for a few seconds and then moves on. I stretch over to read the card. It only has our names and an address written in its left column: the address of Nonno's house in Italy. I recognise the discreet writing. The gradual leaning of the letters on the address is familiar. I follow the movement of the words, jumping from one to the other, knowing, with every line, that this is Grand Maurice's handwriting. Maybe this was the last thing he wrote, a card to us. Maybe this is the last thing that he touched. Then I have to stop thinking. I mustn't imagine the words that Grand Maurice was going to write on our card, all the sentences that he took with him and which went through his head as he slid under the water. I prop the card up, against a book. It stares back at me, never sent, never filled in.

I take the torch from the table. I flick it on. It works for a few seconds then fades. I shake it and it works again.

'Hold the bin bag open please,' Ama says in a weary voice.

She brushes the floor and scoops up the piles of dirt. A long strand of hair hangs off the end of the brush. Ama stops and rubs at a stain. Then she leans her back against the wall and lets herself slide down to the floor. She pulls her knees up against her chest. She closes her eyes and holds her hands over them.

I drop the torch and sit down next to her: 'Are you all right Ama, what's wrong?'

She tries to smile at me. Her voice is shivering, drowning in her throat. 'My love, maybe you should go downstairs and play with your brothers. I'll manage on my own.'

I stand up to go, but linger by the door waiting for Ama to tell me to leave again. She doesn't say anything. She doesn't seem to notice I'm still there. She gets on with cleaning the room. She shakes a carpet out of the window. I hear little bits fall out of it, light rain into the gutter below.

Then Ama looks at her watch and says, 'Machance should be packing up her things to leave now.'

I clamber onto the bed and my thoughts evaporate upwards into the room. I imagine Machance leaving her house in England, the way she left this one, deciding what to take and what to leave. I see her weaving, drained and tired, between her packets and boxes. She goes from room to room, drawing the curtains behind her, cutting out the light, steeping the house in sealed calm. Forgotten apples fall and roll into corners. She doesn't pick them up. By the time she returns, they will have dried up and shrivelled. Then I imagine Pado's colleague, John Betlam, turning up. His waiting car backs up against the front door and sprays the house with acrid exhaust fumes. They hang off Machance like scarves of smoke as she shuts the door and puts her things in the boot. The car sets off down the drive. Perhaps Machance hopes she can turn and snatch a last glimpse of her house. Then the trees drop back and the flatness of the bare tarmac begins. Machance doesn't talk. Shadows of passing meadows invade her absent eyes. Each time the car drives into a village, she sighs at the window, pressing her face into the glass, and a wave of breath clouds her vision. She sweeps along house fronts, peers into doors. Then, as the car crosses town squares, she sits up straight and makes mouthfuls of wishes into the wide façades of churches. She's talking about France, to herself, about Grand Maurice and her return home. I can feel all the loss in the world surging forward with her, hurrying.

Ama taps me on the shoulder without warning, 'Jean-Pio! You've been sitting doing absolutely nothing on that bed for ten minutes! *Mais qu'est-ce qu'on va faire de toi? Vraiment mon chéri.* This is getting beyond a joke!'

Ama hauls me up off the bed and pulls the old sheets back. The bare mattress underneath lets off a damp, trapped smell. Two long dips, the size of bodies, appear in the pattern of the material, either side. Ama quickly unfolds the clean white sheet that she's carrying and wraps it over the mattress. She knocks the pillows together, opens the window wider, ushers me out and shuts the door.

*   *   *

We eat supper quickly. Ama is in a hurry. While we finish our pudding, she goes back to tidying out the rooms upstairs. All of us need a separate bedroom she says, so Pado has transformed the front part of the attic into a bedroom for Duccio. He has hung long swathes of fabric across the beams and made a padded room like a tent, a hidden world up a flimsy step-ladder where no one can disturb Duccio. I try and get a view of Pado's watch from across the table. It's almost dark. Machance must be at the ferry now. I carry my plate to the sink. My head is spinning slightly. I feel queasy. I ask to go outside. What if Machance's ferry sinks?

I kneel on the steps at the front of the house. I bury my head in my chest. I have to save Machance. In my mind, I devise ways she can stop the water from flooding into her cabin. Then I remember how long she takes just to put on her cardigan. How is she going to slip on a life jacket in a hurry? My mind is alight with scenes of sinking ships, ripped-open hulls letting in the waves, and punctured life jackets. I imagine Machance in a daze, snaking her way down the corridors and decks looking for an exit, her long skirt soaking up the water at her feet. Her ship skips and tilts on the crazed sea. My thoughts are crumbling, panic sings through my ears. How is she going to get out? How will she run and wake everyone when the ship goes down?

'*Ma cosa stai facendo?* What are you doing over there?' Pado shouts from the kitchen door.

I look up, bewildered. I quickly pick off a piece of moss from the steps and hold it up to Pado. He walks over.

'Moss?' Pado smiles, taking it from the palm of my hand.

161

'Special moss!' I reply shakily.

'Doesn't look very special to me,' Pado laughs. 'Anyway, it's bedtime for you.'

I enter my new bedroom. It's been cleared and tidied by Ama. There's a black metal bed in the corner with new sheets. A smooth shelf runs along the wall. I get undressed and I lay my head down on my pillow. It has a chemical white smell, a bit like the cleaning liquid for the public loos on the motorways. I feel sick with thoughts again. I try and concentrate on the room, but the image of Machance's ferry keeps on coming back. I only hope Machance hasn't locked her door and fallen asleep. I picture her boat turning and heading out to sea. I feel myself swivel in bed, carried by reeling, foamy waves. The waters rush, hungry. I dig my face into my pillow. I breathe deeply and exhale with every imagined wave. I flick on my side light. I can't think like this. I'll never sleep. I scrape at the metal bed legs, anything to change my thoughts. Still the waves writhe up and down restlessly, kicking and complaining at the burden of Machance's boat. I walk to the other side of the bedroom. The sound of greased, rusting chains creaks up and down in my head. It's going to sink. I clutch my arms one against the other: 'She won't sink.' I say it faster and faster. 'She won't sink.' My mind burns, gnaws. I'm fading, waiting for the first bodies to float between the cars, the deck a mass of corpses, some with eyes of a previous life, others with life jackets and cleaned-out faces as if they never lived. How long did Grand Maurice struggle against the waters? What did he think as the lake overwhelmed him and he sank into the mud? Did he have the same face as Aldo Moro in his car boot when he plunged to the bottom? 'She won't sink, she can't sink.' I say it ten times, louder and louder, then again and again, until I can no longer pronounce the words. I separate them out, but again unwanted thoughts slide into the gaps between the words and I have to rush and open the window. The night hangs unfinished in front of me.

I fall asleep clasped to my pillow. In the morning, I sprint downstairs. Ama is alone in the kitchen making herself some coffee.

'Why isn't Machance here?' I scream at her.

'What a way to begin the day Jean-Pio! How about "good morning", for a start?' Ama looks tired.

'Why isn't Machance here?' I repeat.

'I'm sure she won't be here till this evening. It's a long drive from England. Come on, sit down and have some breakfast!'

I drink some water.

The day passes slowly, nudging forward reluctantly. Ama keeps us busy with tasks. Pado wonders how his colleague is getting along with Machance. I dare not ask where they are, in case they're nowhere, drifting lifeless with the currents of the sea. I have to keep my mind still all day. I have to keep Machance afloat. I concentrate on the work I've been given. I water the flowers Pado has planted. I wipe the kitchen windows with a torn napkin Ama has found with Machance's initials embroidered on it. I soak the napkin in soapy water and make sure the panes are clean. Then I wrap the napkin into a ball and hold it in my pocket all day, clasping its initials so that Machance arrives safely. Ama races Pado through the garden, showing him things to do and suggesting different ways to repair the broken gate. The house, it seems, is pleased to have Ama around, relieved to feel her familiar touch, to live once more. She winds it up like a tired machine, giving it reason to start again.

After supper, we're sitting out on the lawn, which Pado has tried to mow. The grass sprouts up in unequal patches, with deep slashes in the dry mud where the plants have been cut to the ground. Ama is worried. There is no sign of Machance. Pado reckons we should have gone to the post office again and rung, in case she decided not to come over to France after all. I'm thinking of the ferry grinding along the sea bed, packed with drowned people who'll never arrive anywhere. I know the journey from England doesn't take this long. Ama hands out some biscuits. Giulio crumbles one onto his lap and then flicks the bits into the air. Pado takes the rest of the biscuit from him saying it's a waste. Then some headlights bump up the drive, a rising, piercing glow, unveiling the vineyard. A silver car stops down by the gate, pointing its lights at the front of the house. Two blurred faces sit inside. We jump up and walk towards the car. Ama takes off her shoes and runs a little to get there before us. Machance steps out of the car. We swarm around her, kiss and greet her. She stands in the middle of us, motionless and small. We ask her questions, look for her luggage. Then she breaks through our welcoming arms and makes her way towards the house, swerving like a moth,

in and out of the beams of light, hands sheltering her hollow
eyes. She stops and searches for something in her pocket. She
pulls out an iron key. The door is already open.

A light goes on in one of the windows of the first floor.
Machance has reached her bedroom. Ama drops what she
is doing and dashes across the lawn and into the house. We
unpack the rest of the car with Pado. His colleague, John Betlam,
wants to set off straight away. He has to get to Clermont-
Ferrand before midnight. We pile up bags and boxes on the
grass next to the car, wedging them between bushes and vine
stakes. Pado quickly swaps news with John and thanks him for
helping out with Machance. The car starts up again. The headlights leap away from the house, leaving a suspended shadow
behind. We help Pado carry the luggage inside. Ama comes
back out and heads for the last cardboard box left by the gate.
She holds it up high so she can see her way forward, but then
she trips. In the dark, we hear cardboard splitting and ripping as
it's dropped to the ground. Bits of paper scrape and flap in the
night breeze. We run to help her. Our feet knock against objects
in the grass. Photos of people in gilded frames lie all around us
on the lawn. We narrow our eyes to find the faces staring up at
us, trying to recognise smiles and stares. Ama kneels down and
gathers the photos together. She puts them back in the ripped
box, using one arm to bind the cardboard together. She presses
the box against her chest, the frames and glass chiming discor-
dant sounds inside. She fumbles through the dark, running her
free hand over the grass to make sure no photos are left.

*   *   *

The following morning, we wake up to Ama talking, making us promise to be especially nice to Machance.

'She didn't have a good night. She's going to need special care today,' she repeats to us. Ama pulls three croissants from behind her back and wiggles them in front of us as an incentive.

'Yes,' we promise in unison.

I already knew that Machance was going to need help today, the way she did yesterday when her face made wishes into closed churches and I had to stop her ferry from sinking.

'She doesn't like it here, does she?' Giulio says.

'She loves it,' Ama answers. 'That's the problem. She's always loved it here. Coming back is just very hard for her, very hard.'

Ama leads us out to the big basin in the stable next to the kitchen. She undresses us and prods us in under the tap. The tap splutters out some grit-filled cold water. With a tin cup, Ama washes our hair and throws soapy water all over us. She sends us off into the garden with towels to get dry. We haven't got far when we see that there are people walking towards the house. We run in and warn Pado. The visitors stand in a tight bunch in the doorway. They're looking for Machance. Ama tries to persuade them to come back another day. 'Maybe tomorrow or the day after? She's not really up to seeing visitors.' They say they've already been waiting two years.

Pado reluctantly ushers them into the kitchen and pulls out a few chairs. He uncorks a bottle of wine and serves a few glasses. The visitors take up various chairs at the table, fingering their hats, scanning the room, sniffing discreetly at their cloudy glasses. One of them tells me I look just like Grand Maurice.

'What a tragic accident,' they sigh with leaden mouths.

Machance appears and they scrape their chairs across the tiled floor in the rush to stand up.

'*Nos condoléances*, our condolences,' they say all at once, solemnly.

The words catch Machance by surprise. She cowers slightly before stepping forward. She takes their hands, one by one, gently enveloping them in her own.

'*Merci*,' she repeats.

The visitors huddle round. They unravel their questions and stories, gradually, laboriously. Machance replies to them all with a lifeless gaze. One of the visitors is Monsieur Luzille, the village mayor. He has a folder with some forms. He shows them to Machance. She peels them out of the file noiselessly and lays them on the table.

'I'll deal with these another day,' she stammers.

Then Monsieur Luzille delves into his case and brings out a plastic bag with an official seal. 'The police gave me these last year when they closed the case, you might want to have them back.' He lays a see-through bag in front of Machance. A folded penknife, a roll of string and some wire are lined up under the plastic, pressing against it, pushing outwards. Machance draws back in her chair, sliding her hands off the table. She stares at the bag, packaged and taped.

Ama directs us out of the room. 'Go into the garden boys!' she says and we can barely hear her voice. I turn and look at the plastic bag through the closing door. It takes up the whole gap. Then the door shuts.

16

Beneath the steps to the front entrance are the cellars, a darkened mirror of the house above, an open pattern without doors. The cellars have a central clearing and, from this, a silent spread of damp alleyways fans outwards. The clearing has one feeble shaft of light which drips without sound. We explore the shapes of leaking water and mould with torches and candles. We divide up the territory. Giulio has the part with the freezer. I have the wine cellars. Duccio takes over the longest and darkest corridor which has mossy floors, the oil tank and the date '1850' to mark the point where the river flooded and filled the cellar, carrying bottles and labels away. We find the alcoves and holes we used for playing hide-and-seek with Grand Maurice. I'm sure that if I look hard enough I'm going to find something special that belonged to Grand Maurice and, when I do, I'm going to keep it for ever.

Machance stays in her bedroom the first day. She only comes down for lunch and her worries clamp and distort her face as she wanders about the house.

'It wasn't my choice to come here,' she says to Pado when he tries to cheer her up.

'You'd be more miserable on your own in England,' Ama tries.

Machance nods, 'Of course,' to make sure everyone stops talking about her. Then she sets off again on her own. Doors open and close throughout the house. Machance's footsteps pause, then start up again, cushioned in remembering.

It only takes a day for Ama to realise that Machance is not in a fit state to look after us whilst she's in Germany. Pado says he'll cope, but Ama heads off back to the post office and finds the number of an agency in Poitiers that provides *au pair* girls and house help. The morning Ama leaves for Germany, Marie-Jeanne turns up. She's from Bordeaux. She stands at the door with a brown leather suitcase and asks for Ama. Giulio runs off to find her. I stand in front of the girl, smiling. She doesn't seem to want to smile back, or even ask me my name. She's eyeing the house up and down, travelling through the layers of lifting dirt and over the stairs that crack with Machance's every footstep.

Ama finally calls her in and announces that Marie-Jeanne is the girl from the local agency who is going to look after us. Ama thanks her for coming at such short notice. She introduces us quickly.

'This is Duccio, the eldest – he gets on with it on his own. This is Jean-Pio, he's a real dreamer, if you know what I mean, aren't you darling? He needs to drink a lot of water.' Giulio gets a pat on the head: 'This little one is no trouble as long as he rests in the afternoon. *Généralement il est adorable.*'

Marie-Jeanne doesn't look at me or Giulio. Duccio has her full attention. She doesn't ask any questions. Ama looks a little surprised. She remains very polite though, even if you can tell she isn't absolutely sure about this *au pair*. Ama hasn't got much choice though. It's either this curly-haired girl who doesn't smile or Machance or, worse still, Pado popping in and out of his research work. Ama can't afford to worry about us when she's translating, swapping one language for another, non stop.

When Pado drives Ama to the train station in Tours, Marie-Jeanne is nowhere to be seen. Machance is convinced she is already cooking up trouble somewhere. Ama wanted to wish Marie-Jeanne good luck and tell her that there are some yoghurts on the top shelf of the fridge and that Giulio likes the peach ones and Duccio won't eat spinach and I mustn't be left on my own in my room because I gaze out of the window and do nothing. Pado has to hurry Ama to the car. She can't stop crying. She doesn't want to leave. Not now that all the travelling has ended and we've settled in the house. She covers her eyes with her fingers, spread out like two tipped fans.

'Good luck,' she whispers to us with a kiss.

Ama holds Machance tight. 'Be brave!' she whispers into her ear. 'Please! For me.'

Pado is trying to work out the quickest way to the station on the map. He consults with Duccio. Then Ama gently takes the map from Duccio and strokes his hair. As they drive away, I can see Ama muffling her cries inside the black, red and yellow lines of the map, and the map doesn't even show the box hotel rooms that await her and the frustration of translations that never say anything or of travels that still can't end.

Marie-Jeanne strolls into the kitchen. She's been down to the village to get some cigarettes. Machance points at her fingers locked around a cigarette. 'I'm afraid you'll have to do that out of the window or outside.'

Perhaps I should show Marie-Jeanne the picture of the man who smoked sixty cigarettes a day with the purple piles of tumour growing out of his greying skin. Giulio tells me I shouldn't bother. He reminds me of what happened with Michael's cigarettes last time in England.

Machance sorts out the food Ama has left. She lines up the bowls and plates on the table. She opens the cupboards. All her old things have gone, brushed and cleaned away by Ama into dark bin bags with no order. Machance opens tins and lifts up lids. Stark, recently-washed surfaces glare back at her. There is a bowl of broccoli, packed to the top and sprinkled with little white specks of garlic. The hairs from Machance's chin, caught in her nails, skim the green broccoli like record needles. Hairs reading invisible, sound-filled grooves. Machance makes herself some tea and drinks it as if each sip were slowly dissolving her presence away. She feels us staring at her, waiting. She asks Marie-Jeanne to read to us, upstairs, while she prepares the food, but Marie-Jeanne has such a strong accent, and all three of us look so disappointed, ten minutes into our

171

story, that she throws down the book and storms out of the room.

Duccio already has a few theories about Marie-Jeanne. She's obviously homesick because you don't throw books down on the floor like that.

'We did look bored,' I say.

Duccio reckons that she's a bit funny in the head too and she definitely doesn't floss her teeth and, what's more, she flushed the loo without washing her hands. Giulio confirms that he saw her leave the loo without washing her hands. All she did was run her palms along her skirt. Now her hands are roaming about the rooms, travelling like patches of flies across the house. She'll be sliding them down the banisters, rubbing them on the door knobs and scraping at the kitchen plates, all with fingers filthy from yanking the chain above the loo which, Pado says, is a tassel of bacteria hanging in the air like a diseased sword. Then if she goes into the kitchen, she'll be checking no one is there and then opening and closing the containers in the fridge, picking at the food, sliding it out of the plastic and sucking her fingers dry.

It begins to rain, a heavy rain that already has the full heat of summer in it. Machance trundles past us to her bedroom. We can hear her trying to close her high window, the latch swings down against the frame, out of her reach. She calls out for me to give her a hand. Her voice runs down the corridor, hurried by the rain outside. We look at each other. I don't want to go into her room because of all the photos of Grand Maurice, her parents and lots of other dead people she brought with her in the box from England. Finally I get up and amble down the corridor. I stop in the doorway to Machance's bedroom. Books and objects litter the floor and a suitcase lies open across the bed. My eyes can't stop looking at the photographs: poses, gazes and laughs of people who are no longer. I clench my fists so as not to get any thoughts. I dig my nails into the palms of my hands. Machance pushes me a chair. She helps me onto it. There is rain dripping onto the window ledge, bouncing off the wood. I slam down the window latch. The rain bashes against the glass. I stay on the chair, listening to the downpour rapping the pane above my head.

I try to prevent myself from seeing the photos again, but they spring up in front of my eyes, wherever I look. There are pictures of Grand Maurice in all corners of the room, photos of him forty years ago, twenty years ago, two years ago, portraits of him as a young boy, snaps of the house here. Machance sits on her bed and pats the cover so that I sit down next to her. She chooses a picture from the crowd standing on her bedside table and holds it up for me. It's a photo of Grand Maurice as a child with his grandmother. He is dressed in a sailor's uniform, with a hat covering his hair. The grandmother is carrying a parasol and wears a long dress that touches the floor. Machance wipes the surface of the photo with the corner of her sleeve and looks at it again, closer this time.

'There is a whole story behind this photograph,' she says slowly. 'Grand Maurice's grandmother was going blind, but he couldn't accept it.' She points to something that looks like a mole on Grand Maurice's chin. 'See that?' Machance smiles to herself. 'He put that dot on his skin, just for his grandmother.'

She tells me that one afternoon when playing in his grandmother's attic, Grand Maurice found a beautiful butterfly that had got trapped trying to get out of the window. It lay motionless, in perfect condition, on the window sill, its legs caught in a spider's web. He cleaned the butterfly, dusted its wings and put it in a box. It still didn't stir. He went downstairs to show it to his grandmother. She wasn't there. He called and called. No one came. Eventually he found his grandmother in the garden. She was sitting with a group of friends on the lawn.

He said to her, 'Look at this butterfly, isn't it beautiful?'

His grandmother turned, smiled blankly and then joined the others in conversation again. He pulled at her sleeve. 'Look at my butterfly,' he kept on repeating and still no one took any notice of him.

He stood there for a while not knowing what to do. He tossed the box from one hand to the other. He looked at each of them, eating and talking. He repeated his grandmother's name. Yet she didn't stop talking. So he ran to the end of the garden and stood on his own facing the skies. He opened up the box and threw the dry butterfly into the wind. It fell to the ground. He tried again, blowing it gently on its way. Each time, the butterfly simply floated to the ground without moving. Its wings caught on the grass and, the more he picked it up, the more damaged it became. Then it began to rain, there and then, on a sunny day. It began to rain hard.

He was holding the butterfly in his hands and the rain was pummelling its body, black powder coming off its cracked legs onto his palms. He tried to protect it from the rain. He cupped its head and wings. From time to time, he'd wipe his face and it too smeared with butterfly, black powdery ink all over his mouth and cheeks. He walked back to the house. His grandmother was fretting, bringing in her guests, protecting her hair from the sudden rain. There were people behind her carrying plates and checking their shoes for mud. He stood in the hall with the mirror on one side, and his grandmother on the other. He could see his face was a wet grey-and-black smudge and yet his grandmother was still staring at him, fraught about her guests.

'What am I going to do?' she kept on saying to him. 'Are all my chairs still outside?'

He looked at her and he couldn't speak because she hadn't seen the butterfly and because now his face was black with dead insect and she hadn't even noticed. She grabbed him by the arm and led him clumsily to the piano. 'Play something for the guests, quickly.'

He played the piano, facing the guests, and they clapped and smiled.

When he left, no one asked about his butterfly or wondered why his face was black-and-grey. He walked back outside and stood in the rain. The drops spilt onto his face, almost washing it clean.

He took the remains of the butterfly back up to the attic and laid them on the window sill by the spider's web. He opened the window. The rotting wood of its frame snapped loudly and from the cracks in the roof came a rush of butterflies. All above him, butterflies were emerging from their chrysalises. He stood fixed to the spot. He wanted to touch them all as they pushed forward into the light, streaming in from all sides, looking for a clearing to fly into. Soon the room was ticking away with butterflies. They swooped in and out of the stacked furniture, spinning and twirling, round, up and through. More and more of them emerged from the wood, thicker and faster, and the brush of their wings made him blink. With his hands, he guided the butterflies out of the window. When the last one had flown away, he went to his room and looked in the mirror. His face was clean again, washed by the rain, except for one stain on his chin. That part was black, very black, as if the dead butterfly had slid under his skin, slithered in and lost itself inside his face.

When he got up the next day, the stain was still there and the day after too. He would sit through dinners, lunches and breakfasts waiting for his grandmother to say, 'Wash your chin!' or, 'What is that on your face?' She never did. He would walk the garden, with a black-stained face, looking at the sun, feeling the heat on his chin. One evening he was sitting opposite his grandmother as she combed his hair and sang him songs. He kept on leaning his head back and pushing his chin up towards her. Still she didn't see anything. She combed and combed his hair. She even stroked his cheek and said nothing about the stain.

That night, he took out an ink pen and drew a small outline around the stain. It was a hard, black line. It was so strong that his grandmother had to see it, even if she was going blind. The next day, he waited at breakfast knowing that she would say something. She didn't. He went upstairs and drew another bigger, blacker line. The same went on for many days and, each morning as he woke, he would stare out of his window and draw the outline of the first cloud he saw on his chin. Some days it was a scribbled shimmering line. Other days it was bold and, other days still, it was a rainy haze across his skin.

By the second week, Machance says, Grand Maurice was checking all the mirrors in his grandmother's house. He wanted to see if some of them maybe didn't reveal the stain. Some were in dark rooms and he had to search to find the mark on his face. Others were next to windows and flooded with light and the thin shape of black clouds, darting across his skin, appeared as clear as day. He still wanted to make his grandmother see, force her to say, 'What on earth have you got on your face?' He wanted her to call him over and hold his head in her hands anxiously. Then the weather cleared and the days of blue sky never seemed to end. Each morning Grand Maurice would wake and look at the sky and he could see no clouds, nothing to draw onto his face, no shapes to carry him away. So he stopped outlining the patch on his chin with ink and, when he looked at the sky, he invented clouds instead. He imagined clouds of all shapes and sizes, enormous white mountains drifting across the blue and he waited for it to rain. Then his parents came to pick him up and, as he ran out to greet them, his mother said, 'What's that on your chin?', took out her handkerchief and wiped the stain away.

*   *   *

Machance stops as she began, unaware that she has told me anything, as if Grand Maurice's story had spiralled out of the bedroom itself, alone, unaccompanied. The wool of Machance's jersey rubs against my shoulders. I can feel its roughness through my shirt. That's all I can think of.

I wander off to find Giulio. We delve into Pado's piles of medical magazines.

'Duccio says Marie-Jeanne is strange,' he tells me between pages.

17

Ama turns up exhausted after her conference in Germany. She hasn't enjoyed being away.

'Translating is not a way to live. Thank God all that's over now.' She holds us tight.

'Pleased to have me back?' she whispers in our ears. She strokes Machance's hair. 'How have you been *Maman*?'

Pado comes in from the car with Ama's folders and a bursting briefcase. 'Shall I take your stuff upstairs?' he asks.

'Where's Marie-Jeanne?' Ama wonders. 'Has she been helpful?'

Duccio starts explaining that she never made any food and then gets cut off by Machance describing her smoking habits and Giulio complaining about the way she reads.

'What do you mean she smokes?' Ama is furious. I try to explain from the beginning and then everyone takes over. 'Stop, stop, you're all speaking at once. Why didn't she cook? Why couldn't she read properly?' She calls out to Pado, 'Gaspare, what's been going on here? I can't believe this!'

Pado attempts to calm her down. 'I really don't think she was right for the job, that's all,' he says brightly.

'See what happens when I'm not here?' she sighs. 'All you had to do was ring the agency and change her for another *au pair*, for goodness' sake, couldn't you even do that?'

'Forget it, anyway, you're back now,' Pado replies.

I want to add that it's not as simple as all that. I've seen Marie-Jeanne alone in the garden, moving reluctantly along the garden tracks, kicking the gravel like lumps of loneliness. Ama prepares the supper and lays out some plates on the table. Marie-Jeanne appears and complains that Duccio hasn't had his bath.

'Oh, *bonjour*! Have you enjoyed your holiday?' Ama starts sarcastically.

Pado takes Ama aside and whispers that if, for once, Marie-Jeanne wants to do something useful, she should do it, especially as we haven't yet told the girl that she's been more of a burden than a help.

Ducio looks uncomfortable, 'I don't need anyone to give me a bath.'

'When you're twelve you can think about having a bath alone,' Ama tells him.

Pado thinks he's old enough to begin getting in a bath on his own, but Ama has always been worried we're going to reach for the light switch with wet hands or go to sleep or worse still jump in the bath without checking the temperature and slide into boiling water.

When Marie-Jeanne takes Duccio for his bath, he looks at us in a certain way and Giulio thinks about it, as the food cooks in the oven, until something in his head makes him tell Ama that Duccio isn't happy. That's just before the oven bell goes.

'What are you talking about?' Ama asks, surprised.

I could have told her too that Duccio didn't want to go. Giulio insists, 'I'm sure Duccio wants to get out of the bath now.'

'Well, he can,' Pado objects, but Giulio knows he can't so he takes Ama by the hand and leads her up the stairs. The bathroom door is shut, not locked, and all Ama has to do is push it casually open. A little shove of the index finger.

From downstairs, we can suddenly hear a scraping commotion along the floorboards. Pado leafs through his report not aware that the ceiling is swaying from side to side with taps turning off, towels sliding violently off racks, naked skin shivering in the cold. 'Little scrubber!' Ama yells, enough for Pado to look up for a second, confused.

Then the bathroom pours out its load, splashed clothes, wet footsteps creasing the carpet into wide grooves along the floor. I'm counting the steps it is going to take before Marie-Jeanne's door is flung open, before the explanation begins.

Giulio said Marie-Jeanne didn't turn round. She let Ama push her in maddened strides, eyes shut, towels round her feet, hands searching for somewhere to go. Ama is disgusted by the girl's naked body clinging to the carpet like a soggy mass. She drags Marie-Jeanne's suitcase from behind the door. Everything from the drawers, the cupboard, the top of the table, is shoved in. She stuffs in dresses, trousers, boots and knickers on top of each other, unfolded and stamped down with outraged fists into the bursting bag. Ama empties shelves, clears out under the bed. There is to be no trace left. Marie-Jeanne vaguely tries to stop her, her nudity pressing against Ama's furious arms as they knock over scent bottles and lipsticks. Ama coughs up her words. She swallows her cries, presses her hands across her mouth, but, each time, an image comes back into her head to stay.

Machance has stopped serving the food. There's no point. The noise of forks and knives has been replaced by the thudding of footsteps down the fragile stairs: Ama leading Marie-Jeanne by the collar. Out without a word, and into the car in the dark, suitcase on lap. Giulio and I run out to watch the car leave. Ama drives off, with the girl in the back not sure whether to use her hands to close the door or try and wave goodbye. Giulio doesn't even attempt to wave back. That's because he saw it and I didn't. He saw the bathtub and Marie-Jeanne naked, holding Duccio between the legs. Not only that, his mouth was stitched speechless.

I don't understand. 'Who was having a bath? Duccio or her?'

'Both, and she had water up to her shoulders.'

No one's moved the plates by the morning. They're still in the same position as the night before. Ama is too dismayed to do anything and no one has even dared talk to her since the car shot off down the drive with the back door hinged to Marie-Jeanne's shaking arm. Her plate is still in the fridge, untouched, except for the sauce where Machance has run a long bony finger across the surface, breaking the congealed oil. I walk past the table and into the kitchen. I'm trying to see where last night went, whether the seats cling and breathe with Duccio's bewilderment. Duccio is spending the day in his room. Ama brings him some sporting magazines and a board game. He doesn't want them. He chucks them down the stairs and both Giulio and I know we had better not pick them up in case he turns on us.

Pado says it's an experience like any other. 'Was bound to happen one day. Rather a randy seventeen-year-old girl than an old man in the street.'

That doesn't make Ama laugh at all. 'It's the kind of thing that can screw a child up for ever.'

'Come on!' Pado teases her.

'It's no joke,' Ama snaps.

'What are you doing in there Jean-Pio?' Ama shouts suddenly, her voice pouncing on me, interrupting Pado.

I'm counting the packets and bottles on the shelves in the larder, gazing into the kitchen at the plastic bag full of Grand Maurice's things, still sealed with police tape, at the end of the table.

'Tempers die down slowly.' That's what Pado tells us.

It takes at least two days before things become calm again. In the meantime, the early summer winds are piling up leaves and blades of cut grass in front of the house. Machance is as dispirited as the day she arrived. She goes out for long walks in the morning and returns in the evening, bringing dusk back with her into the house. She walks past the table and up to her room without appetite or

183

word. 'I'm tired, just so tired,' she says when Ama attempts to talk to her.

Pado thinks it's her grief over Grand Maurice coming out.

Ama is worried. 'She's not eating anything, Gaspare,' she panics, when Pado tries to convince her it's normal that Machance should want to spend time alone.

'She needs to go over things. It was bound to be hard for her back here,' Pado reassures her. 'Besides, she must be eating something.' Otherwise she'd never be able to walk for miles and miles with nothing except the fields to distract her mind. I've seen her in the kitchen, though, hovering above the food, smelling the tastes in the air, but never eating.

One morning, when Machance is sitting on a bench at the end of the garden, down by the vines, Pado hands me a piece of toast with jam and an apple.

'Here, take this to Machance.'

I look at the bread in the palm of my hand, floating on its warmth. I'm not sure she's going to want it. We have to try. If not, as Ama says, 'she might shrivel and slip away into nothing'.

Machance doesn't notice me arriving or even turn when I call her name.

'Machance!' I shout, 'It's me. *C'est moi.*'

Machance isn't hungry. She holds the piece of toast at arm's length and the brown grains of the bread seem to harden a little with her every refusal. I manage to get her to bite into the apple. She churns the flesh fast so as not to taste it. She takes the toast from my hand and puts it down on the bench next to her. The jam rolls off the edges. 'No, no, you have to eat it,' I insist.

'I can't. *Je ne peux pas*,' she repeats, 'I can't.'

Then it's as if her mouth is silent again and the words she speaks come from nowhere. I sit down, peering into the grass with her. She tells me that looking into the grass is like staring into the bedroom carpet in the morning. She says that as she lies awake in bed she can get lost in the thousands of little carpet threads, twisted and curled before her like these blades of grass, each thread a hundred colours and each colour different from the next. She can follow the threads revolving and snaking their way in patterns, towards the dust, the stains and the smells that trickle into themselves. That's when the faces from the past start appearing in the tiny intricate shapes of grit, each face guiding you into the carpet, rising up out of nowhere, out of lines that disappear, out of shades and pockets that come and go as you blink.

Machance talks to me about Grand Maurice. I already feel the thoughts that swim through my ears and mind when she describes him, when the sound of his name burrows away at me. I get up to leave, but I can sense her words catching on hooks inside me. My thoughts spark off, falling like muddling dominoes. Machance knows I'm behind her, hovering, she doesn't have to look round. She fidgets on the bench. I don't want to talk, not now.

'It'll be all right,' I whisper to her, to myself.

Machance doesn't hear. She wants to talk. She tells me that soon after Grand Maurice got his foot caught in the rabbit trap, he couldn't take a single step without crying out in agony. His foot was continually swollen and sore. He would spend days rooted to the spot to avoid moving. He stayed in their bedroom most of the time and, all the while, Machance had to find ways to help him. She bought him a stick and special shoes. She encouraged him to walk more. She sought the advice of doctors. She changed his clothes every day, moved the furniture from room to room. The garden and fishing were Grand Maurice's only joys and Machance urged him to plant new flowers and trees. He built the greenhouse and the stone wall next to the vegetable garden. He would sit on the wall for hours, rearranging the stones, listening to the garden. Then, occasionally, he would take the car and go off fishing down at the lake. When he returned, they would sit and eat crayfish together, with Grand Maurice cracking each piece of shell like a memory ceasing to be. Then one day, he told Machance he wanted to walk all the way to the lake. She was delighted. She handed him his stick and watched him disappear into the vines. She thought about going with him. She thought she might shout, 'I'll come too, wait!', but Grand Maurice wouldn't have heard. He was already too far away, digging deeper into the land, limping and leaning on his stick, unable to pause for fear that the pain in his foot would take him if he stopped. That was the day he drowned.

'He loved you all so very much, particularly you,' Machance finishes, her words drying up into silence. I feel fear, absence from myself, dulling solitude. I'm loved by someone who's gone, never to be seen again, drowned in a lake.

'Each day is harder for me, not easier,' Machance breathes slowly. 'I miss him so much. Too much.' She knocks her heels against the bench. Shaped bits of dried mud fall away from under her shoes.

I turn and run back to the house. I find Ama going over some translations for Pado. She is flipping sentences, moving and shuffling words. I watch her write fast and think to rub out a word and then another and start again.

She looks at me. 'What's wrong? You seem a little agitated darling.'

'Machance isn't happy,' I blurt out.

'I know,' Ama says, reaching out and squeezing my arm, 'we have to look after her.' She leaves her hand on my sleeve, clutching at the fabric and I don't know if it's for me, for her or Machance.

18

Duccio has a fine black hair on his top lip. His first one. Ama tells us she noticed it a while ago and quietly hoped it would go away. Pado wants him to shave it off. Ama is adamant that it must be plucked. If it's shaved, it'll only grow back stronger.

'Shaving stimulates growth.'

Ama fumbles through her make-up drawer to find her tweezers. She clasps them onto Duccio's lone hair. He winces and kicks out as she yanks at his skin. The hair finally gives and she carries it to the window to get a better look in the light. She blows the hair across her palm. It slips through her fingers before Pado can examine it. Duccio has a tiny red welt over his lip. He rubs it furiously. Ama leafs through her address book to find Elizabeth's number: 'Time is running out.'

By the afternoon, Ama has been to the post office in the village. It's arranged: Elizabeth is coming straight over from England to paint Duccio.

The next day Pado drives to Poitiers station to collect

Elizabeth. She should have got off at Tours or Chinon, but she fell asleep on the train. Ama says that's pretty typical. Elizabeth makes no attempts to apologise when she arrives. In fact she's glad.

'Lucky I ended up in Poitiers. I had a whole hour in the car with Gaspare!'

Ama grumbles something and Duccio walks away in a sulk as soon as Elizabeth starts pulling her spindly easel out of the boot. It is smeared in dry paint, blues striped with pink, yellows and reds. She unloads her boxes, bags and brushes. A strong smell of turpentine wafts off each successive item. Ama takes Elizabeth to her bedroom. She has placed clumps of flowers in jam jars on the bedside table. Ama shuts us out of the room. 'Go off and play, go on! We have things to discuss.'

We can hear the two of them chatting away inside. Giulio reckons that Ama is telling Elizabeth how to paint Duccio. We'd better not tell him in case he gets more upset. We suddenly hear a snapping noise and press our ears against the closed door. Giulio thinks it must be Elizabeth's jaw clicking, the reason her husband left her. I can hear a noise too. It sounds more like her unlocking and locking her case. We'll have to check again later, during supper.

Machance has laid the table for dinner with the knives and forks so far under the sides of the plates, you can't see them. She can't understand why Giulio and I insist on being opposite Elizabeth.

'Since when is she your best friend? *Franchement vous êtes idiots,*' she shakes her head.

189

We persuade her that we only want to be near Elizabeth so we can make her happy. Ama told us, 'Things haven't always been easy for her.' Dinner is very disappointing though because we can't hear Elizabeth's jaw click at all. I try and listen carefully, to no avail. Giulio has a better idea: we should ask her to pronounce certain words.

'Do you prefer "Ouch!" in English or "*Aïe!*" in French?' he asks.

She looks at us oddly, but thinks about it. She prefers '*Aïe!*' Her jaw doesn't click as she says the word.

By the time we wake up the following morning, Elizabeth has already set up her easel on the lawn at the back of the house and had a long conversation with Pado about the freshly-dug flower-beds. Pado and Madame Joignet's son, Marc, have spent days cutting the grass and replacing withered flowers. Marc wasn't very happy about it at first. Grand Maurice, he says, never cared for elaborate lawns or anything like that. He liked to see wild plants and flowers everywhere, sprouting out of the middle of the lawn. Machance and Ama are discussing what Duccio should wear for Elizabeth's portrait. Ama is pleased that Machance is showing interest in something. Elizabeth originally wanted an outdoors, bare-chested look. After the Marie-Jeanne episode, though, Ama thinks that would be unwise. She can't decide then between Duccio's red shirt and the trousers she bought in Paris last year or simply his scruffy everyday clothes. If his clothes are too pretty it'll detract from his face, Elizabeth stresses.

'He has to appear strong, a noble savage look,' she adds.

Machance sighs impatiently. 'What is a noble savage look?' she wonders.

Elizabeth is about to launch into a description of what she means when Giulio comes downstairs to tell everyone Duccio is not leaving his room. He has a message for Ama: 'If he's made to sit for a painting, he's going to cut all his hair off.'

Giulio says it's true. He's got a pair of scissors in there and his door at the top of the step-ladder is closed. Ama rushes off upstairs, closely followed by Elizabeth.

Duccio has his door firmly locked and he's even put a chair up against it. Ama pleads with him from the bottom of the step-ladder.

'Please darling. It won't take long!'

Ama rattles the ladder from side to side. Duccio says he's going to climb out of the window and run away if she doesn't leave him alone. Then Ama has an idea. She tells Duccio he can have a go-cart or a bicycle if he comes down and sits for Elizabeth. The door springs open and Duccio climbs out of his attic room. Ama knew he would. She hugs Duccio triumphantly. He pushes her away. He's not going to give in that easily. He wants to find out when exactly he's getting a go-cart and what it's going to look like. Ama says she'll have to discuss it with Pado first.

Out in the garden, as Elizabeth is rearranging her easel, Ama tries to persuade Pado about the go-cart without Duccio hearing.

'What bloody go-cart? They're far too expensive,' Pado protests.

Ama puts her hands over his mouth. 'Go on. I'm sure we could afford one, only a basic one!' she says, kissing him.

Elizabeth is doing some preliminary drawings, wide black scratches of Duccio that half puncture the paper.

'It's going to take some time,' Elizabeth tells us as we gather round expectantly. 'Anyway, I need to get inspired first!' and she gets up, paint tubes and brushes falling off her lap. Pado lends her the black, rickety bicycle he's found in the stable. She sets off down the vineyard towards the village.

It's a melting hot afternoon. Machance goes to sleep on a chair under the laurel tree by the kitchen. Ama is busy sorting Elizabeth's preliminary drawings. She spreads them out on the lawn. Little insects hop on and off the white grainy sheets. We chase them away. She holds the sketches up and asks us what we think. A couple of hours later, Marc arrives, looking awkward. He asks to speak to Pado.

'*C'est urgent.* Quick!' he tells us.

Pado wonders what the matter could be and comes running out. Marc takes him to one side and whispers something in his ear. Pado looks concerned, then breaks into a giggling grin.

'*Mais, c'est grave*, it's serious,' Marc insists.

Pado tries to agree, 'Of course, *oui, bien sûr*,' but he can't stop laughing.

Ama desperately wants to find out what's so amusing. Marc won't tell her. He doesn't think it's that funny at all.

'What? Come on, what is it?' Ama keeps on yelling at Pado.

We all join in. Eventually, Pado manages to control himself and, once Marc has gone off to see Machance, he tells us that Elizabeth has been spotted cycling topless through the vineyards.

'Topless!' Ama lets out.

Marc says that Elizabeth was first seen down by the Girauds' farm. She then went up past Henri Parriard's vines and down to the river where it runs along the main road to Tours. By the time she had reached Claude Charvel's vines, Marc's cousin had already rung him to tell him to go up to the top of the hill to see for himself. Marc said he was on his way up there anyway and, as he came up the hill that divides his vines from his cousin's, he saw this blonde woman cycle past in the distance with her top off and her breasts hanging loose. He thought she must be a German tourist from the nearby campsite, but as he came closer he saw that it was Elizabeth with her T-shirt tied around her head like a scarf. He couldn't believe it. He was so shocked that he hid behind a tree and turned his eyes away as she went by. Pado's not sure how much Marc would have turned his eyes away. Even so, Ama says, it must have been a bit of a surprise for him. 'Poor man.'

Machance is outraged.

'*C'est une honte*, I can't believe it,' she's keeps on telling Marc. Ama tries to calm her down. Machance won't let herself be calmed. 'You've only been here a short while and already this happens.' Ama makes her a cup of her *tilleul* tea and pours a glass of red wine for Marc. She steers the conversation towards the garden and soon they are all talking about how they are going to cut the top of the walnut tree at the back of the house. Suddenly Elizabeth pedals through the vines in the distance on her way back to the house. Marc gets up to leave. He doesn't want to be here when everyone starts getting upset. Pado says there's absolutely nothing to get het up about.

'Let her do what she wants. For goodness' sake, she only gave her knockers a breath of fresh air!' he says, and then he's off laughing again. Machance reckons he wouldn't be very amused if one of his guests had cycled naked through his village in Italy.

'I'm not sure Nonna would have been that delighted either,' she adds.

Elizabeth is facing a large welcoming party when she glides across the lawn and lets the bicycle drop gently onto the grass.

'Goodness, I'm pooped!' she exhales. 'It's so beautiful here! I wanted to see more and more.' There's a transparent line of sweat running down the back of her neck onto her shoulder blades. It flows like a silent tap, emerging from the depths of her blonde hair, trickling, meandering across her skin.

Ama launches straight in with: 'Please don't cycle topless again, Elizabeth. It's caused a few problems!'

Elizabeth is a little taken aback. 'What! How on earth do you know that? No one could see me. I swear.'

'The trees have eyes here,' Pado joins in, gesturing towards

Marc who is sloping off down the garden on his way back home.

'I'm sorry. I really am.' Elizabeth smiles feebly at Ama.

'It's my mother who's worked up. Not me. Maybe you could tell her you didn't mean to offend anyone.'

'Of course I didn't mean to offend,' Elizabeth insists and slouches off to see Machance.

Machance has her back turned to her. She simply nods as Elizabeth rolls off some apologies about the countryside being so stunning and how she felt so free she could fly. 'Fine, fine, *c'est bon*,' Machance says in a drained voice, 'but if you want to fly again, please do it in the courtyard at the back of the house!'

'I might take you up on that!' Elizabeth answers. That's not really what Machance wanted to hear. Ama is relieved however.

Elizabeth doesn't go cycling again, yet the whole village has got to know about her. Machance can't believe so many people managed to see her in the vineyards. Pado reckons she was gone at least three hours. That certainly left everyone lots of time to have a look. Apparently Marc's cousin also rang some of the Parriard family and Jean-Marc Parriard then rang through to his friend Fernand on the other side of the *route nationale* to Tours and he was also ready with his tractor by the side of his vineyard lane to have a good view.

Elizabeth sticks to painting now. She wanders the garden for her inspiration. She has made several quick, preparatory portraits and has chosen the pose she wants. Duccio is to sit on the grass, his knees up against his chest and his arms wrapped round the front of his legs. He is to gaze dreamily into the air like a young warrior before the on-slaught of battle.

'Ridiculous. *Complètement ridicule*,' Machance huffs to any-one who wants to hear.

Monsieur Luzille, the mayor, walks over to see us nearly every day now. Pado is sure he's only coming on the off chance that Elizabeth might be sunbathing nude, but he seems to have things to clear up regarding the upkeep of the paths and vineyards surrounding the house. He hopes to speak to Machance and always ends up talking to me as he waits for her to come out of her room.

'I was very fond of your grandfather' he tells me each time. Once, when he's about to walk back to the village, he holds me back by the arm. His breath smells of wine and the stubble framing his mouth sounds like sandpaper when he speaks.

'I used to sit here and chat with your grandfather,' he sighs, pointing at a large tree trunk a few metres away, 'but that was before he got his leg caught in that blasted rabbit trap. He never felt much like talking after that.' I don't answer. I don't move, so that nothing can enter my mind or start it going, not even the noises or brightness of the garden.

Elizabeth is painting all day, every day.

'This place really is heavenly,' she whispers to Ama as she spreads herself out on the grass beneath her easel.

Ama has brought her a cup of tea and a glass bottle of orange juice for Duccio. Elizabeth squashes the tea bag inside her cup with the end of a pencil. The water turns a dark brown. Duccio gets up and stretches his legs.

'Why don't you come and have a look?' Elizabeth calls to him as he wanders off. He's not interested in the painting and, besides, he's too busy waiting for Pado to return from Poitiers with his go-cart. Giulio thinks that if he hangs around Elizabeth long enough, she might do a quick sketch of him and he'll get a go-cart too. Elizabeth turns the portrait and sizes it up from different angles. Duccio paces up and down by the gate looking out along the vineyard tracks.

'He's more beautiful than that,' Ama grumbles, studying the painting.

Elizabeth shrugs. She says it's hard painting a face that doesn't want to be painted. 'The important thing is to get his feelings across anyway.'

Ama corrects Elizabeth. 'No, I want physical reality. I want his face the way it is now, before it's too late. You have got that haven't you?'

'I can see you're not a painter,' Elizabeth laughs.

I'm thinking it's already a bit late to catch Duccio as he is now because he's changing so fast. He's no longer interested in hotel listings or his great sporting geniuses book and whenever anyone talks to him, he just gets worked up and walks away.

Elizabeth doesn't want anyone to look at the portrait for the last few days. She keeps it carefully wrapped up in the stable and won't let us near.

'I need to work on this alone,' she tells Ama each time she gets curious.

Pado says he might well pop down in the middle of the night and have a peek at the painting.

'You'd better bloody not,' Elizabeth warns him jokingly.

She turns the key of the stable door and drops it into her pocket, to make sure. Duccio locks his new go-cart up too. With a knife he has scratched his name underneath it in bold letters: DUCCIO MESSINA.

Ama wants to cook lasagne for Elizabeth's last night. She tries hard to get Machance to help. She's not interested. Machance says she'd even prefer to eat her dinner upstairs in her bedroom. Ama hides her disappointment. She can't get worried because this is a special night: Duccio's painting is finished and we're going to have him installed on the sitting-room wall for all to see. Elizabeth puts the finishing touches to the portrait in the stable. Giulio and I are laying out the knives and forks on the table Grand Maurice built under the creeper-leaf awning. Pado hands us huge wine glasses. They ring like bells when you gently tap them together. Ama brings out the food using a ripped dress for oven gloves. Elizabeth is sad to be leaving. 'I can't believe I'll be in London tomorrow. I've had such a wonderful time.'

Everyone is chatting and I'm asking Ama if I should take Machance something more to eat.

'We mustn't bother her darling,' Ama reassures me. 'She's too tired. She wants to be left alone.' I know because I saw her spent face as she climbed up the stairs to her bedroom, the see-through plastic bag of Grand Maurice's things hooked to her hand.

                              *   *   *

Then Ama asks Elizabeth to bring out her easel and show
us her painting. Duccio lets out a deliberately loud sigh of
boredom and drums the table.

'Ah, come on, you look great,' Elizabeth teases him as she
disappears off to the stable.

'I can't wait.' Ama fidgets nervously in her chair.

Elizabeth needs a hand with the easel. Pado helps her set
it up at the end of the table. The portrait is shrouded in a
white cloth.

'One, two, three!' Elizabeth sings, dancing round the table,
with the corner of the cloth in her hand. She yanks at it. The
white linen falls to the ground in a lump.

The painting is Duccio, all Duccio, Giulio and I agree.
The lawn in the background rises up and fills the canvas
with a murky dry green, a grass halo above Duccio's head.
Pado stands up to examine the canvas close-up. He squints
at the paint, pointing his finger at the details.

'Get out of the way!' Ama says, gesturing with her arm.
There's something impatient about her voice. I can tell.
Duccio has got up and walked off.

'Did you actually look at him?' Ama suddenly questions
Elizabeth.

Elizabeth is fussing round Pado and explaining the pose
to him. She can't hear what Ama is saying.

'Excuse me, did you actually look at him?' Ama repeats in
a slightly louder voice.

'Who?' Elizabeth worries, turning to face Ama.

Ama points at Duccio sauntering across the lawn. 'Him!
The person you were meant to be painting.'

Elizabeth sits down opposite Ama. 'What are you talking about, Ava?'

'That's not Duccio. That's not my son.'

'But, we agreed.'

'No, you agreed to paint what you saw and you haven't. That portrait. It's . . . I don't know. It's someone else. Look at the scowl on his face.'

Ama wants Pado to back her up. He rather likes the painting though.

'It's got punch, *molto forte*,' he pats Elizabeth on the back. 'It's definitely Duccio.'

'But there's nothing beautiful about him there. He's like some urchin off the street,' Ama argues, her voice rising.

'Urchin? He looks wild and unpredictable. He's fabulous,' Elizabeth assures her. 'I feel he has something of your father in there, that pensive, brooding look Grand Maurice had.'

'My father!' Ama is furious. 'What did you know of my poor father? How the hell does he come into all this? I don't understand you Elizabeth. I can't believe you could do this to me.'

'I told you I wanted to get his feelings across. I have. You asked me to paint your son and I've done it. Everyone else likes it, except you.'

'I trusted you!' Ama stands up. She sticks an accusing finger at all the flaws she can see in the portrait. She pokes at the head, the eyes, the posture, the colours. 'Everything is violent. The colours are so shocking. Where's the truth in it?'

'What's a painting without emotion?' Elizabeth challenges her.

'I think it's your emotions that you've painted. You've gone and painted your own anger. That's what it is.'

200

'My anger? What are you on about?'

'Your bitterness, Elizabeth, that's what I'm talking about. Look at what's happened to you since your husband left!'

'Hang on Ava! Hold it! What's going on here? What's got into you?'

Pado urges us to start clearing the table. We gather up the dishes and take away the glasses. Ama holds on to hers. Elizabeth is taking down her easel to put it straight in the car. When we reach the kitchen, Giulio says he heard Elizabeth's jaw click. He really did. A distinct 'click'. Duccio zooms past us on his go-cart. We want to have a go.

'No way!' he shouts back.

He pedals down the vineyard as fast as he can to get away from us and the portrait where he's covered in green grass and a snarl that made Ama cry. We watch him bounce over the stones, his black hair covered in clouds of sand. It's dark and he has slipped into a haze by the time he reaches the end of the track. Pado puts the car keys and Elizabeth's train ticket by the front door so he can find them first thing in the morning.

19

The rooms upstairs fill with the new furniture Ama has bought from the flea market in Poitiers and the cellars clear themselves of their clutter. I sift through old bottles and boxes, searching. Duccio won't allow light in the cellars now in case I find something before him. He bans candles, torches and matches. We have to feel our way around and get used to the black, dank shadows of the walls. We mould into our space. We overcome our fear of the dark and cut ourselves off from the noises upstairs. We are led by the subtle echoes of each other's footsteps and guided by the memories of our games with Grand Maurice. We rarely speak, except to ward off an encroaching brother or to name a new find. The days merge into long covered passages where we lose all notion of time.

'What are you doing down there?' Pado asks from time to time.

He doesn't come and see. He has a new book to write. Machance occasionally rattles the door, on the way to her room. Ama calls us for lunch and dinner. The rest of the day, she doesn't care. Sometimes she seems happy. Like never before.

*　　*　　*

Machance tells me that Grand Maurice spent months building the greenhouse and dry-stone wall near the vegetable
garden, even though the rain and wind have destroyed
most of what he put up. Ama thinks we should rebuild
the greenhouse to grow seeds. Pado says that's not a priority,
we still have to make sure the house is weatherproof for the
winter. Inside the greenhouse, in amongst the rotting planks
and cracked pots, is a wooden box with some gardening
tools on top. For a while now, I've been thinking I should
open it. When Duccio and Giulio are down in the cellars
one afternoon, I prise it open and splinter the top. The
metal pegs inside have gone rusty. There are a couple of
large glass bells slotted into each other, a pair of rubber
boots and a measuring tape. The weeds inside the box have
turned white and curled up, thick against the lid, to suck in
the light.

I pull out the boots and turn them upside-down. A small
metal sweet tin drops out. I twist it open and find a few
coins. I close it again and put the tin in my pocket. I try
on the boots. They're huge and bulging to one side on the
right boot. They crack and fold under my weight. I head up
the garden, falling over myself. I'm laughing because I can
hardly walk and Giulio runs out to follow me.

'Let me have a go,' he keeps on saying.

I'm laughing so much I can't stop. Pado looks out of the
window and I can see him smiling to himself too as I twist
and stumble in my crusty oversized boots. Giulio shouts so

much about wanting to wear them that Ama and Machance come outside. They stop in their tracks. Ama spins Machance towards the door, trying to direct her back into the kitchen. It's too late. Machance pushes her away and lunges for me, eyes fixed and dazed.

'*Mais qu'est-ce que tu fais?* Give me those boots immediately!' she screams.

I struggle to get out of them before she reaches me. She looks frightening all of a sudden and Giulio is running for cover too.

'Mother, please,' Ama is saying, 'it doesn't matter!'

I scramble out of the way. Machance scoops up the boots. Her fingers gouge the earth under them, ripping the dry grass in two.

'What? What?' I'm saying to Ama as she looks at me dazed. 'What have I done?'

'Can't you see that these were Grand Maurice's boots?' Ama shouts back, furious. Machance stands still, a boot dangling from each hand, long black sleeves of remembrance racing through her head. Ama holds Machance's shoulders from behind and lets her sob gently. I'm looking at the right boot with the swollen shape. I can see Grand Maurice's foot distorted from the rabbit trap. I can see him lying here with us now.

I run off down the track towards the vineyard. I didn't know. I didn't realise. I still see Ama's face glaring and yelling. Giulio wants to come with me. I run faster. I don't want anyone with me. I dart through the garden, under the tight, clipped hedge that marks the end of Machance's land. I follow the trail down to the river, near the white chalk lane towards the village. The evening air is mine, just mine. I throw pebbles into the bulrushes and watch the ripples grow and then head off back towards the top of the hill. I've been here a few times now, up above the house, at the point where the sky cuts the tops of the vines. The ripening grapes snare the dark heavy smells of the earth. The grass is bursting with insect rustling. The evening sun is so hot it almost bores holes in the stones pushed around the vineyard stakes. My ankles are tingling and crumbling. It's as if Grand Maurice's boots are still gripping on to me, prodding and prompting unwanted, biting images. I wore Grand Maurice's boots. I put my feet in them! I feel dizzy and confused. Maybe Machance believes I did it on purpose? I didn't. How could I? I didn't know they were Grand Maurice's boots. I imagine Machance crying again, clutching the dried old boot with the swollen ankle. Maybe Grand Maurice wore these boots the day he died? Maybe he put them carefully in his box with the tin of coins, said goodbye to Machance and headed off down to the lake to catch crayfish? Perhaps he had put the money to one side to buy something later and the coins in the tin are still there waiting for him to return? I run to clear my head. I can't go back to the house and face Machance. I gulp at the air. I'm swimming inside the vineyards, in and out of the rusting brown wire and the yellowing leaves. I want to push out deeper, where the vines mingle in concealed labyrinths. I want to be lost. From here to the edge of the world, nothing but rows of vines. I run, faster and faster. I leap and spring off the stones and clumps of root. I'm in a warm light. The horizon is full of it, warmth like a veil of sunlight.

*   *   *

I take the tin of coins from my pocket and drop it into the earth. The lid rolls off. Ten-franc, five-franc, one-franc coins grip each other in sharp rustiness. I break them apart and put them back in the tin. I bury Grand Maurice's tin in the earth. I tie a bundle of pulled-up poppy stems onto a stake nearby to mark the spot. Here is Grand Maurice's money, his waiting money. From here I can see the whole village ahead of me and our house to the side. I can see a few lights on in the village. It must be time for supper. I'm not going back, not yet. I'm going to look for Marc down on the Joignets' farm. His tractor is parked across the gateway. The kitchen door is locked. I walk to the back of the building. The dog sets off barking, yanking at its chain. The collar eats into its neck and nearly throttles it as I stand and call Marc. Madame Joignet appears out of the barn.

'Don't tease the dog!' she shouts. She comes over towards me. She's carrying some grain in a bucket. 'What are you doing out at this hour?' she asks. I mumble some reason and she doesn't seem to question it. 'So you're looking for Marc?' she asks. I nod. 'He won't be back for a while. Why don't you help me feed the chickens in the meantime?'

I follow her to the chicken run down by the barn. There are about a dozen brown hens and a few white bantams in a dug-up pen, hemmed in by hedges and a barricade of corrugated iron patched together with car radiators. Madame Joignet gathers up the grain in her hand and scatters it across a plank on the ground. The chickens come scuttling forward, fighting and pushing for food.

'That's my favourite!' Madame Joignet says, pointing to a small white hen. 'It hatched on my birthday last year.

Go on, pick it up. It doesn't mind.' I lift the hen up. It sits happily at the end of my arm. I stroke its clean white feathers and its chest. 'See how tame she is!' Madame Joignet smiles. She's rummaging through the chicken house, fishing out eggs from long wooden boxes filled with hay. 'Wouldn't you like to take some eggs back home for your grandmother?' she offers, handing me three in her cupped palm. I don't want them.

'Now let's check the wretched cat hasn't had her kittens,' she sighs, pulling me away with her. 'I have to make sure I find them before they are too old. It's horrible drowning them when they've become all friendly and fluffy.' I drop the white hen.

'What do you mean?' I cough.

She tells me that she's got far too many cats around the farm and that they only end up fighting and breeding again and then you have to feed them. 'A complete mess!' she fusses. She shows me a heavy linen sack she has ready.

'I simply put a few stones in the bottom, tie it up and throw them over the bridge into the river.' She can see I'm horrified: 'Oh, don't worry, they don't feel anything, they're only a day or two old, scrawny, little pink things. They can't even see properly.'

I look into the sack. Six large, rough stones weigh against the bottom, pressing into the linen. The gaps between them leave enough room for a kitten, a pink life between each stone, waiting to be sealed in and drowned. The stones must tumble and slash the kittens as they drop from the bridge towards the water. And then, when the sack hits the water, the stones snap together in a rapid crush, pushing the last movements of life down into the river. The sack fills with swallowing water and slowly sinks to the river's bed where it sways with the currents. I peer into the sack again, pushing my head and arms down into the darkness inside to touch the stones. I dig into the bottom of the bag. My shoulders rub against the rough surface of the linen. Nothing can survive in here. My head suddenly hurts. I struggle to lift my hands out quickly. Grand Maurice's drenched, floating belly and Aldo Moro's bruised corpse rise up out of the bag with me. I push the sack away from me, with a rapid kick of the foot. I feel my body tingling. I search for thoughts to save me. I look at my fingertips, powdered with minute shapes of sand from touching the stones. I wipe them down my trousers.

Madame Joignet pulls me away. 'What are you doing? *Viens*, leave that sack alone.' Then she points to a crate filled with hay she has prepared for the cat. 'See, if I leave a bowl of food, the cat will come and have her kittens here.' To prove her point, she turns and calls, 'Boulette! Boulette! I bet you she'll be here by tomorrow.'

She puts a few finishing touches to the crate, adding a bit more straw. 'Right, let's go.'

I don't want to go. I can't go! What if the cat comes back and has its kittens right in front of Madame Joignet? All she'll have to do is drop them in the sack and fling the whole lot high over the bridge. I feel muddled, sick with panicked blood.

'I'm going home now,' I say to her. She looks at me, surprised.

'Oh, *d'accord*, but I thought you wanted to see Marc, he'll be here in a few minutes.'

'I'll see him tomorrow,' I nod, waving her goodbye.

I make my way towards the gate. Madame Joignet reaches her house first. When she's fiddling to open the door, I charge back to the barn behind her back. The dog barks. She doesn't look up. I lie down next to the cat crate, waiting. It's late now. Marc drives in, parks his car and enters the house. The glow from the windows gives me enough light to see. The first thing to do is to get rid of the cat food. That should stop the cat from coming. I take the plate outside and bury the contents under a spiked piece of tractor engine. I keep one morsel back in case. The chickens are moving uncomfortably, listening to my noise. I mess up the crate, but I can't make it too obvious. I hide some sharp stones under the hay to stop the cat from settling down. I sit waiting, my legs stretched out in front of me. Maybe Ama and Pado are going to come looking for me. I can't go home. Not now. I can't let the kittens die.

I hear a long howling from a cat. I sit very still. The noise gets louder and louder. A cat emerges and stands in front of me. 'Boulette,' I call softly. I chuck it the bit of meat I kept back from the plate. It eats it up hungrily. The cat's belly is huge, sagging along the grass. It walks towards me, rubbing itself along my shins. I stroke it. The cat sits for a while, panting. Maybe it needs water? There is none here. I pick up the plate and race off to the chicken run. I scoop up some water from the chickens' bowl and take it back. The cat has got into the crate.

'No!' I shout at it, 'Shoo!' I pour some water over its head. It doesn't move. It only licks the drops falling over its fur. 'Please,' I beseech it. I kick the crate, gently and the cat hisses.

Its belly takes up most of the crate. The cat doesn't seem to care about the sharp stones under the hay. It settles down and rests its chin against the edge of the crate. I pick up some mud and shower it in fine dust. Again it hisses angrily. I can't believe this. It's going to have its kittens here, all ready for Madame Joignet to kill. I have to move the cat. It's the only way. Very gently, I lift up the crate. Dry mud and shreds of hay fall through the holes underneath. The cat looks nervous. I begin to run. The cat stands up. I'm running so fast the cat keeps on wobbling and falling down again. I get to the edge of the wood. The cat's leg has slipped through the bottom of the crate. It lashes out furiously at me as I try to disentangle it. Its claws sink into the skin on the back of my hand. I'm bleeding. The cat limps off into the woods and lies down under a bush. I wait for a while. The cat looks settled. I carry the crate back to the barn and put it back where it was. There are specks of blood on the straw. I cover them up.

Ama and Pado are out in the garden with torches. I can hear them calling my name. Their long beams of light fly over the tops of the trees and criss-cross the lawn. I have to make something up quick. I'm not sure what. I'm bleeding. It'll have to be that I fell over. I look at my hand. It doesn't look like I fell over though. It's obvious that something scratched me. Three thick red lines are dug across my hand. I'll say I found a dog and that it was lost and that I wanted to help it and then it scratched me and ran away. I think about the story a bit. It sounds convincing.

*   *   *

210

'I'm here!' I shout. The beams stop and then bound towards me.

'Where the hell have you been?' Ama shrieks at the top of her voice.

'Are you all right? Jean-Pio, are you all right?' Pado overtakes her.

'You can't slip off like that. You had us worried sick!' Ama wrings her hands. Their torches swivel and flip like fireworks.

'Sorry, I got lost,' I say. 'I didn't realise it was so late.'

Pado puts his arms around me. 'Don't worry. You're back now.' He kisses me on the head.

'Where were you? What were you doing?' Ama demands.

I start telling them the story about the stray dog and Ama gasps. She turns to Pado horrified: 'Rabies, Gaspare, what about rabies?' Pado shines the torch onto my hand. No doubt about it. The lines look like animal scratches. 'Stray animals are the worst too. Did it bite you or scratch you Jean-Pio?' Ama fusses.

Pado takes me straight to the house. Duccio, Giulio and Machance are all sitting at the table. 'Where have you been?' they ask in unison.

Pado is boiling a kettle and Ama has gone off to get some antiseptic lotion. They bandage my hand and almost burn my skin with cream and boiling water. Ama shoves some cheese and biscuits down me.

'Now, off to bed. We'll be seeing a doctor early in the morning.' I want to tell them it doesn't matter. It was Madame Joignet's cat. I can't.

*   *   *

Ama wakes me up at seven the following morning to tell me that Pado already has the car running downstairs. She pulls some clothes over me, makes me brush my teeth and hands me an apple and a piece of bread.

'Run along!' she says.

Pado is looking at the map. Apparently, the best doctor in the region is in Châtellerault.

He drops the map onto my knees. 'Follow that yellow line and keep an eye out for the turning to the right.'

Pado tells me I probably shouldn't be eating in case I get car sick. We throw my bread and apple out of the window.

'Some lucky birds will get that,' he tells me.

I only hope that I threw the bread far enough onto the roadside. What if some sparrows come and eat my bread on the tarmac and get mowed down by a car? I turn to try and have a look. I can't see that far back.

'So, *figlio mio*,' Pado smiles. 'How are those headaches? Do you still get them?'

Why is he asking me this now? I don't understand. I shrug my shoulders: 'Sometimes.'

'Sometimes?' Pado repeats.

'Yes, sometimes,' I reply. I see the sign to Châtellerault on the right.

'Should we mention them to the doctor?' Pado asks.

'I'm fine,' I say. 'The turning to Châtellerault is right here.'

'Strange not travelling so much any more, isn't it?' Pado adds.

'Strange.'

'Don't worry Jean-Pio. This doctor is meant to be very good.'

We draw up in front of a large building with a doctor's plaque. I look up at all the windows, guessing which ones might belong to the doctor. It can't be the apartment with washing spread across its balcony, nor the one with geraniums hanging from the shutters, or even the one with bird cages attached to its window latches. A doctor wouldn't have caged birds. Pado takes me up some stairs and it is the apartment with the bird cages.

'*Bonjour Professeur*,' the doctor greets Pado.

'Hello!'

The doctor and Pado sit and chat for at least ten minutes whilst I examine the bird cages fastened to the shutters. The birds hop endlessly onto their perch and down again without a break. I try to make them look my way. They're too bored to see anything.

'Do you like animals?' the doctor asks.

I kind of nod so as not to be rude, but I know he's wasting the birds' lives, making them go up and down in a tight cage every day, for ever, until they die. He takes Pado to his bookshelf.

'Look,' he says proudly, 'I have a copy of your book on respiratory diseases.'

Pado tells him it's an old edition and there's a more up-to-date version.

'I'll send it to you if you give me your card.'

The doctor searches around the top of his desk and hands Pado a visiting-card. Then he asks to see the scratches on my hand. He rolls up my sleeve and takes some blood.

'Look the other way,' Pado says, stroking my head. I don't. I watch the syringe filling with blood. The doctor checks a few other things and writes a short medical history.

He tells us that rabies only exists in certain areas of France, certainly not near here. He has a map in a drawer of his desk. The red patches correspond to areas where animals have been found with rabies. When that happens, all cats and dogs are destroyed in the area unless they have a certificate of vaccination. Hundreds of cats and dogs gone, in a matter of days.

He takes my blood pressure. Pado watches him attentively.

'Seems fine to me,' the doctor says, wrapping up his equipment.

'He also gets headaches,' Pado adds, casually, without looking at me.

Why did he say that?

The doctor gets interested. 'Oh, I just read an excellent book by an Italian professor, Alberto Devoti, he's doing some impressive research into headaches. Have you heard of him?'

Pado nods, 'Of course.'

'How do the headaches start?' the doctor asks me.

I'm staring at Pado because I can't believe he told him about the headaches when I said it didn't matter. I don't know what to say. I stare at the doctor with vacant eyes. Then I explain that sometimes the headaches hurt like being out of breath. At other times, they build up from behind the ears, with a stretching of the heart, till they blur the eyes and envelop my whole face. He can't really make head or tail of what I'm saying. Pado juts in to give more words, but it's not my words that are wrong. The doctor fiddles with my neck and behind my ears.

'Let's take a look inside your ears,' he tilts me to one side. The sudden jab of the metal makes me wince. 'Sorry,' he says, 'is that very sensitive?'

'It hurts a bit,' I reply.

'Sounds like there might be something wrong with the ears to me.'

'Come off it,' Pado laughs. 'There's nothing wrong with them, no infection, nothing. I've checked already.'

'It's not necessarily an infection! You see it might be some form of migraine from an allergy to food or dust, or it might be a minor malfunctioning in the ear. That could be due to an infection from a long time ago or quite simply from receiving a blow from a football on the side of the head. Anything. He might just have a ringing in the ears. Do your ears ring?'

'Allergies,' Pado changes the subject. 'That's an interesting point. Maybe.'

The doctor looks at me with a big smile. 'You look like a healthy chap though. *Tu m'as l'air solide*, Jean-Pio.'

I gaze at the ground, waiting for this to be over.

'Well, aren't there tests we could do for allergies?' Pado suggests.

'Well if you do think it's an allergy, then I'd keep him off dairy products. That normally does the trick for children his age. Food intolerance is more common than you think.'

Pado wants to know more. The doctor hands him a book. 'This has all the answers. Brilliant book, *vraiment intéressant*, straight from the United States,' he says.

I could stand up now. I could tell them both that there are no allergies, that there is no pain other than the drilling fear of a thought that could sweep us all away unless it's stopped. I could tell them that now, here. They wouldn't understand. How could they understand that any thought can become a bad thought, a danger, a danger for us all, a panic that can come when you don't expect it, any time, anywhere?

'Come on. Let's go.' Pado smiles at me. 'Thank you for your time. We'll keep you informed of his progress.'

The doctor gives me a friendly squeeze on the arm. 'Don't worry about the headaches. They'll go if you eat properly and don't think about them!'

He asks me what school I go to. I tell him I've never been to school. He looks a little surprised.

'We've never been in one place long enough for school,' Pado explains. 'Still, look at him, he's been to nearly every country in Europe. He speaks English, French and Italian fluently. Not bad for an eight-year-old!'

The doctor shows us to the door. 'I'll be in touch if I see anything in his blood,' he says waving us off, 'but don't worry about rabies.'

On the way back, Pado is thinking aloud. 'Maybe school's not such a bad idea, at least for a while,' he says.

'Are we going to go off on conferences again?' I ask Pado.

'Not for the time being, Jean-Pio,' he tells me. 'I'm sure one day we will have to, but please don't tell your mother I said that.'

When we get back to the house, Ama is on her own in the kitchen preparing food. She has a plate of aubergine slices next to her. Each slice is coated in a perfect white crust of salt.

'Where is everyone?' Pado asks, looking into the room next door.

Ama is jittery. She carries on sprinkling salt over the aubergines. She tells us Machance took Giulio and Duccio to Grand Maurice's grave in the cemetery.

'I couldn't face going I'm afraid. Not today.'

'But you still haven't been, Ava,' Pado says, stroking her hair.

'I know. I know. Please don't get at me. I didn't feel up to it. Not with my mother, for the first time.' Then Ama turns and divides the aubergines into smaller slices.

I'm relieved I wasn't there. I don't know how I'm ever going to go into that cemetery and stand over a grave and know that beneath the stone is Grand Maurice's body hauled up from the bottom of the lake. What will Duccio and Giulio look like when they return? I turn and leave for the garden and vineyards.

20

Ama walks down into the cellar. It's the first time she's come to visit us there, so we know something is up. She tells us that we have to go to school. She and Pado have decided. On Monday, after a weekend of scraping around for pens and rulers, we walk to the village school with Ama. She is wearing her straw hat against the sun. The headmistress, Madame Tressetout, comes out and chats to Ama.

'*Bonjour les enfants*,' she smiles.

Ama negotiates a two-week period of observation with Madame Tressetout. She agrees: for the first two weeks we can just sit and watch the classes, taking in our new environment and subjects. I can only really take in the noise of trouser belts being fastened and skirts falling to the ground as my desk is next to the lavatories. I know who washes their hands and who doesn't. Madame Tressetout stands over me, repeating sentences, but I haven't been listening.

My bench partner is Laurent. He has a broken nose and a bicycle. He can pedal up the steepest hill in the village without stopping and has a little satchel on his back in which he hides dried corn leaves. He picks them before summer and dries them for smoking. His whole attic is littered in them and, each time he smokes, his eyes nearly pop out. We rush about his farm down by the river, chasing ducks, spying on the people in the houses and farms nearby. He tells me about his neighbour, Pierre Jacquet, who has little statues of all the dogs he has ever owned. They line the paving to his vegetable patch in a perfect row. Pistolet, Henri, Chantilly, Papi and Camomille all died years ago. Henri was the greatest, Laurent remembers, but he went sliding under a car and ended up like an olive without a stone pushed against the back teeth and brought up again. I know that if he really ended up like that then he can't be trapped inside his statue the way Laurent insists. He says that, one day, he's going to climb over the fence and scrape the statue around the eyes to check Henri's inside. He wonders whether you can feel hair and smell dog inside the solid stone.

Laurent's mother sells rabbit *terrines* and eggs at the markets in Loches and Châtellerault. I watch, speechless, as she pulls rabbits out of their hutches and knocks them over the head with the curved handle of a trowel. They fight against death, but always become still if she brings out the knife for their throat. I stare, unable to move, sick rising in my mouth. Laurent's mother once asked me to give her a hand. I couldn't speak so I couldn't refuse. She passed me a sleek black rabbit with a thrust. I held it at arm's length. She tied the back legs together as I closed my eyes. She was pulling one way as I pulled the other. I clenched the rabbit's warm coat out of comfort for myself. I felt the wriggles grow and then fall. It was a day for betrayal, a day to beat thoughts back, every minute.

Laurent's mother sometimes asks me to stay for lunch. We normally have one of the rabbits she's killed that day. It comes in a casserole hidden in sauce. It has herbs between its legs and potatoes piled high on its bald head. If I've seen the rabbit alive, I whisper to it with every mouthful. I say: 'Forgive me' and, all the while, Laurent is looking at me with a full-stomach grin. As I chew, I gently rock my head to clear it of thoughts. I don't want to remember the soft frightened eyes, the bucking back paws. I shake my head so much it hurts. It's as if my mouth is loaded with fur. I can feel the swilling tough meat fluffing up into grey hairs, then black and brown. They spike at my lips and tickle my throat. Laurent's mother eats her kill hungrily, her fork digging away at her plate. I turn away from her. I can't swallow. I can't. My mouth has become a paste of hair and I can feel the heartbeat of the rabbit beating away in the pan. I ask to leave. I run to the garden latrine, my mouth gorged with meat. It is a hut with pictures of naked women lying on cars. One of the women on the walls is leaning to one side with her leg cocked. She has the look of a rabbit. The latrine has two corrugated holds for the feet, a swinging metal chain and a deep gaping opening in the ground. The mouth of the installation is wide enough to fall down if you slip. I spit all my food out, down the hole.

*   *   *

Madame Tressetout doesn't take any notice of Laurent in the classroom. She doesn't like him because he's from a family with lice, no electricity or running water and his mother wears a torn apron all day long. Laurent never changes his clothes either, or polishes his shoes. During school checks for lice, Madame Tressetout slaps his ears and says 'typical' to me if she finds some eggs thick in his hair. The day I catch lice, she says it doesn't matter and shrugs her shoulders. She sticks me under a boiling tap until the plug is blocked with minute creatures and eggs. She squirts chemical lotions on my hair, gluing strands to my ears. When I walk home, I smell like a sweet stand at a fun-fair. Laurent says that if I tell Ama about the lice, she won't let me go to his house again.

Laurent carries a rabbit paw round with him at all times and he gives me one too. Mine is white with a brownish tinge. I don't want it at first. He insists. He says it's for good luck. The claws have been taken out specially. Laurent's father has tied a bow on it for me. On the bow is a picture of Notre Dame Cathedral in Paris. It was wrapped around an Easter egg before. I bury it deep in my pocket.

21

During break time at school, Laurent gets together with Pascal. Pascal doesn't say much, but everyone leaves him alone because he's huge. His father is huge too and his mother also. Pascal says he doesn't believe that I can speak English and Italian. 'How come you speak French then?' he sneers, as if he's proved his point.

Laurent insists I can speak English and Italian and that I'm teaching him some words too.

'Go on, say something then,' Pascal urges me. I don't know what to say. He pushes me.

'How about – Hello it's a sunny day – or – My name is Pascal?' I try in English.

He looks at me blankly, unconvinced.

'Anyone can speak gibberish,' he laughs.

Laurent gets angry with him. 'Jean-Pio speaks English and Italian and you're a fat *connard* if you don't believe it.'

Pascal is going to smash Laurent's face in now if I don't say something else fast.

'How about "Madame Tressetout has got big tits and a

big arse",' Pascal snorts at me. 'Go on, say that in Italian and English!' He waits. 'Ugh, I bet you he doesn't even know the word for tits and arse in Italian or anything,' Pascal taunts me.

Laurent is staring at me in panic. I can't let him down.

'Okay,' I say, 'but you have to swear not to repeat it to anyone.' They swear. They listen as I reluctantly spell out the words. When I've finished, they fall silent.

Pascal says: 'How do we know he's not making it up,' but he knows really. I speak my sentence again. Then they make me repeat it once more. Laurent promises me another rabbit paw if I do.

'*Signora Tressetout*, teyetes, teets, tiiites, aarrse, harse, *couloo, culo*,' Laurent tries after me. They screech with laughter.

'What about "pussy"? How do you say that?' Pascal asks.

I try and remember all the words Pado uses in the car when he's driving. Madame Tressetout suddenly calls out to me across the playground.

'Come here Jean-Pio!'

'*Culo*,' Pascal whispers. I sprint back to the classroom. Pascal follows me. He can hardly run he's laughing so much. 'You'd better tell me what "pussy" is later,' he winks.

Madame Tressetout explains that Duccio hasn't left his classroom during break time. He's too busy reading the books from the geography lesson.

'But he likes geography books,' I tell her.

'Fine,' Madame Tressetout says, 'but he's got to get some fresh air too. Ask him to come outside, from me.'

I enter the classroom. Duccio is in the corner with a pile of books on his desk.

'Madame Tressetout says you've got to go outside!' I say to him.

He looks up at me, then down at his books again.

'I'll do what I want.'

I dare not add anything more. Even Pascal says Duccio will hit anyone who annoys him. I go back outside. Maybe Giulio might be able to persuade him.

'He's coming,' I gesture to Madame Tressetout, before searching for Giulio amongst the trees at the back of the playground.

At the end of the lessons, Laurent tells me I must come back to his home as his chicks should be hatching. We slip out of the school and jump on his bicycle. He pedals and I hold on to the seat at the back. We're off into the vineyards, skidding down the gravel paths, skirting along the ditches.

His mother greets us: 'Get a move on or they'll all be out of their eggs!'

The hen refuses to let us near her. We can see the feathers covering her chest bulging with movement as new lives crack out of the eggs. Laurent gets fed up with waiting and pushes her to one side with a stick. She lashes out and pecks. We have time to see some cracked shells and a few tiny heads. A couple of unhatched eggs are left. We wait an hour, and then another. Laurent smokes at least three rolled-up corn leaves before the hen decides to get up and leave. She bustles off, clucking to her new brood of barely-walking chicks. There is one egg left unhatched. Laurent says there's always a dud one, either unfertilised or a chick too weak to break the shell. He heads off to follow the hen. He leaves me staring at the unhatched egg, alone in the middle of the nest. I pick it up. It's warm to the touch. If I put my hand out straight I'm sure I can see it shaking slightly. I put it to my ear and I imagine the soft knocking of a beak against the shell. I take a penknife from the shelf in the barn and gently pierce the shell at the top. Then with my fingers I flick away the pieces until I see the membrane underneath. I can see viscous wet feathers pressed up against the shell, a minuscule heartbeat flickering to be let out. I finish removing the shell and a sodden chick, with a head it can hardly lift, comes rolling onto the straw. I can feel my hands almost giving way in disgust because it's so fragile and strange: its sticky feathers, its heavy large head, its beak that taps at the air. I lift the remaining shell off its back and support its wilting head with my fingers. I gently pull at its wings to let them loose and uncurl its feet. Laurent's mother comes to see what I'm doing.

She tells me I should have let it die in the egg. 'What are you going to do now? It'll only last a couple of hours. You shouldn't interfere with nature!'

I say I'll look after it, I promise I'll do everything to keep it alive.

'But it can't live,' she protests. 'How can something like that live. It wasn't meant to survive, look at its head, its glazed eyes. Give it to me, *allez, vite!* I'll kill it and put it out of its misery.' I run away from her fast.

'Have it your way,' she laughs, 'but don't come crying to me when it dies.'

*   *   *

Without calling Laurent, I put the chick in my top pocket and join the track towards the river, back home. The chick falls, almost lifeless, into the folds of my shirt. I run, in a crazy zigzag, all the way to the house. I avoid the bumps and stop, from time to time, to check my pocket. The chick's feathers have dried and its mouth is opening with a desperate longing for air. I blow gently into my pocket. Back at home, I run up to my bedroom, checking Ama and Pado can't see. They mustn't find out that I've brought something back to life. Maybe it has a disease? I plug in Ama's hairdryer and send waves of warm air over its contorting, weak body. It begins to lift its head. I fetch a little box and pinch some cotton wool from the bathroom. I carry on with the heat and soon it's stumbling across the box. Machance walks past my door.

'What are you doing with that hairdryer?' she asks. Before I can invent something, she is in my room, bending over the box. 'You'll need some very small seeds if that's going to survive,' she explains. She sits down and tells me that she used to know a bit about chickens and they need to have special fine feed in their early days. 'I'm sure Marc has got some on the farm. Go and ask him. I'll wait here and look after it.'

I don't have time to thank Machance or warn her not to tell Ama and Pado. I race down the garden, off towards Madame Joignet's house. Marc is on his tractor at the end of the vines. I tell him about the chick and the grain.

He drives me to the farm on his tractor and scoops up a pot of chick feed and sends me off again. 'Good luck,' he smiles, 'but don't be sad if it dies.'

It won't die, I repeat to myself, running home. I clutch my

rabbit paw. I squeeze it with all my might. It can't die. No thoughts of it dying. It won't die.

Machance has plugged in the hairdryer again, 'It needs to keep warm.' The best way though, she reckons, is to put it near a light bulb. Machance helps me sprinkle some grain in the box. The chick doesn't react. It potters about, stopping to shiver from time to time.

'I've named it Giscard,' Machance tells me. 'At least you'll remember who the president of France is.'

'Giscard!' I call to it. 'He doesn't know his name yet,' I say.

Machance giggles. It's the first time I've seen her laugh since she arrived.

22

You always know when there are unwanted visitors in the house because Machance sits in the kitchen sighing long spluttering sighs. They start with little bursts and then rise and fall with long hisses that swell up from her feet, through the stomach and into her mouth with a spurt. The kitchen fills with exasperation that lingers like a nasty smell above the cooking.

It doesn't stop the visitors from coming though. They rush to see Pado every Sunday after church. They come over the top of the vineyard into the long grass, in groups or alone, rumbling down the paths. They need medical advice, examinations, even prescriptions. Ama wants to stop this roll of free patients who knock impatiently with muddied fingertips on the kitchen window. 'Stick to legionnaires' disease, Gaspare. You gave up general medicine years ago!'

'I know,' says Pado. 'You try telling them that! Anyway it's never anything I can't handle, sore throats and colds.

I've already seen most of the people on my walks about the village.'

Some Sundays, there's practically a queue outside the laundry-room that has become the clinic. Ama begrudgingly lays out clean towels on the table and a folded apron serves as a pillow if people need to lie down. Duccio, Giulio and I sit and guess what people might be coming for.

'That woman has got an arthritis problem. That man's got a urinary complaint and she's suffering from heart problems.'

Is anyone, I wonder, coming for headaches? Someone here must be swapping bad thoughts for good thoughts, desperate to tell someone for the first time. Maybe this wide-faced woman or that man sitting in front of Pado going on about his feet, his knees, his chest, his arms, his hair, anything, just to stop himself talking about the thoughts in his head.

'There's nothing wrong with you,' Pado will say to the man, 'really, I can assure you,' and Pado will tap away at his skin to check again, not realising that the man's whole body is stretching with thought after thought in a frenzied desire to shriek and wrench out the undesired words and images knocking at his ears in a shrill voice that can never be spoken or known. That's when the man will get up to leave and, only as he's turning the door knob, he might say: 'There is just one thing,' and then he'll say nothing, never anything, because no one could understand.

We never know if our diagnoses are right or not. If no one's looking, we sneak up to the laundry-room window and peer inside. Pado is chatting away, taking people's pulses, asking them to take off an item of clothing. People wriggle and curl out of their clothes to produce a bare arm, a thigh and more. One day, we sit speechless as the woman from the village cafe undoes her bra, hangs her breasts in Pado's hands and cries.

Ama goes mad the day she finds a glass jar of broken bone and chipped, cracked teeth in the laundry-room.

'I thought you said you only gave advice? What the hell is this disgusting thing?'

'I do give advice,' Pado protests, 'but this was a particularly interesting case I thought I could use in my work.'

'I'm going to throw it away Gaspare,' Ama seethes. 'Do you realise what you're up to? Send the person to a specialist.'

Ama marches off with the jar, towards the bin. Pado struggles to wrestle it from her grasp. Ama won't let go. 'This is the last straw, Gaspare, look at yourself! You're more interested in this rotting bone than your own family!'

Pado sits Ama down on a chair in the kitchen. 'Listen to me, will you. I'm not exaggerating. This bone is a very interesting case. It's decomposing in an unusual way. I want to have it analysed in Tours. I really don't understand something. It will help the man who brought it in and it'll help me in my work too.'

'What bloody man?' Ama huffs. 'Who is it?'

'Allow me to do my work, please!' Pado insists.

Ama eventually puts the receptacle of yellowing bone and teeth down. 'Okay, have it your way, but I'm not having you fiddling around with all these diseases that, quite frankly, you're not trained for! And no more people on Sundays!'

*   *   *

230

One afternoon Pado sets off alone in the car to Tours to have the bone and teeth analysed. Duccio and I are trying to work out who brought them in. We know it was a man now, but who, we can't tell. I reckon it was the man in the black overcoat who complained about having sore legs last week, but Duccio says that whoever brought in that much broken bone and teeth wouldn't be able to walk. That means it might be the young father with the blonde daughter two weeks ago. He had a huge bruise across his face and a limp. We eventually decide that it must have been this man.

Pado looks confused and troubled when he returns from Tours.

'Well, what's the matter?' we all ask.

'It's not that simple, boys,' Pado replies. 'As I first suspected, the bone and teeth are not human, but animal. Now I've got a bit of a problem. How am I going to explain that to Monsieur Talarbe?' Pado searches anxiously for Ama in their bedroom.

'If you'd told me it was Monsieur Talarbe from the beginning, you wouldn't have had to go to all this bother!' Ama sighs, once she's listened to Pado.

'Who's Monsieur Talarbe?' we demand.

Pado picks up the phone and rings Monsieur Talarbe. There's a long pause on the end of the line and Pado keeps on asking: 'Are you all right?'

The man says he'll be over in a few minutes and Pado tells us to go up to our bedrooms.

'And you too,' he says to Ama. 'I think the old boy sounded pretty shaken.'

'Well obviously,' Ama complains. 'You gave the poor man and his wife another false hope.'

'Look ... I wanted to check,' Pado tries to say, then he retreats into himself. He paces up and down the kitchen.

'Will you all go up to your rooms, please! Now!' he orders.

We stand in a ring on the landing upstairs. Ama whispers the story of Monsieur Talarbe's only daughter, who went missing nearly thirty years ago. She would be older than Ama now if she were alive. Anyway, maybe she is still alive, somewhere. No one knows. All Ama can say is that she disappeared one day when out in the fields in front of her house. That's why Monsieur Talarbe is always ploughing his land. You can often see him, sifting through the mud, breaking up clods of earth to see what's inside. Every time he finds something, he takes it to a specialist for analysis. The *Mairie* council even clubbed together to get the Talarbes a metal detector, anything that might help them find their daughter's buttons, her shoes, a necklace or even a tooth with a filling. For them every stone and rock could be their lost daughter.

When the old man appears, we all go to the window to see what he looks like. He parks his car outside the gate and straightens his jacket as he gets out. When he's about to reach the kitchen door, we see him turn and wave back at someone in his car.

'Did you see that?' Duccio says.

We chase down to the sitting-room for a closer look. From there, we can see into the front of the car. A grey-haired woman with a long scarf tied round her neck is sitting in the front seat. She keeps on rearranging her fringe in the mirror and looking around nervously.

Ama tells us to stay put and walks down to the car. She taps on the windscreen and leans in through the open window. Madame Talarbe looks at her, surprised. Then she pulls her scarf up until it covers her face and sobs. Ama reaches inside the car and holds her. Giulio says he wants to go out after Ama. Duccio tells him to shut up. He presses his face up against the window. He can't stop staring at the car, rocking up and down with the weeping woman. Monsieur Talarbe leaves the kitchen and reaches his car. Before getting in, he turns Pado's jar upside-down on the grass and grinds the bone and teeth into the earth with his foot.

23

It's the 11th of November, Armistice Day, and Laurent and I have gone to the church, as we were told to by Madame Tressetout. The pews are crammed with old men hooking medals on their jackets and practising tunes on trumpets. Several of them come up to me and ask me who I am.

'*Ah! Le petit-fils de notre ami Maurice!* Maurice's grandson!' one of them exclaims loudly to make sure everyone realises. I'm pleased to be amongst people Grand Maurice knew, until I see one of the men shake his head. '*Pauvre Maurice*, what an awful accident!' he mutters to himself.

The headmistress's husband, Monsieur Tressetout, takes me to one side.

'Are you ready for this?'

'I know the Lord's prayer,' I say in reply.

'That's not what I mean,' he answers and guides me by the shoulder towards a room at the side of the church. 'Wait here!' he tells me and then goes off to consult with the priest.

The room is sullen, nothing but a wide, wood floor with a bright light shining on top of a cupboard against the wall.

The cupboard has a crest on it. Monsieur Tressetout returns, unlocks the cupboard and prises open a case standing upright inside. A golden cross, almost as big as me, lies in an envelope of red velvet.

'Pick it up,' he tells me. 'Go on!'

What does he mean? Why do I have to pick it up? He guides my hands towards the glittering cold sides tucked inside the velvet. I can anticipate the metallic smooth touch of the cross. My hands shake. I'm suddenly nothing but thoughts. I'm thinking I must clean my mind before I touch the cross, but Monsieur Tressetout clamps my hands onto it, his large palms clasped around mine. Together we pick the cross up. It shudders and wobbles. I manage to balance it against my head. Now I'm standing alone. I breathe in its smell, its clean, polished, fragile smell.

'I want you to carry this cross down to the cemetery and back to the church at the start of the service,' Monsieur Tressetout explains. 'The brass band will play behind you.'

I look at him, suffocating. No, they can't do that to me. I can't carry this cross through the village. I can't even go into the cemetery! What if I get a thought? What if I can't hold it any more? What if I stumble and fall? What if I see Grand Maurice's grave?

I put the cross back in its case. Deep breaths. Calm, then panic, then calm.

Monsieur Tressetout shouts: 'Okay, it's a deal!' and leaves the room. 'Be ready in about twenty minutes!' he adds, before shutting the door.

Through the wall, I can hear the church filling with

families, unknown women's feet clicking across the floor, coughs, the whirl of skirts and coats, old soldiers shaking each other's hands. I can't do this. My body is quivering and I can feel my eyes dimming in fear. I open the doors of the case again. Quickly, before a thought comes, I try and touch the golden cross. A thought about Grand Maurice and the cemetery snaps in first, because I'm thinking I can't have it. It tries to puncture my resolve. I start again. I put the cross back. I rinse my hands in the air. I clear my mind. I squeeze my rabbit paw, fur against my palm, willing myself to think of something else. I need good thoughts: images of Ama and Pado waiting behind the doors or Machance walking the last stretches of the vineyard. I quickly pounce on the cross and sweep it up. It topples against my head, heavy and cold. A banner dancing on top of me. I walk towards the door, short, patient, unstoppable steps. The sound of people milling gets closer. What if I drop the cross? I know that thought. It's the one that's been trying to break into me since I picked up the cross the first time. Ignore it! Ignore it! Step by step. What if I trip up in the cemetery when I see Grand Maurice's tomb? I know that thought too. I must carry on. I have to carry on. Then the cross. What if I'm carrying it the wrong way? What if I stand on someone's grave by mistake and my feet are right above their head and coffin? What if I think of Grand Maurice buried beneath me in the earth? My arms ache. I'm walking round in circles. I can't open the door. Monsieur Tressetout. Where's Monsieur Tressetout? Jesus on the cross. I must think of Jesus on the cross. No thoughts. Pure thoughts, thoughts for Jesus. Jesus's feet are next to my hands, a nail jutting out. I feel the nail. No. Stop. No nail. They hammered it through his feet. They nailed Jesus's feet together, one on top of the other. I knock against the door: 'Please open the door!' The priest is in deep conversation with a short woman.

'Hang on, Jean-Pio,' he tells me.

I can't stop. If I stop I won't be able to keep my mind. I must carry on moving. My hands. I have to move my hands down to stop the nail cutting in to my skin. Then the blood. What about the blood gushing, pouring from Jesus's wounds? I shake my head. I shake it to stop the thoughts. The cross begins to swing. I can feel the top of it twisting above my head, turning me like a dervish. I'm going to fall.

I can hear the short woman mutter. 'He looks a bit shaky.' Then she asks, 'Isn't that Maurice's grandson?'

My knees are giving in, falling away. The cross swivels with me. I can't make it back into the side-room and I can't stay still. Jesus's legs. What about his legs? They pierced his sides and broke his legs. I remember now. My hands are wet with exhausted fear. Jesus's blood is running down over me. The cross sways like a slender tree. I'm faltering. Monsieur Tressetout! Where is he? I must give him the cross back. I turn, a tripped hazy turn, and the cross spills its blood and the bones fall off its back. I'm walking straight towards Monsieur Tressetout. I must clear my mind. Stop it. What if the woman doesn't move out of the way? What if I hit her with the cross? My head burns down the sides, long slashes of heat pushing in from both ears. My eyes are boring their sockets backwards into me. There is warm blood on my hands. No. Stop it. Stop thinking!

Monsieur Tressetout asks: 'What has come over you?' and that's enough.

I push the cross into his chest and crumple.

*   *   *

Madame Tressetout rushes over. 'I bet you he hasn't drunk enough water. His mother warned me about this! It's the same at school.' She checks my pulse and stares into my eyes. I can't see her. I can smell chalk and blackboard on the tips of her fingers. 'Nothing wrong with him. Get him a glass of water!'

I don't want anything. I want to be left alone. I get up, away from her grasp. I want to see my parents. I open the church door. Dozens of people are collecting in clusters, exchanging news. Giulio and Duccio are in the back row. They see me and wave. Where's Ama? I search the rows, up and down, quickly, desperately. I can't see her. I go outside. The school playground next to the church has been turned into a car park. Smooth, hard grey tarmac with no breaks except for the occasional shard of stone. I try to remember what school was like two days ago with Laurent dragging on his corn leaves behind the wall, the familiar opening and closing of doors, the headstands and cartwheels, the legs and arms dancing through the air.

Then I see Machance. She's sitting outside the church on her own. She calls to me. I wander over and fall onto the bench next to her.

'What's got into you?' she says, concerned. She rearranges my hair and straightens out my jumper.

'I don't want to carry the cross to the cemetery and back,' I tell her.

'It's a great privilege Jean-Pio. *C'est important.* You should be pleased to do it,' she assures me. 'You'll do it beautifully,' she adds, patting me on the knee. 'Remember, you're not doing it for yourself. It's for all those men who gave their lives in the wars. Anyway, I'll be standing by the cemetery gate, waiting for you. Don't worry.'

She gets up and walks down the steps. The square in front of the church is filling with more and more people. Cars drive up onto the pavements to park. Bicycles stand chained together between trees. A flag is hanging on the front of the town hall.

'*Enfin*, where have you been?' Monsieur Tressetout fusses when he sees me. 'It's nearly time to go!' He throws a white robe over my head and the priest slips a cloth sash across my shoulders.

'Go on! Get the cross!' they both urge me.

I step into the side-room again. The buzz and hushed voices from the church slip in behind me. I open the case and seize the cross without time for a thought. I lift it high. Then I start counting: 'One, two, three,' and, every step, I count again. I emerge into the church. The band strikes up and the old men shuffle into line behind me. I step round the corner of the altar. A wave of faces appears before me. I mustn't look at Giulio and Duccio. I count again, numbers not thoughts. Then I make my way down the aisle towards the open back door. Laurent is standing there, handing out programmes. I mustn't look at him either. I can feel his gaze stick and cling to the cross like glue as I pass beside him. The cross only just gets through the door.

The music flares up fully in the open air. The trumpet behind me is out of tune and the player keeps on banging it in frustration. I can hear the thump of the metal instrument against his trouser leg.

'Doing well,' Monsieur Tressetout whispers from behind.

I'm counting still. My feet are swelling with past numbers, present numbers, numbers to come, numbers uncounted. I'm nearly at five hundred. The turning to the cemetery is ahead. I can see a bending figure dressed in a black skirt. It's Machance. She is there. Slowly. I must walk slowly. The cross carries me upwards. I can't feel my arms any more. I'm drifting, hovering along. The backs of Jesus's legs hang in front of me, two golden bars shaped like muscles. Machance is smiling. A welcoming, anxious smile.

'Stop by the monument in the middle of the cemetery and put the cross down,' Monsieur Tressetout whispers loudly.

Only a few paces more now. Machance is right up in front of me on the steps. I turn in through the walls. I cross over into the cemetery. I step inside. I stop in front of the obelisk, dressed in flags. Monsieur Luzille is there and the trumpets play a sombre tune. The mayor reads out names, dozens of names. I'm here for the soldiers who were killed, Machance said. My feet tingle with fear. I rest my hands on the horizontal bar of the cross. Jesus's nailed hands are next to mine. The names of the dead come and go. I recognise some of them, the same ones as at school. Bernard, Bertrand, Blenet, Brigeaud, Bugol, Camsarre, Coudert, Cussard, Denis, Doriot . . . I look for Machance. She's gone. The spot where she was standing has been taken up by a wiry man in a hat. He looks at me. I turn the other way. I spy Machance over in the far corner of the cemetery. Her black skirt is resting on the ground, like a lowered flag. She is kneeling down over a tomb, dead heading flowers in a pot. She takes each wilted flower, breaks it up and scatters it on the stone beneath her. Everything in front of me shrinks. The ground swells. I see Grand Maurice's tomb. Right there, for the first time. The names of the soldiers carry on rushing through the cemetery, rooting up graves, slipping into gaps and crevices. I cling to the cross, my eyes fixed on Grand Maurice's tomb. I revolve the twisted crown stuck with a pin to Jesus's head. The gravel between the packed tombs grinds under our shoes. Flower wreaths and garlands rustle. The band strikes up. We're off, back to the church. I count again and again and the names of the dead jump in before each number. I want Grand Maurice's name. Where is his name?

24

Machance thinks we are going to have to get some more chickens to keep Giscard company. She writes a note to Madame Joignet and sends me over to the farm.

'It's not that easy to keep chickens,' Madame Joignet warns after reading the letter. 'What do you want? Laying hens? Young ones to eat? A few bantams?'

I'm not sure; not 'to eat' though.

'And you're going to have to fence off a bit of the garden or make a pen to stop them destroying everything, and then there are the foxes, the pine martens and weasels.'

She tells me she'll see what she can do, especially if it's for Machance.

Two days later Marc turns up and helps Pado fence off a corner of the garden. They drag an unsteady cupboard, full of woodworm, from the house. Marc adds a wing of corrugated iron onto it as a roof. We then secure the cupboard to a post driven into the ground. '*Va bene.* A perfect chicken roost.' Pado smiles with satisfaction.

I place a few fruit crates inside as nests. Marc tells me we are going to need some big stones to weigh down the netting at the back.

'I'll leave that up to you,' he says as he heads off back home.

I know that Grand Maurice's dry-stone wall, by the vegetable garden, has loose rocks. I make my way down there. I try and pick up the first stones I see on the grass. They're too heavy to carry. I yank at a couple more at the top of the wall. Stones rub against stones, giving way, a chalky noise. I pull out a small flat stone and then more come tumbling down. I jump back to avoid them falling on my feet. One stone in the wall is cleaner than the rest. It has no marks of rain or dirt. I tug at it and a corner of paper is suddenly jutting out in front of me. It pokes out like a damaged feather, an unpulled trigger. I touch it and the paper uncurls in my hand. It has handwriting all over it, from top to bottom. Elegant, swerving flicks of black ink crown the words with fragile wisps for accents. The paper has a date printed on it, it's a page ripped from a diary. 18th April 1976. I try and read, but the earth and chalk have eaten away the words. The writing has slipped through holes in the paper. Sentences are worn away, pushed aside to the margins, soaked in grime. There is a bit at the end of the page that looks more complete. It says, 'Today, I don't understand.' I push back the stones and find more pages. I pull out a flimsy sheet from under a lump of clay, with markings like fingerprints. It has the same year: 1976, 24th May. Next to the date is the word 'why', repeated across the top of the page. Then at the base of the page, I can just read the words, 'waste of time'. I know the handwriting, there's something familiar about it. I recognise the way the letters slant and skim the page. I remember the postcard in Machance's room with the address carefully written in one corner. It's the same handwriting, the same curves and lines. This is Grand Maurice's writing. I can't believe it! My hands are shaking. I turn the page over, nothing, I can't read any more of it.

I run my fingers over the backs of the stones. A few more pages are tucked inside a gap. They have the same writing, shaky, faint, tripping off the lines with unsteady hands. These pages are written like lists. One starts: 'Nothing, this week, nothing . . .' The other pages are dated August 1976 and, on them, words and days of the week fasten onto one another in short frustrated strokes of the pen. Beside one date is another list. This part is barely legible, merely the odd word, fractions of ink to start a line. It says: 'The summer is empty.' I sit down on the grass. I know no one is watching, yet I feel that Grand Maurice is here, spilling some unknown sorrow from out of the wall.

I don't understand: hidden pages of a diary from two years ago, words like lists for Grand Maurice, lists to himself, to measure his life, to note that it could have been different, but it wasn't. I feel the weak evening sun on my hands as I dig for more stories on the tattered pages that come from nowhere. There's nothing left in the wall. I read and re-read the scrawled writing. I lie back on the grass and stare at the clouds. I invent new words to chart the sky, thoughts to calm this moment. I listen to the wind beat through the pages ripped from the past, layers of regret and disappointment. My eyes melt into the air. My face is shot with blue and banks of white cloud to cover my dismay. Perhaps I should go and get Machance or Ama, tell them that Grand Maurice was suffering because little pieces of paper were calling to him from these stones. I know I mustn't. Not this. This is something you shouldn't see, something else that pushes like thoughts at your temples every day to keep you silent. I walk up to the house and sit down on a kitchen chair, near the door. From there you can see the rows of packets and tins in the larder beyond and the beams on the ceiling like floating columns above. Giulio turns up and asks me to go and play with him. I don't want to. Duccio doesn't want to play with him either. He's found a place in the garden with quartz rocks that you can chip into sharp pieces. He says he's going to take them to school and see if he can sell them. I'm left alone. The room is running away with images of Grand Maurice overturning stones, reciting sadness to the world. Ama comes in and nearly walks into me.

'What are you doing on that chair?' I try to tell her that I'm resting. She's not pleased. 'For goodness' sake, Jean-Pio, do something my love, don't just loll around all day long, staring into space. I've told you I can't bear it. I really can't.'

25

Madame Joignet comes over carrying two large cardboard boxes with holes in the top. Machance and I greet her excitedly. I spring open a top and ten frightened hens cower beneath me.

'Turn the box upside-down, that'll get them out,' Madame Joignet laughs.

I stroke them a little. They huddle in the corner. Finally I do as she says and tip the box onto the grass. The chickens bunch together shivering with fear in the middle of their new territory.

'What about the other box?' Madame Joignet asks. 'Aren't you going to open it?'

Machance nudges me, as if to say she's known about something all along. I quickly lift up the cardboard flaps. Inside are a couple of black ducks. Giulio and Duccio have come running out to have a look. We stand there amazed as the ducks wiggle their way across the grass and start nibbling away at the ground.

*   *   *

That night, over dinner, I announce that we have to find names for the new chickens and ducks. Ama says we should opt for local French names. Giulio wonders why we don't call them after ourselves. One duck could be Pado, the big white hen Duccio, and so on.

'They're only animals!' Pado complains. 'They don't need names.'

Machance smiles to herself, absently. Ama is pleased to see her light up a little. She says, 'As you're doing so well, why don't you eat a bit more of your fish.'

Machance shunts and flicks it with her bread. When no one is looking, she picks it up and dumps it on my plate.

'Machance!' I'm about to protest, when she puts her finger to her lips, telling me to be quiet. I stare at the fingered piece of fish on my plate. I want to give it back to her, tell her she's got to eat. She's looking at me insistently. I eat it, knowing that it's thanks to her that I got any chickens and ducks.

26

Machance is not well. She stays in her room most days now. Ama and Pado say it's all right as long as she is eating. She's not. I know.

'Machance,' I shake her. 'You've been in bed for a week!'

I list the reasons for her to get up. I go through them with her. She has to stop this numbness from settling inside her. I guide her to the side of the bed and put her shoes in front of her. 'Come on, please. Let's go and see everyone downstairs!'

She presses against me with her spoon-like fingers. 'No, no Jean-Pio. Let me rest!'

Even if she can't get up, then she mustn't stay like this, wrapped in muffled words. I pummel the sheets to release their noise. I want to burst in to her mind. Then perhaps she might talk again. Her stillness might suddenly change into words. Saliva has leaked onto her pillow. It has left a mark. She lays her cheek against the moistness, her breath pressed, restricted. She pushes her head further into the sheets. She drives her face into the whiteness until it hurts.

I pull her back. 'Machance!'

She cries inside, because there's nothing left to cry about loudly. A sickness of words flows into the room, braided patterns on the ceiling, looking for meaning. They unravel down the walls in phrases of resentment and impotence, sentences she cannot punctuate, feelings she cannot stop.

I take dishes to Machance, up in the bedroom. I hold them to her face so she can breathe in the smells. She fiddles with the food, smudging it backwards and forwards across the white plate, wearing it down, until nothing is left. I bring apples and biscuits out of my pockets. She pushes them away. She makes me eat them instead. I have to, 'for her, for Grand Maurice,' she says. I sit and eat the unwanted food. I stare at the floor to avoid the photographs, shuffled and reshuffled along the shelves every day. And then the transparent bag with the unbroken police seal, full of unwound string and wire, swirling inside the plastic, stuck to the bedside table.

If I can get her to talk, Machance tells me about Grand Maurice, how they met for the first time and the way they travelled across Europe with Ama as a child. She goes from story to story, cutting off episodes, missing places and names, tripping and stumbling on memories. She meanders through moments that have come to an end, trying to understand. I need to get words out of her. I spur her on. I must keep going, propping her up with bright images and thoughts to fight this shuttered emptiness. Then she whispers 'enough' and lays her head back against the wall.

She kisses my hand. She holds back the past on her tongue. She swallows desperately, and the harder she swallows, the more parched her mouth becomes. Her lips settle on my hand, two dry burns.

27

Laurent says someone has told him something about Grand Maurice, but he's promised not to tell me.

'Who?' I beg of him, 'who?'

'I can't repeat it. I promised,' he argues.

I know that with Laurent all you have to do is offer him something and he'll give in pretty quick.

'I'll give you some money,' I say.

He looks at me suspiciously: 'What money? How come you have money?'

'I just do,' I reply, 'but you can't have it until you tell me what they said.'

Laurent thinks about it for a while. 'Okay,' he agrees. 'Give me ten francs now!'

'I don't have it here,' I explain to him, 'you're going to have to come with me.'

I jump on the back of Laurent's bike and he rides like mad down the village hill, past the river, towards our house. He slides to a halt at the bottom of the lane and nearly knocks me off the back.

'I'll wait here,' he says.

'It's not here!' I tell him. 'We have to go up into the vines.'

He can't cycle up the vine rows because of the pruned branches and mangled wire strewn across the ground. He pushes his bike behind me, asking me, all the way, whether I really have any money at all. We stop by the vine stake where I tied the knot of poppies. I tell him to turn and face the other way while I unearth the money. He does so half-heartedly, trying to look all the time. I throw some mud at him and he keeps still. I quickly find Grand Maurice's tin. I prise open the lid and carefully take out a ten-franc piece and then bury the container again.

'Here,' I say, handing the coin to Laurent.

At first he doesn't want it because it's rusty. After he's inspected it a bit more, he accepts: 'Okay!'

'So who is it?' I ask.

'Guess,' he tries, even if he can see I'm getting impatient. '*Bon, bon*, calm down! It was my father!'

'What does he know about Grand Maurice?' I sneer.

'I promised not to tell!' Laurent retorts.

'All I have to do is ask him!' I smile back. I can see he's scared because his father doesn't need much of an excuse to smash his face in.

'You wouldn't dare ask him,' he says.

'I would,' I answer, and Laurent knows it's true.

'Okay, I'll tell you, but you have to give me another coin!'

'Another coin!' I shout. 'I'm not giving you any more money, you liar, *sale menteur*.'

'Something else, then.' Laurent is following me down the

vines. 'Give me something else then. How about one of your T-shirts?' he asks.

Ama would notice immediately if I gave him one of my T-shirts. I'm thinking I could show him Mr Yunnan. I bet he's never seen someone's bones wrapped up in three cardboard boxes. Then he'd tell me anything straight away.

'I have one thing I can show you,' I say, 'but you can't tell anyone at school. Swear!'

'No, I want something. I don't want to see anything.'

'This is special,' I add to convince him and slowly I can see his curiosity getting the better of him. By the time we get near the house, he has agreed.

We put Laurent's bicycle down by the gate and walk across the lawn. Pado is lying on a deck-chair in the sun. A full cup of coffee is balanced on his half open report.

Ama is down in the vegetable garden. I take Laurent straight to the sitting-room with the high shelves. He can't believe the house is so messy.

'We haven't sorted it out yet,' I tell him as he leans into every room to look at the piles of furniture and the cases of books.

I get him to hold a chair under me as I climb up to the shelf and bring down Mr Yunnan's three boxes. I hate touching the boxes, peeling off the tissue paper and seeing the white scrubbed bones, waiting for thoughts to enter me. I take the smallest box first, the one with the skull. Before I open it, I ask Laurent what it is that his father has said. He looks awkward.

'My father,' he whispers, 'lent your grandfather his crayfish net the day he died and he broke it by wiring too many stones onto it. My father told me "no wonder he drowned" because he didn't know how to lay a crayfish net properly. It was far too heavy and that's why it all got caught up in his bad foot and pulled him to the bottom of the lake.'

My head is dancing in a violent rush. What is Laurent talking about? Grand Maurice never used a net. He always used our old bicycle wheel. That's the way we did it, a bicycle wheel with bits of meat on it. I'm standing on the chair with the box in my hands. I can't feel anything. The room bloats below me, the parquet puffing and springing out of sequence and shape. Laurent taps on the box. 'Come on, get a move on. Show me what's inside.'

I mechanically open the lid of the small cardboard box and lift off the scrunched wrapping paper. Laurent examines the contents.

'Is that real?' he stutters, gawping at the skull.

'Mr Yunnan is his name. He was shot in the back of the head,' I reply in a flat voice.

I point to the break above the neck and cover up the head and reach for another box. Again, I lift off the paper. Laurent checks out the hands and the ribs. Then I get the last box and Laurent can't believe that legs and feet can look so fragile. He waits as I put the boxes back in their place. I don't say a word. He utters a rapid goodbye and I watch him out of the window as he picks up his bike and races away. I sit down on the long blue sofa and stare at the wall with its damp stains that spread along the contours of the bricks. The paint is ruptured and splintered in the corner. Crumbling brick pokes through. How many stones did he put in the crayfish net? He would never have used a net and stones. We had our bicycle wheel. It was the best method in the world. That's what he always said.

28

I'm in the main classroom at school and I can see Ama running towards the school with a distraught face. What's she doing here? She knocks on the window when she sees me and makes her way to Madame Tressetout's office. I dash out to meet her and, all the time, I'm hoping she speaks to me in French and not in her loud English. She hassles me to get ready as fast as possible. Laurent is watching me out of the corner of his eye. Pascal too. Ama hasn't got time for details. We have to get to the hospital. Machance is ill.

Ill? 'How ill?' I ask.

Duccio and Giulio join us and we rush about picking up our books and satchels. Ama starts up the car. Everyone is looking at us from the school windows.

'Lucky Ama's not wearing her straw hat!' I whisper to Duccio. He doesn't laugh. Nor do I. I just said it to stop thinking, to say something, something instead of this.

Basically Machance didn't come down to breakfast after we'd left for school and Ama went up to see her and found her gasping for breath in bed. She called a doctor immediately and he took one look at Machance and rushed her off to hospital. Pado tried to convince him otherwise, arguing he could care for her at home, but the doctor warned that it was no longer a question of simply getting food down her throat. She needed strong medication.

'What will the doctor give her to eat?' Giulio asks.

I'm wondering too. I reckon they'll give her apples like we did. She can roll them around in the palms of her hands and take her time to eat them. Ama is twitchy. She changes gears with violent shoves whilst scouring the roads for signs to the hospital. At the hospital she rams the car into a parking space so hard that Duccio falls off his seat. She asks us to get out and wait on the front lawn. Pado turns up afterwards in Marc's car. He sits with us outside. 'Not to worry *ragazzi*,' he tells us. He explains that Machance has got a bit weak recently because she hasn't been eating properly. 'Nothing serious.' A short stay in hospital and she'll be back at home in next to no time. Ama comes out and Pado goes in instead of her. The doctor wants to talk to Pado alone. Ama tells us the same as Pado. 'It's only because she's a bit weak. We're going to have to take very special care of her now. She has to eat.'

We drive back home from the hospital. Pado follows behind us. We stop off at Madame Joignet's to give Marc's car back. Pado joins Ama in the front of our car. He starts asking Ama about supper. She says she's not interested in eating.

'Don't you start!' Pado teases her.

Ama doesn't find it funny at all. She looks at him astounded. 'Great sense of humour!' she snaps.

Dinner is quickly made.

Ama keeps on repeating things like: 'Did you see how shocked the doctor was? He couldn't believe we hadn't called him in earlier. Couldn't you tell my mother was ill, Gaspare? You're meant to know about these things!'

Pado says that he'd been telling her for ages that Machance had bad depression, but she hadn't wanted to listen.

'Depression!' Ama huffs, 'I'm not talking about bloody depression. The doctor says she's completely undernourished as well as other complications.'

'They're all connected to depression,' Pado replies, 'and you should know that.'

Ama shoves a bowl of pasta into the middle of the table and, with a crooked fork, drops helpings of tomato-stained spaghetti onto our plates.

'Eat up, boys,' she says drearily. Duccio wants to know if we're going to see Nonno and Nonna in Italy soon.

'The travelling is over,' Ama lets out before Pado can answer. 'We're here to stay!'

Duccio eats his food and reads a book at the same time. No one stops him. I stare out of the window. No one notices. Ama begins stacking up the dishes in the sink. She runs the hot tap full blast and watches the jet of steaming water pound the bottom of the sink. She washes out a saucepan with tarnished, burnt food inside. Pado winces as the metallic rim hits the enamel of the sink.

After dinner, I wander off alone outside. I check the wire

nailed to the chicken house and the level of the water bowl. The chickens squint nervously at me from their perch. I pick Giscard up and stroke his glimmering back, rinsing my hands of thoughts through the feathers. The other chickens edge away. How am I going to look after them all without Machance? Pado makes me wash my hands when I get back into the house and gives me another lecture about psittacosis, then all the other diseases you can get from birds.

'Hygiene is vital,' he tells me as I climb into bed. 'You have to be very careful!' He hangs around my bedroom door for a moment before closing it. 'Any new facts to tell me?' he asks.

'No, Pado,' I reply and he doesn't insist.

'She'll be back soon,' he reassures me. '*Buonanotte caro. Goodnight.*'

I find it hard to get to sleep. I peer out of the window onto the dark garden. Pado and Marc's new paths aren't so new any more. Thistles have sprung up in their middle and the clean edges are blurring with the rest of the lawn. I lean my head on the window sill. I can hear Duccio walking to and fro in his room upstairs. He's restless too. I get back into bed. I fall in and out of sleep, I can't get Machance out of my dreams. She's everywhere, talking and calling to me, crowding my room with her voice and image. A dream keeps on coming. I see Machance leaving her hospital and moving into a square room, on the top floor of a high building, nowhere I know. She lines up photographs of all of us on her mantelpiece. Grand Maurice's photo is in the middle, a portrait of his face, cut off at the neck, framed and cushioned by a wallpaper background. She lays out all her objects. She wipes them. Her comb. Her hair grip. Her long red scarf. Her tweezers. Her wash bag. Her toothpaste. Her pen with the seal of a hotel in Nice. She places her clothes on the back of a chair, skirts on top of cardigans. She puts the toothpaste in her pocket.

Machance slots a tape into her music machine on the mantelpiece. The song reminds her of something, so she skips to the next song and then to the next because each song has an association she can't suppress. Finally a loud catchy tune comes on and she drums to it with her fingers along the mantelpiece. She sees herself in the full-length mirror of the bathroom opposite. There's a noise outside. She runs to the door. She peers through the eye hole. There's no one. She returns to the bathroom and looks in the mirror again. She dips her hands into the basin and runs the water in a trickle. It spills and slips along her wrists, warm, oily water, brown with grit from the unused pipes. She brings her face up close to the light and tugs at a grey hair on her chin. It slides out of its follicle, and a dark stain appears in its place. She pushes at it, softly at first, then she squeezes her nails into it. Her skin breaks and bleeds. She turns to the window. The street is still silent and deserted. Then there is another noise from the stairwell. A shadow is moving up and down outside, under the gap in the door. She wrenches it open. There's nothing. She rushes down the stairs and into the street. A few people start appearing, but no one can see her. She staggers to the edge of the town. In front of her are vineyards. She searches for grapes to eat. There are no grapes. No leaves on the vines.

She reaches into her pocket and brings out her toothpaste. She sits and squeezes the white paste out of its tube and into her mouth. She calls to me and my mouth moves with hers. There are stones engraved with reproach here, stones which suck in the light to leave the clouds bare. She picks some up, rubbing the earth off them to feel their bellies. There are no messages, none at all. If she had words, not thoughts, she would grab these stones and write all over them, words to cancel out her loss and expel the bitterness. She throws the stones onto the earth.

She spots Grand Maurice. He is sitting on a wall, his feet over the edge. He appears unable to move backwards or forwards. His back is upright, as if fastened to the air. He has a measuring tape and his walking-stick hangs from his hand. He stands up and parts some bushes. He cuts away at the grass. He throws the bundles behind him. He tramples the earth with his feet and flattens it with his palm. Then he lies down. He rests his greying black hair against a fallen branch. He checks the angle of the sun, the scent of the flowers and the sounds that come and go in the wind. He turns to Machance and tells her he has found the perfect place to be buried. He invites her to lie down next to him.

Machance runs back to the house, hitting out at bushes, the vines, everything. She blocks our doors with bolts, ties up windows with wire and string, traps branches and leaves, shuts out light. With each turn round the house, she shouts a new reproach and complaint, more and more words pouring out. We all try and break out of the door. Grand Maurice says he is off to the lake. He waves as he goes. I have to stop him. Before I can reach him, Ama falls to the ground. We crowd over her. Pado supports her head with his hands. She stares up at us with shallow eyes. I jump up in bed awake. I'm clutching the sheets. I reach for the light. I race to Ama and Pado's bedroom. I can feel the night coldness of the tiled floor travel through me. I peer through the broken lock of the door. Ama is sitting up in bed reading, the light from the bedside lamp enveloping her hands.

I open the door, slowly.

'Jean-Pio! What are you doing? It's four-thirty in the morning,' Ama protests.

'I have a headache.'

'I thought we'd got over all that,' Ama sighs. She goes to the bathroom and starts filling a glass of water. 'Here, drink this.' I take the glass, but don't drink. I drank three glasses during dinner. I counted. Pado rolls about in bed, grumbling something. Ama puts a finger to her lips: 'Hush. Sssh.'

She makes a little space in the bed next to her. Her eyes are full of sleeplessness. I lie against her pillow and watch her read, turning the pages of the book until daylight.

29

We get up early on a Saturday morning to drive over to the hospital. The doctor tells us Machance has been moved to her own room at the back of the building, on the ground floor. Ama is relieved because, she says, at least Machance will be able to look out onto the garden now. The corridors are long and grey, bordered with stretchers on wheels. I run ahead, looking into each room through the thick round windows in the doors. Old people, young people, with tubes and machines stacked behind them, return my stares. I brush each door with my rabbit paw and, as I do so, I whisper: 'Don't die.'

I find Machance's room before the others and open the door. Machance tries to get out of bed to welcome me. She already has one foot on the floor when Pado swings in, followed by Ama.

'Oh no, stay in bed *Maman*!' Ama gestures.

For a moment I know Machance is wondering why we are there, cramming her room with our concern. She glances at us all in a speechless plea. She sinks back into bed. Without stirring again, she buries deeper and deeper into her mind until she can no longer hear us talking away. We have to leave her to sleep. But she doesn't want to sleep. I touch her arm through the sheet and it's full of a feeling I can't describe. Duccio pulls me away.

Ama busies herself, sorting out the flowers and the tissues by the bed. Pado goes off to find the nurses and discuss the progress charts hooked onto the bed railings. I'm looking at Machance's grey hair spread across the hem of the sheet. Does she stare at the tiny flecks of dirt and dust on the sheets like she stares at the carpet in her room? A spot, a speck, a long dark wisp, a frayed rip, a splinter, a stripped feather, a crease, an odour, a memory, a face from years ago? The thousands of paths and patterns that make up a thought have slipped into her room and I'm fighting for them to keep our minds clean. She turns and opens her mouth to speak to Ama. The words pale on her lips.

Ama is putting up a few photos of us on the mantelpiece opposite the door. She pulls a photo of Grand Maurice out of her bag and then decides against it. She checks to see whether Machance has seen. Her eyes are lost again. When we leave, Machance insists on getting up to see us to the door of her room. Pado says it's good for her to stand up and walk a bit. She has to get her energy back. We retreat down the corridor, turning every moment to check on her. Machance smiles feebly. She stands motionless with one hand wrapped around the handle. We reach the end of the corridor and push through the fire doors. We turn and check again. Machance is still there, the handle jutting out into her hand like a walking-stick. I imagine she will be there for hours. Immobile, she will blend into the walls and slip into their gaps, expecting nothing any more. Maybe no thoughts will come to her again. A series of images only. Faces floating in and out of her. Strong colours inside which she can swim, until they fade. Colours which no longer ask her to act, to step out of herself. No word can stir her now. No noise draws her from within. She is silently dripping with the remnants of the past. A thousand perforations are tapping at the floorboards, splitting open the wood. When we get in the car, I can hear this rain as it dowses the ground. Why have we left her to cry her hurt alone?

'She has to come home!' I shriek at Ama and Pado from the back seat. Duccio edges away from me, brushing off my voice. Giulio looks at me uneasily. Ama doesn't move and then she turns to me. 'I'll speak to the doctor tomorrow.'

'I'm sure she'd be better off at home too,' Pado reassures us.

30

The ambulance bringing Machance to the house gets lost in the vineyards because she's lying down on a stretcher in the back and can't tell the nurses which way to go. Ama is worried because they should have been at the house at least an hour before. Fortunately, the ambulance driver spies Marc pruning and asks him the way. Then Pado can't get the gate open again and Machance has to be wheeled in a chair across the bumpy grass. She's happy to see us all and, as she is taken up the stairs, I can see she is looking forward to the peace of her room. Ama has cleaned it in her absence. Machance is too weak to complain at the change and, inside herself, maybe she is glad. Giulio, Duccio and I have made some drawings for her. I've sketched and coloured in a chicken that looks like Giscard. Giulio has drawn a man pushing back the sun with a long green pole and Duccio has scribbled some cats across a flag stuck on a boat. He doesn't know why.

We're all interrupted in our welcoming party by the hooting

of a large van outside. It's the *France Télécom* engineers who have come to connect the house to the telephone network.

'Completely unnecessary,' Ama moans to us all.

Pado is eagerly clearing a space for them to get to the wall and make their connections. He goes through the various costs and tariffs and looks happy.

'The telephone should be connected in a couple of days,' the engineers tell Pado as they leave.

Ama launches into: 'And what exactly are you going to do with this telephone?'

'What do you think!' Pado replies.

'You know what I mean,' Ama continues, irritated. 'If it's for research and finishing another book then fine, but if it's for organising more of those damn conferences . . .'

Pado calms her down. 'Listen, Ava, I have to get this telephone, that's all. We need money and I can't carry on working like this, cut off from the world!'

The argument ends because we all realise that Machance has been left upstairs on her own. Ama hurries off, slamming the door behind her.

A week later, when Ama is out at the Sunday-morning market in Loches, Pado gathers us together to telephone Nonno and Nonna in Italy. The line cracks and spits and eventually a loud, '*Pronto.* Hello!' jumps back at us. It's Nonna. She's delighted to hear us and we have to wait a few minutes whilst she goes off to find a pen to note down the new number. Then Nonno takes the receiver and asks us when we are coming back.

'Lorenzo, the dog, misses you, Jean-Pio,' he tells me.

Pado talks to Nonno. We can hear him saying, 'Really, how interesting, *va bene.*'

When we've all said goodbye and Nonna has come back on to give us a deafening kiss down the phone, we ask Pado what Nonno was saying. Pado tells us that Professor Alberto Devoti is in all the papers in Italy because he is organising a series of lectures on his research. He has even rung Nonno to find out where Pado is.

31

It's late afternoon. I'm standing in the vineyards. The vines are changing colour, almost moving, losing the shape of their clipped branches, unfurling from the wires that bind them down. I brush the earth with my foot. I draw a small boundary to keep me still. There is a wind so strong that it calls down each row of vines, an echoing, never-ending, compulsive noise. No other sound exists.

Machance is gesturing to me from the lawn in front of the house. A dim, distant figure, waving. Ama is putting a woollen jacket round her shoulders. She hands Machance a biscuit and strolls back into the house. Machance gently eats the biscuit. She looks different.

'The chickens are fine, Giscard too!' I say as I walk up to her. 'I checked them an hour ago.'
   '*C'est bien!* Good.' Machance smiles.
   Then she walks down the lawn and takes me by the hand.

'Jean-Pio, I need a walk. Will you come with me?'

'Walk, Machance?'

'Yes, walk.'

'But aren't you too tired to walk? You only got out of bed the other day!'

'No, I'm fine. I have to walk. Please come!'

'I've never seen Machance like this before. It has to be a good sign. I shout up to Ama: 'We're off for a walk.'

She's delighted Machance wants to get some exercise. She comes running out of the kitchen to watch us strolling across the lawn together.

At the bottom of the vineyard we turn right and right again. We cross over the river. It's a new path for me. I haven't had time yet to search these lanes and ditches packed with late blackberries and the sounds of dry autumn leaves. Machance has a determined stride. I can't believe she can have so much energy after being ill.

'Slow down,' I say to her, 'remember you haven't eaten very much.'

She ignores me, as she seems to ignore the landscape surrounding her.

We walk for at least half an hour. Machance has gone silent. Not a pensive, contented silence, but a lull waiting to break. Something is familiar about this place, I don't know what.

'Where are we going, Machance?' I ask.

'Is it down here?' she answers, pointing to a fork in the track ahead.

'What?'

'The lake, Jean-Pio? Isn't this the way you used to come with Grand Maurice?'

I suddenly recognise this lane, this low wall that separates the fields from the vineyards. I don't want to be here. I can't be here! I look at Machance, speechless. She stops in front of me. She's panting slightly. The sun seems to be coming from the earth below her, a faintly warm, humid rush under the grass.

'But . . .' My whole body feels rigid with fear.

'Is it down there?' Machance asks again. 'I hope you can remember the way?'

I turn from her and start walking ahead, counting my footsteps, the order of leaves on the ground, anything to avoid knowing where I am. But it's as if I'm now walking a beaten, routine path where the meadows and trees serve no other purpose than to map a furrow for my feet. I blindly change direction, slicing my way through tall thistles. Machance struggles behind me, clasping at branches to keep going.

We come to a halt again at the edge of a birch wood. A lane covered in twigs slopes down through a harvested patch of corn. We kick the twigs out of our way. The air has changed. There's a dank smell of mud and soggy wood. Our feet catch on stones. The lake swells up in front of us. The track peters out, its gravel and earth fall into the dark water.

Machance takes in the lake. With her heavy eyes, she circles round it, throwing out lines to the other shore, sounding out its depth, dipping into its waters. She runs a finger through the mud. A dark cut. She ties her hair back. She fumbles clumsily at her face, rubbing her eyes. She takes me by the hand and we walk over to the other side. It's a ten-minute walk, a short distance that seems to go on for ever. The lake shimmers. A few insects skitter across its surface, sending ripples to dissolve against the broken mounds of reed-clogged grass.

'So this is where you used to come with Grand Maurice,' Machance says, as if to herself. I look at the nettles and reeds. Everything is the same as before. The place where we laid down our boxes still has the same scuffed tree trunks. The water curls and plays with the shore as before, not quite reaching the cracked pattern of dry mud on the edge.

'Is this where you fished?' Machance asks.

'Yes, over there,' I point to a break in the bushes at the side where the grass has grown up high. 'And we hooked our fishing stuff onto the branches of those trees,' I continue, trying to find my words, gesturing to the trees behind us.

Machance looks round. Her voice is fragmented and shivering.

'Well, at least the police have taken all your nets away. They couldn't leave them lying around. Maurice should never have used them on his own, not with his foot. The police told me. *Mon pauvre Maurice.*'

I stand still. What nets? We never used nets! Grand Maurice always fished with our bicycle wheel. It's the best way, the only way. Machance's breathing glides over the water and spins backwards like skimming stones. The trees shroud her in towering shadows. The sky is too blue today. I imagine our bicycle wheel must be at the bottom of the lake now, encrusted with rust, moulded in slime, lost where Grand Maurice placed it the day he died. I follow the brushing movement of the water. Machance leans on a rock, spreading out into the lake. She scrapes up a sprig of silver birch. She twists it absently. She snaps off the leaves. I walk up to her, watching the little bits of crumpled leaf fall about her feet. We stay together, in front of the lake, without a word. Machance holds on to my sleeve. Her fingers grip at my wrist. Then she turns away. The birch twig is left clinging to her jumper, sticking into the material. I pick it off, unwinding it from the strands of blue wool. I drop it back into the nettles and grass. Machance's shoes are covered in rotten leaves and mud.

We walk back up the bank, through stubs of reed. We pass by the trees. I search for the branch where Grand Maurice slung our ropes and bicycle wheel. A bird springs through the thickets and undergrowth, out into the woods. Machance keeps going. I look up into the trees. My eyes drift into the irregular mesh of twigs and bark above me. The sun plays with a circular groove of shining metal, high up on a trunk. It shoots a sharp light down onto the ground. I squint upwards. Above me is the bicycle wheel, strapped to its branch, in its usual place, eroded, undisturbed. I stall, leaning against a tree, my head churning up the earth beneath me. I cling to the bark to stay still.

Machance turns and faces me. Did she see it? Did she not see it?

She doesn't say anything and my eyes are begging her not to talk. Not now.

'Are you all right?' she whispers, moving forward. Suddenly

I don't know. I don't know anything any more. My mind is full of stones. I want to shout at her: 'Why? Why, Machance? What was he doing without our bicycle wheel? I don't understand!' My words are gagged by stronger thoughts. I can see Grand Maurice carrying his borrowed net, crammed with stones and wire, wading into the centre of the lake. I can see him getting lower in the water, until the muddy waves are lapping at his neck. He doesn't swim. He just carries on walking along the lake bed, until his head merges into the colour of the water, until the sun and lake become reflections of each other.

Machance says she'll make her own way back. She doesn't want me to wait. I follow the path home. Slowly at first, then running, running fast so as not to walk, counting so as not to think.

Everyone is settling down to dinner as I arrive at the house.

'Where's your grandmother?' Ama asks anxiously.

'She's on her way,' I reply, out of breath.

'Is she all right? Where have you been? Maybe you should go and fetch her in the car Gaspare?'

Pado wants to know where we've been before he sets off.

'I don't know,' I answer. 'You can't take a car there anyway.'

'Why didn't you walk back with her?' Ama insists, surprised.

'I don't know,' I stammer. I wash my hands at the basin, facing the wall.

Then the door opens and it's Machance.

'You should have started without me!' she smiles.

Ama stops and fixes her in the eye, 'You should go walking more often, you look much brighter.' She kisses Machance on the temple. Duccio pulls up a chair for her.

Before the end of dinner, Machance turns to me, 'Don't you think we should check on the chickens and ducks?' She tugs the back of my chair, 'Come on, let's go.'

It's dark outside. We walk slowly over to the chicken house, checking the fence. Our two shadows merge on the earth in the light from the kitchen windows. The hens are all in their shelter in a neat row. Machance puts her hands against my back and presses softly.

'Thank you for taking me to the lake. I had to go one day. I couldn't have done it without you.'

I reach into my pocket to touch my rabbit paw. I pass my fingers over it, up and down, pushing through the fur to feel the bone. I drive my thoughts into the paw, a severed foot packed with the secrets of the drowned.

32

Ama storms out of her bedroom and runs down to the kitchen. She stands by the window, twisting its handle backwards and forwards. She runs her fingers along the glass, a dull smudged noise.

'What's wrong?' I say.

'Don't ask me. Ask your bloody father!' she snaps back.

Pado is banging his way down the stairs, a bag on his back and a suitcase in his hand.

'Try and speak some reason to your mother!' he says, walking past me.

He drags his case to the car and chucks it onto the back seat.

Giulio runs after Pado. 'Where are you going? Are we leaving?' he keeps on asking.

'I'll tell you in a minute,' Pado gestures.

Ama stays at the window. Her hands have stopped moving. She keeps them flat against the glass.

*   *   *

'Still sulking?' Pado asks Ama when he comes back in through the door.

She doesn't reply. She keeps her back turned to the room. Duccio has joined us. We sit. Pado speaks loudly and clearly so Ama can hear.

'Boys, I absolutely have to attend a conference in Italy. It's important for my work. There's nothing I can do from here. Your mother doesn't seem to agree, so please be good and look after her while I'm away. I'll see you all in a couple of weeks. Any messages for Nonno and Nonna?'

'I want to come with you!' Giulio yells.

'You can't miss school. Come on, be good boys!'

Pado kisses Ama's frozen neck, in the gap between her hair and her shirt collar, opens the door and heads off towards the car. I dart across the grass after him. Duccio and Giulio wait with Ama. Pado is checking his bag for his passport. He finds it tucked away in one of his files.

'Right! *Avanti!*'

He opens his window to say goodbye to me again.

'Please come back!' I blurt out.

He smiles, 'What are you talking about, Jean-Pio? Of course I'll be back.'

I run to the front of the car and clamber onto the passenger seat. We drive down the vineyard. He stops the car at the turning to the village, 'Now out you get!'

The car turns into the village, towards the motorway heading south. It's quickly gone. I stand next to the ditch that runs along the verge. The grass is damp and crushed. Any reminders of the sun are deep in the ground now. The leaves around me have been kneaded into the earth by the rain. A few have become transparent, small empty screens that fold inwards. Pado must be through the village by now. I walk past the chicken pen. I can see the hens bunched together at the gate, pushing angrily at the wire to reach me, waiting for their food. They jump up over each other, squawking and quarrelling, a mess of colours, streaks of brown, white and black. The ducks lurk in the background, with Giscard, expecting their bits of bread. I have no bread today. Ama has her hands flat against the glass of the window and Pado is steering his way down to Italy.

One hen has slotted her head through the wire of the gate. She strains her neck to reach the new earth on the other side, pressing her whole body against the wire. Her beak almost touches the ground on the other side. She pushes again, but the gate won't give. I grab hold of the latch. The hen scrambles away, yanking her neck backwards out of the wire. I stand there with the gate open. The chickens twist their heads upwards, dozens of flat eyes like upturned floating fish, looking at me. I feel uneasy. My mind is bursting with a rising headache, fusing with the walk to the lake and the sound of Pado's car on its way down the drive. I don't want to think like this any more. I don't want to think of anything, not today, not ever. I clutch at the wire of the gate, running my fingers over the rusty lines. Thin marks of red metal powder come off on my skin. I push harder, I don't know why. The wire slices into me, the two shades of red, rust and blood, mingle across my palm. No bad thoughts, no good thoughts. Nothing.

* * *

The chickens surge forward, converging on the open gate. They swarm over my feet. They stop at the edge of the open field. Then they cross through the gate, gradually, hesitantly. They spill into the long grass, picking at the undisturbed earth, climbing onto tree trunks, hunting in flower-beds. I rush to stop them. I shout their names, lunge at their wings to catch them. Then I give up. I don't have the strength to run. I can't go on. I walk out towards the vines. There are chickens everywhere now, spreading in a multicoloured blanket across the lawn and orchard. Some break away and stick to a patch of the vegetable garden, some rush back to the gate, lingering, not daring to step forward again. Others slip under thick hedges to hide.

33

Giulio and Duccio think they've found a new alcove in the cellar. They're taking down hammers and shovels to have a look. I'm not interested. Ama follows me through the house and garden telling me to do things.

'What's got into you recently, moping around all day, spending so much time with those bloody chickens! Why don't you go and play at Laurent's? And don't forget to close the chickens' gate again. I had to spend at least an hour rounding them up.'

Ama doesn't know that Laurent has even more chickens than me. In fact, he has about fifty of them and a seagull rescued by his uncle on the beach in Brittany and a one-legged jay which walks with its wings. He doesn't count any of his mother's rabbits as his own because when he did she always killed them first. Laurent shows me the rabbit skins his mother has hung up to dry. They line the walls of the barn in packs of ten. In a metal bucket are layers of rabbit paws for the cats to chew on. Laurent says I can choose a new one if I want. Ama hasn't discovered the paw I carry round in my pocket yet. I'm going to have to find a good excuse if ever she does.

Laurent's uncle is hanging around the farm. He asks Laurent for one of his corn leaf cigarettes. He retches and coughs and tells us it's disgusting, but that doesn't stop Laurent. I've been trying to tell him for ages about the photographs I've seen in the books at home and how Ama and Pado's friend in England, Michael, is going to die because he got frantic when I flushed his cigarettes down the loo. He says he doesn't care. I shouldn't care either. What's the point?

Laurent wants to show me something down at the rubbish dump near his house. We both hop on his bicycle. The dog follows us, barking and nipping at our ankles. We swerve across the fields, sloping to one side. We lean the bicycle against some trees. There's a stench of rotting waste everywhere. Laurent throws a crushed fruit juice can at a rat. It disappears down a hole. The ground is soft or hard depending on the waste underneath our feet. We jump up and down on a blue sofa with thistles growing between its springs. The cushions are slashed. Laurent tells me he did it with his knife last week.

At the end of the quarry, up against a pile of crates, Laurent has laid out a plank across some tyres. The top of the plank is lined with old wine bottles, carefully spaced apart.

'Just watch this!' Laurent smiles at me.

He takes ten steps back and delves into a stock of small rocks ready at his feet. He hurls them against the bottles. The first bottle smashes into pieces and topples the next one over with the ricochet. Laurent picks up more stones and misses the third bottle, but knocks the top off the last one.

'Go on, see if you can do it,' he says, chucking me a few stones.

Together we fling stones at the bottles. A few of my targets smash, the bottles shatter and propel glass shards through the air. I try again. This time I miss them all. I pick up a large stone and hurl it with all my might. It slams against a piece of wood and dents it. I feel hot. Laurent feeds me some more stones. 'Go on! Do it!'

My mind is rippling. I have to do it. I have to smash these bottles or else. Or else what? My mind fills with possibilities I don't want to imagine, with scenes I don't want to see. My thoughts crush one against the other. Images of the lake, of Grand Maurice, Machance and Pado. What was Grand Maurice doing? What was he doing? Then I suddenly stop. I'm not going to let the thoughts in. I can't think like this. I'm not going to have these thoughts any more. I run behind the plank and knock the bottles off with a stick. They crash to the earth.

'Stop!' Laurent runs at me, 'You can't do that,' but I can't stop.

I swing the stick at all the bottles. I send them flying, filling the dump with sharp whips of noise. I smash and pummel the remaining parts with a rock. There is cracked bottle everywhere, broken colours of green and blue, transparent and opaque. I kick bits up in the air. I stamp on them again. Jagged glass cuts through the earth. Laurent wrestles the stick from me.

'What are you doing you idiot, *connard*? These are my only bottles!'

'I'm sorry,' I say after a while. I had to do it. I couldn't stop. I don't want to think about anything, ever again.

Laurent sighs resentfully all the way back to his house, 'Where am I going to get new bottles from now? There aren't any left at the dump.'

I don't know. I'm sorry. My hands are still shaking from the impact of the stick against the glass. I'd better head back home before Ama gets worried. It's enough for her to be waiting every day by the telephone for Pado to ring without me being late too.

Laurent's uncle won't let me go so soon. He wants me to describe London to him first. I tell him it's so big that you can drive for an hour and still be in the same place. He doesn't understand. Then he says he's never been to Paris either and I have to tell him that if you take the wrong turning there you can go round and round for hours on the circular motorway. Laurent makes me speak English, then Italian. He guides me through the farm, translating everything. The uncle calls Laurent's parents and I have to go back and translate everything all over again, just for them. I speak long sentences about the car and rabbits in English and then in Italian. They stare at me. Laurent's mother takes me to her kitchen and points at things about the room.

'What's that in English, what's that in Italian?'

I name the objects and then I want to be left alone because that's all in the past now. Now I'm here, in the land in the middle, and no one is to know that I came from a car that never stopped moving.

34

It's the rabbit trap. I know. That's the reason for all this, the reason why Grand Maurice sank to the bottom of the lake. I have to get rid of it. Then the headaches will go.

Laurent says he saw a rabbit trap in the woods on the way to the river once. That has to be it. I'm going to take it apart, smash it up, crush it into tiny pieces. I am half-way down the garden when Duccio asks me where I am going.

'Nowhere, nowhere,' I repeat, but he follows me all the same. 'Leave me alone!'

He won't go. He marches up and down in front of me. I sit on the path and wait. He gets bored, kicking up the gravel with his foot. A stone lands on the grass. Ama says that's the way the lawn mower gets broken, but neither of us remove it. Duccio heads back off to the house. When he's not looking, I take the track to the river. It is carved with puddles of stagnant water, cut through by tyre marks. I find a jar. It has powdered mud inside it. The label has fallen off, leaving a gluey frame.

The woods are not wide. Monsieur Luzille has some land behind them. I can see the back of his house through the trees. He has a couple of goats on tethers. They look up as I pass by. I pace up and down, over and over again. I follow little animal tracks in the hope that they might lead to the trap. I lift up branches. I kick away leaves. Nothing. I start again, this time skirting the outside of the wood, looking in. Maybe Laurent never even saw the trap?

I hear a noise behind me. The sound of a twig cracking. I crouch down. It's Duccio. What's he doing here? I duck behind a tree. He turns quickly, calling my name. He has a long stick in his hand. He thumps it against the bushes and tree trunks, deep resounding punches against the bark. I lower myself even more, till my head is touching the damp leaves on the earth. Then Duccio is bounding over towards me, thrusting his stick in the air like a lance: 'Seen you, seen you!' I stay on the ground. What am I going to do now? He stands over me, his shoes a few inches from my face.

'What are you doing down there?'

'Nothing,' I reply.

'What do you mean "nothing". You're lying on the ground!'

I jump to my feet. Duccio looks me up and down. He checks I have nothing in my pockets or hands.

'Go on, tell me what you're doing.'

I tell him I'm collecting special leaves for the chicken house.

He asks to see them. I pick up some leaves and hand them to him.

He laughs. 'I don't believe you!'

He flicks at the earth with his stick. Mud flies up. Duccio says he'll wait until I tell him what I'm doing. I start collecting leaves. He knocks them out of my hand. I pick them up, clean them and then stash them in my pockets.

'Come on, stop lying. What are you doing?' Duccio flicks at the earth with his stick again. He looks impatient. I don't know whether I should tell him or not. Maybe I should? Maybe he could help me? He doesn't want to leave.

'Okay,' I say, 'but you can't tell anyone.'

'What?'

'Promise that you won't tell anyone.'

Duccio rolls his eyes to heaven. 'You're so boring . . . All right, I promise.'

'You swear?'

'Fuck off, what is it?'

I look at Duccio. His long black hair is covering one of his eyes. The other is blinking in the light. I can't read his expression. I'm still not sure I can tell him anything. He's scratching away at the undergrowth with his stick.

'Come on, hurry up,' he urges me.

I walk past him towards the bushes next to us. I part the branches and look under the leaves. 'I'm looking for the rabbit trap,' I tell him without turning round. 'We have to find the rabbit trap.'

'What rabbit trap?'

'You know, the rabbit trap. Grand Maurice's rabbit trap.'

Duccio leans towards me. 'What do you mean? What are you talking about?'

I start explaining about Grand Maurice and his foot.

'I know all that you idiot,' Duccio sneers angrily.

'Well, we've got to find it. We've got to find the rabbit trap. What if someone else gets caught in it and is never the same again? What if they have to sit there bleeding, counting their teeth for days on end with their foot cut in two?'

'What are you on about?'

'What if someone dies because they get their foot caught and no one ever finds them, ever?'

Duccio is throwing his stick up in the air, swirling it above his head.

'You're mad. You're completely mad.'

His laughter bolts through the woods.

Duccio follows me across the woods. I scrape away at piles of fallen leaves and search under trees. I find a narrow track with some feathers.

'Are those from a flying rabbit?' Duccio teases, prodding me with his stick.

He refuses to help. He walks behind, chuckling, marking the mud with the pattern on the soles of his shoes. Then abruptly there's an area of flattened ground between some trampled shrubs. The twigs have been cleared to make way for a small opening, in between some leaves. 'Give me your stick,' I say to Duccio.

I skim off the leaves. A jagged piece of metal pokes through. I brush away some twigs. It's definitely a trap.

'This is it!' I shout, jubilant.

Duccio peers down at it. The jaws of the trap are like glistening knives, lethal jigsaw pieces, waiting to connect. The trap is fastened down by a metal peg, rammed into the earth. A few clumps of fur are still on the soil, traces of a recent kill. I pick up the strands of fur and run my fingers over them. Duccio takes back his stick and clears the rest of the leaves away. The trap emerges, clean, gleaming. Duccio stabs his stick in between the clasps of the trap.

'Don't do that!' I push him off.

Duccio laughs. 'What are you going to do? Pick it up?'

I find a rock and drop it on the trap, lift it up and start again.

'You can't destroy it. It's not yours.'

Duccio tries to stop me.

'Let me go!'

I push him away and pick up the rock again. It bounces off the trap without denting it.

'We have to break it,' I shout at Duccio. 'Quick, we have to break it!'

'You really are mad!' Duccio screeches.

He leaps over the trap, dancing, throwing his legs up in the air, showering me with earth. He kneels down in front of the trap and jabs his hand in and out of its jaws.

'Stop it! Stop it!' I'm screaming. 'Don't do that! Duccio, please!'

Duccio swerves his arm in and out of the trap. 'In and out, oops. Nearly! And in and oops, ooohh.'

I'm pleading with Duccio. 'Please. No. No!'

'Go on. I dare you,' Duccio smiles, 'you try.'

He carries on, snaking his wrist inside the trap and then moving it swiftly out with feigned gasps. Then it snaps. It snaps so hard that Duccio shrieks like a rabbit being slit open. He's clamouring for breath. His eyes are rolling, rushing sockets of fire.

'No. No!' I'm scrambling towards him.

The jaws of the trap have lacerated his jacket sleeve. He can't move his arm. His hand is stiff and reddening.

'Get me out of here! Get me out of here!' he yells.

I try and pull the trap apart. It's blocked and rusty down the sides. I yank on the peg. It won't budge. Duccio is crying, striking the ground with his leg to get free.

'Hang on. Just hang on!' I scream.

I jump to my feet and run to the house. My heart is thumping, my head spinning. What have I done? Why? What have I done? I should never have told him about the trap. It's all my fault! I can't believe it. I trip over a tree root and pick myself up again. I reach the garden and scream for Ama. There's no one in the house. I go from room to room. Where are Ama and Giulio? Where's Machance? My head is gorged with thoughts, the worst thoughts, the ones that leech onto your throat so you can't breathe.

Duccio is stuck in the trap! I look out of the top window into the garden. Machance is near the vegetable garden with a basket, dead heading roses. I yell at her in cracked words. She looks up. She drops the basket of roses and rushes up to the house. By the time I get down the stairs, she is standing, frantic, in the kitchen.

'What have you done Jean-Pio? What have you done?'

I can barely speak. I stutter something about the wood, the rabbit trap and Duccio. Before I can finish, she has dragged me out of the kitchen door. Together we charge across the lawn, down the track and into the wood. Machance is panting, out of breath, coughing. We can hear Duccio shouting. The brambles whip at Machance's legs as I run behind her. Duccio has almost managed to get his arm out. There's a strip of his sleeve left between the clasps of the trap. Machance tears the fabric without a word and frees Duccio's arm. The fabric remains inside the trap, hanging, lifeless, on severed threads. Duccio rubs his arm. There's only a nick in his skin. He managed to pull his arm out in time. Only his sleeve was really snagged. His words are shaky. His eyes are pierced with confusion.

Machance keeps on looking at me in disbelief. Duccio examines the fine cut on his arm.

'It's all his fault,' he spits as he heads off to the house.

I'm waiting for Machance to get angry at me. I'm waiting for her to grab me and pull me off to see Ama. Instead, she strokes my head, making long, gentle furrows in my hair. She stares at the rabbit trap out of the corner of her eye.

'I only wanted to help, Machance.' She brushes the thorns and bits of bramble off her skirt. She doesn't reply.

'I wanted to destroy the trap so that no one ever got hurt like Grand Maurice! You said he was never the same after the trap. You said so yourself!'

Machance finishes flicking the thorns from her skirt. She shakes it to make sure. 'It wasn't this trap, Jean-Pio. We had that destroyed four years ago.'

She holds her face tightly turned downwards. I wait for her to look up. She doesn't.

'All that's in the past now, Jean-Pio. You can't think about that any more.'

She folds her arms, as if clutching herself. Her hands are already chapped by the cold.

I run off. Machance doesn't stir. She shrinks into the distance as I leave the wood. From the edge of Monsieur Luzille's land, she is a disappearing speck of blue. Her grey hair floats above her, a falling leaf on its way to the ground. What have I done? It's all my fault. It's all because of me. Duccio could have lost his hand. Machance is crying now, I'm sure. Her sobbing is going to fill the woods like the noise of drying twigs and grass crackling in the sun. I wander towards the vineyards, up the hill. A few drops of rain fall around me. There's a rush of damp cold, a sudden shadow. I reach the vines. My mind is swilling with thoughts, hounding me, throbbing. I'm rooted to the spot. I can't move.

I have to get rid of these thoughts, expel them from me. I can't even swap them for better ones now. There are no better ones. I don't even want to think. I can't go on. The earth is splitting, giving up on me. I lie down between the rows of vines, my head on a flat rock. I look into the sky. The clouds link onto each other, drawing out a heavy chain of shapes. They pile into a mass pressing down on me. Images bore away at my temples. A raindrop falls on me. Then another. I see a tiny drop pouring down from the sky and smashing against my face. It splashes my eyes and trickles down my cheek. I try and pick out one raindrop from another. At first, they mingle in a sheet of water. Then, I catch one. It falls so fast I can't follow it all the way. It soaks into a transparent pane of sky without a trace. I latch onto another and it disappears the same way. Soon I'm following raindrops in their hundreds as they fall to the ground beside me. I watch them from the moment they appear to the second they hit the earth, ring a circle of water and bounce up again. Tears mingle with the raindrops. I'm crying because Grand Maurice is gone for ever and Ama is right, nothing is going to bring him back now. I'm crying because I have thoughts and headaches that have no name. I'm suffering because I'm the only one who knows that you don't need stones and nets and wire that tie round your feet if you catch crayfish with a bicycle wheel. A raindrop falls on my hand, then another and another. I can feel them slide down my palm. My clothes are wet. The earth under me is swelling with water. A puddle is forming by my head. I stare into the autumn rain streaming down in swathes of black light, knocking and puncturing my eyes. Thoughts are still coming, hard, drilling. The raindrops dilute them, wipe them away. Soon, I'm watching the rain, slotting pain and sorrow into each drop before it falls. I'm sending out names and embedding them in the sky, inside the drops, deep inside. Grand Maurice, the cemetery, Aldo Moro, the capsized ferries, Mr Yunnan, I send them all, each in turn, into the rain. Every drop holds a memory. Every drop contains a thought to be washed away. I scour and wipe the corners of my mind. I press my nose against the stone and touch a soft, shallow dent in the sand where the rain has shot the earth. I dredge up the unwanted thoughts that cripple me. I draw them out of me, out of my head. I chase them into the skies, away. I can see and feel nothing but rain in my eyes and mind.

35

Ama has put some bread and cheese on the table for lunch. She knows what happened with Duccio and the trap, but she's not saying a word about it. Instead she tells us about her plans for the house. She sketches an outline of the house on a scrap of paper and, with her pencil, springs from room to room, imagining new colours, installing lights and bringing down walls. Then she moves on to the garden and her hands divide up the table to map out new flower-beds and cut hedges down to size.

'What do you think *Maman?* Would you mind?' Ama says, turning to Machance. 'Perhaps we could even build a new greenhouse?' she ventures.

Machance doesn't seem to mind. 'If you want,' she joins in. 'A better greenhouse might help. We could get rid of that crumbling old wall in the garden too.'

Ama gets up and starts taking the food off the table. We diligently follow her to the sink with our dirty plates.

'Don't worry. Off you go!' she says to us.

*   *   *

Giulio waits for me by the door and then, together, we run to the chicken pen to check on the hens. Giulio wants to remove the ivy growing up through the floor of the chicken house. I leave him to it. I make my way over to the vegetable garden. At the wall by the greenhouse, I kneel down and twist Grand Maurice's frayed diary pages out of the stones. I tug at the paper gently, careful not to rip it. I lay the sheets inside my trouser pocket. The bottom of my pocket fills with dirt from the wall, powdery specks. I push the stones back into the wall. Each in its previous place.

Walking through the village, I can hear people eating at their tables, watching television, stacking up plates and pans. A few windows are open, filtering in the gentle breezes of November that swell the air. Fallen leaves have been swept into piles in the corners of gardens. A white metal table has blown over in the wind. An upright chair stands alone, stranded. My shoes grate along the road beneath me. I look down and follow the tarmac as it fans out past the church and up towards the vines, a river that feeds and connects into other roads, into other streets and motorways everywhere, to Pado winding his way across Italy.

At the church, I turn left. The cemetery wall appears, solid and packed with moss between the bricks. I walk the whole way round to the gate. The handle is smooth, washed by the turning of sorry palms. The gravel rolls and jumps out of my way, spilling onto the slabs of the graves either side of me. Names everywhere. Photo portraits bleached into the arches and crosses. Grand Maurice's tomb is in the corner. I pick the dead flowers off the plants Machance has left. I place them in a small pile. I take the diary pages from my pocket. I clean them, blowing the grit into the air. I fold them in two. There's a hollow at the point where the gravel meets the tomb, a narrow, clean gap. I slide the paper deep inside, under the stone. I sweep the gravel flat with my hand.

Acknowledgements

Thank you to my mother, Dominic, Piers and Peggy for their enthusiasm, to Koukla MacLehose for her unfailing belief, to Carmela Uranga for her devotion and inspiration, to Petra and Paddy Cramsie for their constant friendship, to Laurence Laluyaux for her conviction, to Peter Day for his laughter, to my perceptive reading friends: Cesca Beard, Gina Bullough, Kate Brooke, Cressida Cowell, Charlie Fane, Sophie Janson, Faith Mowbray, Sista Pratesi, Ranwa Safadi, Gigi Sudbury and Romilly Walton-Masters.

And Emily, of course.